Love
SCENE
A Crush NOVEL
ELOUISE EAST

Beta Readers: Emma Brown, Mike Van Eimeren, Jess Waugh-Bacchus, Tammy Basile

❀ Created with Vellum

CONTENTS

LOVE SCENE

DEDICATION

Be true to yourself.

LIST OF CHARACTERS

(ALPHABETICAL ORDER)

Analise, Bartender at Crush, Kade's girlfriend, Friends with Crush group

Asher, Childminder, Sean's boyfriend (Instant Desire),

Ava, Police officer, Samuel's sister

Carlie, Vaughn and Emma's daughter

Carter, Samuel's brother, Lia's husband

Casey, Paramedic, Luke's boyfriend (Life Support),

Catherine, Samuel's mother

Charles, Samuel's father

Charlie, Bartender at Crush, Josh's boyfriend (First Kiss),

Colton, Woodworker, Ioan's boyfriend (A Crush for Christmas),

Dane, Zak's son

Devon, Manager of Infinity

Don, film director for Lynx Films

Elsbeth, Actor, played Eric's love interest in film

Emily, Accountant, Eric's sister, Friends with Crush group

Emma, Eric's friend, Vaughn's wife, Carlie's mother

Eric, Actor, Siblings: Emily and Ethan

Ethan, Architect student, Eric's brother, Friends with Crush group

Gregory, Samuel's colleague

Ioan, Carer at nursing home, Colton's boyfriend (A Crush for Christmas)

Joey, Police officer, Friends with Logan and Ava, Kade's police partner

Josh, Charlie's boyfriend (First Kiss)

Kade, Police officer, Friends with Logan and Ava, Joey's police partner

Kenzo, Retired Army, Veteran Centre volunteer, Zak's boyfriend (Covert Strength)

Kristen, big part of Vaughn and Emma's life

Lia, Carter's wife

Logan, Detective Sergeant, Casey's brother

Luke, Personal Trainer, Casey's boyfriend (Life Support),

Maggie, Samuel's personal assistant

Max, Interior designer, Trent's boyfriend (Primary Seduction)

Mikey, Eric's little at the beginning of the story

Milton, Samuel's ex-husband, now with Gregory on and off

Noah, Zak's brother

Ryan, Eric's lawyer

Samuel, Lawyer, Siblings: Trent, Carter, Luke and Ava, Parents: Charles and Catherine

Sean, Architect, Asher's boyfriend (Instant Desire),

Tom, Owner of Crush

Trent, Teacher, Max's boyfriend (Primary Seduction), Samuel's brother

Vaughn, Actor, Eric's best friend, Emma's husband, Carlie's dad

Wren, film producer for Lynx Films

Zak, Woodworker, Kenzo's boyfriend (Covert Strength)

CHAPTER ONE

ERIC

Eric Clarke always entered Infinity through the front door, much to his own amusement. Granted, he wore a mask, covering two-thirds of his face, but he was still identifiable to those who were obsessed enough with him. There were a lot of people waiting to get into the club, many of who jeered and laughed as he bypassed the queue. The thrown remarks, such as, "You'll never get in," and "You'll look like a fool," made him smile. He rested his thumb on the sensor next to the door, and when he was given entry, several gasps were heard, and then the mumblings began about who he was.

Infinity was a unique club—one of a few around the world—that catered to those who needed privacy, security and complete confidentiality. Every member of the club had been vigorously security checked, and only those who the owners decided were suitable were allowed entry. The use of thumbprints made everything easier. On rare occasions, like tonight, there was an open night, giving the public limited access for a limited time.

Usually, Eric stayed away on those open nights. It was too easy for him to be identified without his mask, but he had no choice; this was the only night he would be able to attend for a while.

After entering, he closed the door firmly behind him, shutting out the numerous calls for his name, then strode to another door set off to one side. His thumbprint was required again before the door clicked open.

"Good evening, Mr Clarke."

Eric smiled at the older man and held out his hand. "Good evening, Devon. How have you been?"

Devon Everett was in his forties with muscles that went on for miles. Eric knew he'd been in the military, but he had obviously continued with his training, even though he was retired. Devon's face reminded Eric of Sylvester Stallone, but he had the personality of a kitten, which was jarring when you first met the guy.

"I'm good, thanks. We have everything set up ready for you in room seventeen. We're just waiting on your partner, Mikey, to arrive."

"Perfect. Am I all right to head there now, and he can join me when he's ready?"

"Of course. You know your way. Have a good evening."

Devon clapped him on the shoulder, and Eric made his way down the dimly lit corridors, the lack of any kind of scent or sound unnerving, and through the maze to his allocated area. His thumbprint gave him entry to the room, and he grinned as he saw the contents.

Several shelves lined the walls on the left, holding everything from books and cuddly toys to general knick-knacks you would expect to find in any home. Next to them sat a large, comfortable-looking, two-seater sofa with a small coffee table in front of it. To the right stood a small bed and changing table with some shelves holding nappies, changes of clothing, dummies, blankets and any other item he could ever think of needing for a little. A larger bed was tucked into one corner of the room.

A small bathroom was situated through an alcove to his left, which held a bathtub, a shower cubicle, a toilet and a small sink. There was another small sink by the entrance door with a fitted fridge underneath.

Eric wandered around, touching every now and then before stopping and crouching in front of several large boxes next to the sofa. Lifting the lid on one of them showed him a train set, another held building blocks, and yet another box had a tea set. His gaze lifted to the shelves he'd seen initially, scanning for what he hoped to find and nodding when the colouring books and pen pot were found.

He stood again, resting his hands in his pockets as he surveyed the space. He'd never been in this room before, but it was just what he needed. Devon required a definite thank you after tonight. Eric hoped his partner would be as suitable as the manager expected him to be.

The sofa was as soft and inviting as it looked, and Eric made himself comfortable with a book from the shelf, wishing he could remove his mask to make it easier to read, but he needed to speak with his partner before he did. As soon as he'd opened the first page of the book, a click sounded, alerting him to the fact his partner had arrived.

Eric didn't change his position. He kept his demeanour open and calm, hoping to show the newcomer he was approachable.

A golden-haired slender man entered, carrying a small bag. As soon as he saw Eric, he paused, then beamed. "Daddy!"

The man bounced on his toes but didn't move from where he stood inside the closed door. It was unusual for his partner to immediately drop into being little, but it seemed Mikey was closer to the surface than some others were. Usually, there was a discussion before they began, but it appeared as if Mikey was ready to go. Eric wasn't worried because Devon always made sure each partner knew what he needed from them.

Eric smiled and stood, resting the book on the coffee table. "Mikey, come here, sweet boy. How has your day been?"

"A bit tiring, Daddy. I had lots of learning to do, and it hurt my head." Mikey rubbed at his forehead as his mouth turned down.

"Well, I know exactly what we can do to help you. Shall we get you a little more comfortable?"

Mikey bit his lip and glanced up at Eric from under his eyelashes. "Daddy?" he whispered.

"Yes, Mikey."

Mikey's finger touched his own cheek. "Can I see you?"

Eric had forgotten he still wore the mask, and now that he'd seen Mikey, he felt more comfortable and lifted it off and placed it on a nearby shelf. There was no hint of recognition, and he knew Mikey wouldn't have been told his identity—that was Eric's decision— so either Mikey didn't know who he was or didn't care.

"Thank you, Daddy!"

"You're welcome, Mikey." Eric moved a step closer. "I think it's time for some relaxing time, sweet one." He lifted his hand and cupped Mikey's face, brushing his thumb against his cheek. "Shall we see what clothes you can choose from?"

Mikey grinned and nodded, grabbing Eric's hand and pulling him along as he strode to the shelves.

When Mikey stopped and put a hand over his mouth, muffling a squeal, Eric chuckled. "See something you like?"

"Daddy," he mumbled from behind his hand, "They have yellow ones!"

"All right, Mikey. Go and get on the changing table, and I'll bring along your things. Put your bag under the table, then you know where it is if you need it."

Eric watched as the little guy tripped over and pushed at his bag until it fit under the changing table. He hoped there was nothing in there that could get broken. Turning his gaze back to the unit, he picked up the yellow t-shirt with rainbow unicorns on the front, the matching yellow shorts and a nappy. Mikey was lying on his back with his legs draped over the edge of the table, his hands fidgeting with the drawstrings on his trousers.

"Mikey?" He waited until their gazes met. "Let's sit you up so we can take your t-shirt off. We can get you into the yellow one, and you can look at the pictures as I change you."

"Okay, Daddy."

Eric lifted the hem of Mikey's t-shirt and tugged it over his head before replacing it with the chosen outfit and helping him to lay back down. Mikey automatically lifted his legs to allow Eric to remove his trousers and pants, which he folded and placed on the shelf underneath the changing table. He watched as Mikey ran a hand over the glittery top and smiled. Picking up the nappy, he spread it beneath Mikey and encouraged the little one to rest his legs down again.

"There we go. Snug as a bug," he said once Mikey was redressed.

Mikey giggled, the sound sending waves of happiness through Eric. This. This was what he wanted: the joy and freedom to take care of another person, to be their everything, to take the burden from them. Someone allowing him to do this for them meant more than anything else to him. He could do without sex, indefinitely if necessary, but this was a need he couldn't repress.

"Shall we see what there is to play with, and then you can have a snack in a little while?"

"Yes, please, Daddy."

Eric led him over to the boxes and took the lids off so Mikey could see. He had a feeling he knew what the little one would choose, and he was right. "Let's get the trains out."

"Can we put them on the table?"

Eric nodded. "Sure thing."

They worked alongside each other for a while, getting the track out and making a route that would fit on the small surface. Mikey took a long time to choose which train he wanted, checking over each one until he was satisfied with the green one.

When Mikey was happily watching the train go around the track and chattering to himself, Eric moved to the sink and fridge. There wasn't a full kitchen in the room, but there was a small counter next to the sink and fresh fruit in the fridge. Eric washed his hands and made a small bowl of fruit, keeping an eye on Mikey while he did. Once the fruit was ready, Eric filled a sippy cup with water and tightened the lid to prevent spillages.

Leaving the snack on the side, he took the drink over to Mikey. "Here you go, little one." He crouched and offered the cup, which Mikey took eagerly. Eric ruffled his short curls, chuckling when Mikey pulled a face.

"Could I have some juice, please, Daddy?"

Eric tilted his head. "Tell you what, drink the water, and when it's snack time, you can have some juice with it."

Mikey scrunched his nose but nodded.

"Good boy."

With the sippy cup empty, he returned it to the counter before sitting next to Mikey once more. They spent some time with the trains, adding a few blocks to make a bridge over the track in several places, much to Mikey's delight.

Every passing second released more and more

tension from Eric's body. Nothing existed outside of these four walls, and it was freeing.

After a few more minutes, Eric asked Mikey to tidy away so he could have a snack. Mikey jumped straight to it, throwing everything into the boxes.

"Mikey! Please don't throw the toys. They don't belong to us, remember. We have to be careful with them; otherwise, no other little boy or girl will be able to play with them, and they'll be sad."

Mikey's head lowered, and his bottom lip trembled. "Sorry, Daddy."

"It's okay. Just be careful as you put them away, please."

After that, Mikey took care and replaced the lids on the boxes before sitting on the cushion Eric had placed on the floor beside the table. When the boy was settled, Eric put the bowl in front of him with the previously agreed juice and sat on the sofa with a bottle of water.

He watched, entranced, while Mikey ate the grapes, strawberries and blueberries with a small crease of concentration between his eyebrows. As he studied him some more, he realised Mikey was eating them in order: one grape, one piece of strawberry and one blueberry, then back to the grapes again. Eric smiled as he drank his water.

Not long after, Eric noticed Mikey was fidgeting even though he had some fruit left. "Have you had enough, Mikey?"

Mikey shook his head. "I need to pee-pee," he whispered.

Eric moved closer, sitting on the floor next to the little guy and rubbing his back. "That's okay. Would you like to use your nappy or the toilet?" Each little was different, and Eric hadn't asked. The rule was each partner would be honest if it was something they didn't want. Mikey hadn't disagreed with Eric putting a nappy on him, so Eric had assumed he would be fine with using it, but not every little was.

"I…I've never pee-peed in a nappy before," Mikey mumbled to the floor.

That wasn't an answer. "Mikey, would you like to try using your nappy? You don't have to, but it would make me so proud if you wanted to have a try." Eric didn't want to pressure Mikey, but it seemed to be something Mikey was interested in trying, even if he couldn't voice it himself.

Mikey nodded.

"I need your words, sweet one," Eric coaxed.

"I'd like to try," he whispered.

"Good boy. I'm going to choose a book, and we can read a story while you get comfortable." Eric stood and picked a train book. Hoping to make Mikey feel more settled, he scooted Mikey forward on the cushion. Sitting behind him with his legs spread on either side, Eric allowed Mikey to rest back against his chest, and both were able to see the story.

As he read the story about a train going on an adventure up a mountain, Eric felt Mikey tense and relax several times, and he made sure to surround him as much as possible. When he heard Mikey sigh and felt him relax more solidly against him, he smiled.

Once the story was finished, Eric rested the book on the table and wrapped his arms around Mikey's waist. "Do you feel okay?"

"Yes, Daddy." He squirmed. "It feels weird." He giggled.

Eric chuckled. "I bet it does. I'm so proud of you, Mikey. You're such a good boy for your Daddy." He pressed a kiss to the side of Mikey's temple. "Let's go get you changed."

Eric cleaned him up and replaced his nappy. "Are you feeling sleepy, Mikey?" he asked after Mikey stifled a yawn behind his hand.

A slight flush tinted Mikey's cheeks as he nodded.

"Would you like to sleep in the small bed and have a nap, or would you like to sleep next to me for a while?"

Mikey bit his bottom lip. "With you, please, Daddy."

"All right. You jump into bed, and I'll get more comfortable before I join you," Eric said.

"Okay!"

He rolled off the changing table, making Eric's heart clench in panic for a second before Mikey giggled and stood, skipping across the space to the large bed. He watched as Mikey crawled across the duvet and slid himself under the top until all Eric could see were his eyes and a mop of curls on the pillow.

Eric shook his head and smiled, striding across to the bathroom. He sorted himself and washed his hands before returning to the room. His t-shirt was removed and folded, as was his trousers, and placed on the arm of the sofa, then he climbed into bed next to Mikey, who immediately turned and burrowed himself into Eric's side.

The warmth from the little one was like a furnace, but Eric didn't mind. Within seconds, Mikey was asleep, his soft snores blowing warm air across Eric's skin. Eric sighed to the ceiling, his mind calm and centred for the first time since he'd last been in this situation.

He didn't sleep while Mikey did. Eric enjoyed the peacefulness and satisfaction that came from taking care of someone. It meant he knew as soon as Mikey stirred.

"Did you have a nice sleep, Mikey?"

Mikey hummed sleepily and rubbed his cheek against Eric's chest, his curls tickling Eric's chin. When his nipple received a wet lick, he jolted and huffed a laugh.

"Is there something you want, little one?"

"Hmm." Mikey pressed his hips against Eric's.

Smiling, Eric said, "Let's get you changed, and we can snuggle in bed, all right?"

They quickly went through the motions of cleaning Mikey up, but this time, Eric didn't replace the nappy, knowing what Mikey wanted. Once he was free, Mikey streaked, naked, across the room to the bed, then jumped on it before sliding under the covers again with a giggle.

Eric laughed and finished sorting the changing table, washing his hands before returning to the bed. He slid next to Mikey and wrapped him in his arms once more.

Mikey latched onto him, pressing close until there was no space between them. Eric stroked a hand along Mikey's spine, getting closer and closer to his ass with each pass. By the time he was stroking to his thighs, Mikey was making small noises and humping against Eric's legs.

"Do you need something, Mikey?"

"You, please, Daddy."

Eric crooked a finger under Mikey's chin, lifting his face to him, then pressed a kiss to his lips. He took it slow at first, taking each of Mikey's lips between his own before licking across them, requesting entry. When Mikey opened, Eric deepened the kiss, sliding his hand to the back of Mikey's head and moving him where he wanted. He gripped a handful of Mikey's ass and pressed him closer, encouraging him to thrust against Eric's leg again.

Mikey pulled back, panting. "Please, Daddy."

Eric rolled him to his back, covering his body with his own. "I'll take care of you, sweet one."

Eric moved lower, pushing the cover off the bed as he licked and kissed his way down Mikey's chest and stomach, resting between his spread legs. He paid attention to Mikey's navel when he found the boy squirming each time he came close. Licking a strip across to his hipbone, Eric pressed a kiss to each protruding bone, then back to where Mikey needed his attention.

Pearls of precome were waiting for him, and he sucked them from Mikey's tip, earning a moan.

"Oh, Daddy! Please!"

Eric took the head of Mikey's dick into his mouth, using his tongue to lave the underside as he sank down. Mikey's cock wasn't overly large, so Eric was able to take him all the way down his throat, where he swallowed. Mikey's cock twitched, and he knew his boy wouldn't last long. Withdrawing, he swiped his tongue across the tip and reached over to the drawers next to the bed to retrieve lube and a condom.

He pushed his briefs off, dropping them over the side of the bed. Opening the lube, he squirted some on his fingers and moved them against Mikey's entrance, rubbing around in circles until Mikey relaxed enough for the tip of his finger to slide in. Eric watched Mikey's face for any sign of being uncomfortable or in pain, but apart from biting his lip, his gaze was fixed on Eric.

Eric pressed his finger forward until it was easily being taken, then prepped Mikey further. When he was taking three fingers and rolling his head back and forth on the pillow, Eric pulled back and rolled a condom on, slicking it generously.

"Hurry, Daddy!"

Eric chuckled. "Patience, Mikey."

He braced himself over Mikey, leaning down for a kiss as he held his cock at Mikey's hole. Hovering over him, Eric watched his expression as he pushed inside him. Mikey's mouth dropped open, his hands reflexively clenching around Eric's biceps, but no protest came.

When he was fully seated, he paused, kissing Mikey and teasing his lips and nubs until neither could wait any longer. Mikey squirmed below him, and Eric withdrew, pressing in again slowly. As soon as he found Mikey accommodating, he picked up the pace. Sweat began to bead along his back, and he moved closer, lifting Mikey's legs higher and pounding deeper.

"Daddy! Daddy!"

"Come for me, Mikey. Whenever you can. Come for Daddy," Eric gritted out, his own orgasm not far away.

As if he'd been waiting for his permission, Mikey came, long streaks of fluid coating his stomach, and his ass tightened around Eric's cock.

"Fuck! Mikey!" Eric gripped Mikey's hips tightly to his own as he released into the condom, surrounded by the heat of Mikey's ass. He hoped he didn't leave bruises.

As the tension of his climax released, he slumped forward, catching himself on his forearms before he crushed Mikey beneath him. He panted into Mikey's neck, pressing kisses to whatever skin he could reach in between. Mikey's hands roamed Eric's back, bringing him down and leaving a trail of goosebumps along the way.

"Thank you, Daddy," Mikey said with a sigh.

"You're welcome, sweet one."

Eric withdrew, holding onto the condom. He removed it, tied it off and left it to one side to take with him when he left. He'd had a scare once before, which had left him more cautious than ever, and he refused to leave his release anywhere where it could be retrieved by someone else.

He cleaned up in the bathroom and returned to tend to Mikey, who was snuggling up in the covers once more.

"Let me clean you up, Mikey." Eric pulled the cover back, cleaning Mikey and tucked him back in, climbing back into bed once he'd finished. He held

Mikey while they both came back from where they'd been.

"How are you feeling?" Eric asked. From the atmosphere in the room, it seemed Mikey was out of his little persona.

"I'm good, thanks. I loved it all," he whispered.

Eric smiled and smoothed a hand along Mikey's back. "I'm glad. Thank you for tonight."

They spent time relaxing and talking before getting ready to leave. Eric retrieved the condom and wrapped it in tissues, tucking it into his pocket before sliding his mask back into place.

"I bet it must be a pain to have to hide all the time," Mikey stated.

Eric glanced over at him and sighed. "It's…wearing, yes. Thank you for not treating me any different than anyone else. That means a lot to me."

Mikey blushed and ducked his head. "You're welcome. I don't know how it feels to be famous, but you come here for the same reason I do…to be free. What happens out there," he pointed to the door, "is nothing to do with what happens in here."

Eric stepped closer and cupped Mikey's face. "Truer words have never been spoken." Pressing a kiss to his lips, Eric pulled back. "Thank you."

Eric leaned back against his front door, listening to the silence surrounding him. His house was large—to be expected of someone famous—and had never felt like home. There was too much space, too little furniture and too much white. His interior designer had declared his house needed to be minimalist with clean lines, and he'd let her get on with it. He didn't spend a large amount of time there, so he hadn't cared at the time, but every time he returned from Infinity, it made it clear he was alone.

There was no one to greet him, no one to talk to and no one to take care of.

An empty house to go with an empty heart and only partially fulfilled life.

CHAPTER TWO

SAMUEL

"Maggie? Do we have everything we need for those two files now?" Samuel asked with a sigh, flicking through several sheets of paper on his desk, looking for the one piece he needed.

"Yes, we do. There is only the Keenan case and the Benedict case left with outstanding tasks."

Samuel Walker slumped his shoulders and rubbed at his forehead. He wanted nothing more than to throw the Benedict case out the window. "All right. What do we need for the Keenan one?"

"We need the transcripts of the statements both parents made, and according to the file, the telephone records for both as well." Maggie crossed her legs, resting the file on her knees as she scanned the page in front of her. "Oh, and Mrs Keenan called and left a message for you. I would recommend calling her back because I don't think she'll wait until next week."

Samuel blew out a breath and sat back in his chair, linking his fingers over his stomach. "Why does it always seem like there is more work that needs to be done before I have one day off?" He chuckled without humour.

Maggie smiled softly. "Because you're trying to do it all at once."

He ran his shaking hands over his face and inhaled slowly to calm the nausea churning in his stomach.

"I'll be back in a moment," Maggie said, resting the file on her vacated chair and exiting the office, closing the door behind her, muting the sounds from the rest of the office.

Samuel spun his chair towards the window, taking in the rain-splattered glass and dreary skies beyond. Leaning forward, he placed his elbows on his knees and dropped his head into his hands. He loved being a family lawyer, always had, but lately, he'd lost some of his…mojo, as his brother Carter would say. Lately was probably the wrong word. He'd lost some of the love for the job when his ex-husband decided to sleep with another lawyer Samuel had to deal with regularly, and that was five years ago.

Family meant a lot to Samuel. His parents were amazing with him and his four siblings, and he had always wanted to be like them with a big family to care for. He'd thought he was on the way to that life with Milton, but to find out he'd been cheating on him with Gregory…was insulting, to say the least.

Life had become a chore from then, especially as he spent hours, even days sometimes, working alongside Gregory. Every time Samuel tried to put it behind him, it came back when he next saw the two people he detested above all, which was more often than he wanted to.

"Here you go."

Samuel flinched when a cup was placed on the desk next to him. He'd not heard Maggie come back into the room. She squeezed his shoulder, and the soft squeak of leather advertised her return to her seat.

"Thanks," he croaked, pressing his fingers into his eyes before stretching out his neck and facing the mound of paperwork once more.

Taking a gulp of hot coffee, he refocused, and they continued through the Keenan case. Once that was sorted, it only left the Benedict case that was shared with Gregory. The bane of his life.

The two of them spent several long minutes going through exactly what was needed before the weekend and what could wait until after. Maggie left to get some of the information from Gregory, and Samuel concentrated on completing the details he needed. When she returned, the man he tried not to interact with came in after her. Maggie gave Samuel an apologetic look.

"Samuel!" He always forgot how much of a force of nature the man was. "I hear you need some more information from me."

Samuel stood. "Not from you, Gregory, from the file. There is nothing in here from Mrs Benedict. I need those papers so I can make sure everything is in place."

"They're with the secretary. You should have the information in a couple of days."

"I don't have a couple of days, Gregory, and you know it. I need it tomorrow morning at the latest."

Gregory frowned. The expression made his face crease more than usual. He was at least ten years older than Samuel, although his dark hair and clean-shaven appearance made him look younger. The last five years had not been kind to Samuel, unfortunately, and standing next to Gregory made it more apparent than ever.

"The case cannot be delayed because you won't be here, Samuel," Gregory chastised.

"Then find someone else to take over for me. I will *not* be here on Friday. If I don't have the information by tomorrow morning, the case will need to be postponed because I won't get to it before Monday."

He sounded a lot firmer than he felt. Inside, he was trembling, and his head was whirling. The stress of dealing with the man was taking its toll.

"Now, now, Samuel. No need to take that tone. You

could always drop in for an hour or so on Friday. It wouldn't take long."

"No, Gregory. It's my brother's wedding. I will not be here on Friday."

All of them knew it was a lie—he would go in if there was no other choice, but he was determined to stand his ground. He'd lost a lot more respect for the man, who had always treated him as second best. After finding out Gregory had been fucking Samuel's husband for several months behind his back, he'd lost every ounce of respect he ever had. He had no idea why the partners still made them work together, but Samuel was a professional, and he would do the work, even if it killed him in the process.

"Knock, knock."

Samuel closed his eyes, resting his hands on his desk and hanging his head. Just what he needed.

"What are you doing here?" Gregory asked.

"I came to see Samuel. What's it to you?" Milton said, a note of disdain in his voice.

As soon as they had been found out, Milton and Gregory's clandestine relationship fizzled and burned. Milton looked down his nose at Gregory, and Gregory looked like a lost puppy every time Milton was around when they were in the off part of their "on and off" relationship. Served them both right as far as Samuel was concerned.

It was a shame Milton wouldn't get the message

that Samuel didn't want to see him anymore. He turned up every week or so to "check-in with him," so he said. Samuel had no idea why he wanted to do it when they had been divorced longer than they'd been together.

Gregory sniffed and, without looking at him, said, "Samuel, I will ensure the information is with you as soon as possible." He trailed out of the room.

Samuel turned his gaze to Maggie, who raised her eyebrows at him and flicked her eyes towards Milton briefly. He shook his head and grimaced. "Thank you, Maggie. If you can, please check with the secretary about the Benedict case to be sure."

Maggie nodded, scowled in Milton's direction and collected her things before leaving the office without closing the door behind her. She knew Samuel well. He no longer wanted to be enclosed in a room with this man.

"So, Sammy, what are you doing this weekend? I heard something about a wedding?" Milton wandered around the room, dragging his fingers along the shelves in a seductive way that would have distracted Samuel while they were married. Now, it only made to make him roll his eyes.

"Stop calling me that." He sighed and sat down, scooting himself closer to the desk.

"Well?"

"Well, what?"

Milton huffed out a breath. "This weekend? Your plans?"

"None of your business."

"Sammy," he whined.

"Stop calling me that!" Samuel's voice rose slightly but not enough to cause someone to come and check on them.

Milton raised his hands, palms forward. "All right, all right." He came closer, his hips swaying provocatively. "Who's getting married?"

His ex-husband rounded the desk and planted his ass on several sheets of paper, crossing his legs towards Samuel and leaning into his personal space. Samuel ignored him, pretending to concentrate on the paper in front of him until Milton's fingers touched his hair, then he pushed away from the desk and stood, pacing away from him.

Milton was a handsome man, three years younger than Samuel, with sleekly styled black hair and green eyes that pierced right through him. He was charismatic, flirtatious and interested when they had first met, and Samuel had fallen for it. The lion had caught his prey, and Samuel had been none the wiser despite his family's misgivings about the man. His beauty and demeanour had blinded him to the man underneath it all—the man who had only come to light once his affair had been discovered.

"What do you want, Milton?" Samuel asked,

shoving his hands in his pockets and putting the desk between them.

"I wanted to make sure you're okay." Milton rose and skirted the desk once more.

Samuel moved to the door, making it clear he wanted Milton gone. "You don't need to know that information. Please leave."

It was the same words he used every time Milton turned up. Words that were always ignored. Samuel was tempted to get a restraining order, but he didn't want the hassle.

Stepping closer, Milton ran a finger down Samuel's shirt buttons and whispered, "See you soon, handsome."

Samuel clenched his jaw and shut the door behind his ex. His desk chair beckoned, but he chose the small fabric sofa instead, sinking into the softness and resting his head against the back of it. He closed his eyes against the bright recessed spotlights glaring down from the ceiling and breathed deeply against the churning of his stomach.

His life was a mess, and he couldn't envision a way out of it.

"Sweetheart! How lovely to see you! I wasn't expecting you today. Is everything okay?" His mother wrapped her arms around his neck and held him tightly. On a subconscious level, he must've realised this was what he needed because he immediately sank into her embrace, closing his eyes against the relief only his parents could bring to him.

He inhaled her scent, the same perfume his father bought her for every occasion, the one she loved so much. Pulling back, he smiled. "I'm all right. Tough day at work, that's all."

She gave him the look only parents could master when they knew their children were not telling the whole truth and patted his cheek. "We have jacket potatoes for dinner if you're joining us."

"That would be great, thanks." He hung up his coat and slipped off his shoes, the motions of his youth as automatic as ever.

"Go sit with your father in the living room. I'll bring you a drink."

"I can grab one—"

"Go sit." She pointed, and he went. He knew not to argue with that tone.

He entered the large room to the quiet conversation of his dad's favourite station coming through the radio. "Hey, Dad."

"Samuel." Charles Walker rose from his armchair and pulled him into a hug. "Glad to have you here.

How are you doing?" His dad cupped his neck as he always did when he knew something was bothering him.

"Long day. I thought I'd come to see you both before the Friday madness."

Charles laughed. "Yes, madness is right."

"From your side, Charles, but from mine, everything is going swimmingly," his mother teased as she entered with two mugs of steaming liquid.

Even the scent of tea was restorative to a degree, and Samuel felt his muscles begin to unwind, coupled with his parents' company.

"That's because you have Max on your side, Catherine. He is enthusiastic about all the minor details. I'm dealing with Trent, who doesn't care about anything apart from getting to the moment when he can marry Max."

Samuel grinned, understanding exactly what they meant. Max was an interior designer, so creating beautiful events was his job and his passion, but Trent didn't care about the details; he just wanted rings on their fingers.

They spoke some more about the minor details that still needed to be completed, then his mother vanished into the kitchen to finish dinner, waving away Samuel's offer of help. It had been instilled in each one of their children they should take part in the creation of what they would be eating, and each had been taught how to cook despite Trent's lack of ability.

"How are things at work?"

Samuel sighed. "They'd be better if Gregory wasn't there and if Milton stopped visiting."

Nodding, his father rested his chin on his thumb and worried his bottom lip with his finger. "There's not much you can do about Gregory, but Milton shouldn't be there. Can't you ask someone to refuse him access?"

"I have, but Gregory allows him to come and go despite Milton not working there." Samuel set his empty cup on the coffee table, being sure to use a coaster to avoid his mother's wrath.

"If he's harassing you…"

Samuel shook his head slowly. "It's tedious to deal with him. He behaves as if he has a chance of us getting back together, and it's not happening." He stared at the fireplace, not seeing it, and rubbed at his head. He couldn't see a way out of Milton being part of his life, however brief it may be each week. The guy probably spent more time with Samuel now than he did when they were married.

"Do you have a headache?"

The voice startled him, and he blinked rapidly to get his bearings. "Yeah, a little."

"Let me get you some paracetamol before dinner." His father gripped his shoulder and left the room, leaving Samuel with the company of the radio, which was playing some instrumental piano music. Unwilling to be left with his thoughts any longer, he shuffled to the kitchen but paused when he heard the hushed voices of his parents. He knew from experience eavesdropping was not polite, but he couldn't resist.

"—little Charles would've loved being part of this family," his father said.

"He would've. I can't believe it's been over forty-five years since he died."

"Samuel might have found life a little easier if he hadn't been the eldest—"

"What?" There was no way his parents had kept a secret like that. They weren't like that. They had always been open about everything and had expected their children to be too.

They both turned as his voice called through the large space. His father swallowed hard and stepped forward. "Samuel—"

"Tell me I didn't hear what I thought I did?" Samuel couldn't trust his own hearing at that moment. "That you didn't…" He couldn't finish the sentence. His hands shook as he stretched and clenched them. In the back of his mind, he knew that many people didn't like talking about a loss of a child, but why wouldn't his parents tell their children at least? Especially when it affected their lives as well.

"I'm sorry, Samuel. You were never supposed to find out," his mother said, coming to a stop in front of him and grasping his forearm gently. "It was a long time ago, and we thought it was best for him to be…" She trailed off.

"Hidden? Why the hell wouldn't you tell us about having an older brother? You've hidden this for…over forty-five years?" His breathing increased. What other secrets have they kept from him?

"He was living on in our memories, Samuel. We didn't want you getting upset about missing out on a brother."

"How could you do that to us?" He turned to his parents, whose expressions had become pained.

"We thought it was the best cour—"

"That wouldn't fly in court, Dad," Samuel bit out. His heart raced and sweat beaded on his skin.

"I know you're angry, son, but we're not in court now."

"It doesn't make a difference." His voice cracked. "How can I trust you to tell me the truth now that I know you've kept this from me?" He pulled away from his mother and strode down the hallway to the entrance, quickly sliding on his shoes and coat.

"Samuel, please!"

He shook his head, trying to dislodge the buzzing sound that had taken up residence. Opening the door, he paused and said, "I'll be here as planned on Friday." The door closed behind him, and he climbed into his car, pointing it towards home.

None of the journey registered with him, and he soon found himself standing inside his entryway, staring at the floor. He removed his coat and shoes, then wandered to the fridge for something to dim the noises in his head. Three bottles of beer called his name, and he took them to the sofa set under the long expanse of windows. Sitting with his back against the arm and his elbow resting along the back, he stared out across the dark and dismal lamp-lit landscape of Cambridge as he made his way through the alcohol.

He had never believed his parents would lie to him, to them. It went to show no one knew people at all and only saw what others wanted them to. Except when a lawyer was involved, and then all the gruesome details of their family life was spread out before them. As a lawyer, Samuel should've known better, but he believed his family was as perfect as it could get.

How wrong could he have been?

The lights of the city winked out one by one as he sat, working his way through the thoughts and feelings tumbling around inside him. As midnight hit and the streetlamps began to dim, he sighed and stood, stretching his arms above his head. He stumbled his way to the bedroom, uncaring of his need for a shower. Without even removing his clothes, he lay down and pulled the duvet over him.

He had to get through one more day, and then he could relax. For a short time, at least.

Samuel stared at his desk and the papers littering its surface, a couple curling slightly in the gentle breeze coming from somewhere. Although the air was cold, he didn't mind. He was too deep in his thoughts to be bothered by the temperature, especially with the heating negating most of it. Swallowing hard, he grimaced and picked up several pages before turning his gaze to them once more, trying to decipher the information written across them.

The missing Benedict case information had been waiting for him when he'd arrived at work that morning, and he had spent the few hours he'd already been there trying to figure out what they said.

A cup of coffee appeared before him, and he followed the steam's path until he met Maggie's gaze.

"Thought you might need a pick-me-up." She gave him a small smile.

He cleared his throat. "Thanks."

"Anything I can help with?" She indicated the files around him.

Samuel shook his head slowly. "No, I need to get through it, so I know where I stand when I come back on Monday."

"All right. Well, you know where I am if you do."

"Thanks, Maggie."

She left the office, closing his door behind him and cutting the breeze off. Samuel needed to get rid of the thoughts in his head, the reminders of what he'd found out the previous evening. If he could do that and get through the work before him, he would be able to finish on time and enjoy his few days off. Closing his eyes, he inhaled deeply, rotating his neck to loosen the cramped muscles.

When he exhaled, he opened his eyes and focused on the paperwork. Brushing everything aside, apart from what was happening with the Benedicts, he began making handwritten notes for Maggie to type up later that day or the following day, depending on her workload.

Two hours later, his stomach grumbled enough to knock his concentration. Sitting back in his chair, he dropped his pen on the table, a small drop of ink spilling where it landed. Samuel threaded his fingers through his hair and tugged as he closed his eyes. The minute he stopped focusing on the case files, he remembered, and heaviness permeated his body again.

Sighing, he stood, grabbing his jacket from the back of his chair. After telling Maggie he was going to fetch his lunch, he wandered down the street to his usual lunchtime haunt, his hands deep inside his pockets.

The scent of the bakery reached him before he

saw the building, which was nestled around the corner from his office. As he entered Sweet Tooth, he inhaled the intoxicating scent, smiling briefly at the manager, Audrey. His order never changed—a cheese and ham toastie, a packet of crisps, a cake of some sort and a hot chocolate—so the barista nodded at him, and he stepped to the side to wait for his food to be ready.

Samuel leaned against the wall, staring out the window. He needed to get himself together; otherwise, the day he was supposed to be spending with his family would be a nightmare. Every member of his family wanted to know the other's business. Secrets never lasted long. At least, he'd thought they didn't. His parents had proved the statement a lie.

"Samuel."

He flicked his gaze to the counter and saw his order was ready. Swiping his card over the reader, he paid, waved goodbye and strolled back to the office.

The idea his parents had kept something so… monumental a secret was confusing, but he was also bitterly disappointed in them. Before, Samuel had thought they had hung the moon. Now, he wasn't sure what to think, and it was wearing him out.

His heart ached with what they must have gone through. Were they still feeling the same way? Samuel would have to talk to them eventually, but it would probably have to wait until after the wedding. Despite the circumstances of his finding out, he refused to ruin Trent's marital vows.

The afternoon went quickly once he got back into the mindset of work and brushed aside everything else. Nausea and heartburn were his constant companion, but he managed to finish the work he needed to and only had to stay an hour later than usual. He'd already sent Maggie home, but he'd emailed her his thanks, a list of what had been completed and needed completing, and good wishes for the weekend.

Letting himself into his quiet apartment, he resumed his position on the sofa, watching the city begin to power down. The night was clearer, which meant there would probably be a frost in the morning. He made a mental note to leave enough time to scrape the ice off his car before he had to meet Trent at their parents' house in the morning.

Unable to get up the energy to cook, he called for a takeaway, eating the whole carton of chicken chow mein when it came. Washing it down with beer, he, once more, tried to figure out what had gone wrong. Why had they not thought to tell them? Why couldn't he have been brought up knowing he had another brother?

He shook his head and cleared everything away, then drifted down the hallway to his bedroom, where he undressed. Catching his reflection in his mirror, he eyed his body. He'd let himself go when Milton had left, and not taking care of himself had resulted in flabby areas all over his body. Running his hands over his skin, he watched as it rippled with the movement. He frowned, shook his head and climbed into bed.

There was no one to see him, so what did it matter? He was alone and always would be.

CHAPTER THREE

ERIC

The comfortable large armchair-style seat within first-class was nothing Eric wasn't familiar with, but it always held a different meaning whenever he was heading home. Cambridge would always be home, regardless of who he was, how much money he made and how other people treated him.

He no longer lived with Emily and hadn't for many years, but the city he'd been born in would forever be where his roots were. That might change if Emily or Ethan ever left the city, but he'd cross that bridge when he came to it.

His headphones were blocking out the noise of the passengers around him, playing some guitar music into his ears and soothing him as it always did. His gaze roamed across the scene outside his window, which was practically nothing, as they were around thirty-five thousand feet in the sky at that moment.

The director had complained when Eric had asked for a week off to attend his friends' wedding, but he'd agreed after a little persuasion. It was always the same; they argued to get their own way when, in fact, they could easily move onto a different scene to account for the changes. Directors usually kicked up a fuss because they could. Eric, on the other hand, hardly ever asked for things to be changed for *his* benefit. He allowed others to get better amenities and timeframes because it didn't matter to him. There was no one on this side of the world he spent any huge amount of time with, except Vaughn, and most of the time, he was on some project or other, so they had to communicate via phone anyway.

Rubbing a hand over his chest when his thoughts returned to his siblings, he thought about the conversation he'd had before he'd needed to board the plane. It had been around eight in the morning for Eric, which was Emily's lunchtime, he'd been told. He laughed when she'd brought a large sandwich into view and proceeded to devour it as they talked. Ethan had been at work but had left a message to say he'd be there when Eric arrived that evening.

Crossing the Atlantic was a chore he only ever minded when he wasn't homeward bound. Re-situating the headphones, he lost himself in the music he'd brought with him and a brain-training puzzle book. Before he knew it, the crew advised lunch was ready.

By the time he landed, he was weary but happy, and when he saw Ethan and Emily waiting for him in the arrivals area, he grinned and pulled them into a hug.

"God, I've missed you!" he said, breathing in their unique scents—Ethan smelled of his cologne, Emily of Lavender.

"You're certainly a sight for sore eyes. Are you eating enough?" Emily said, a crease forming between her eyebrows.

Eric laughed. "I have no choice in the matter. My chef makes me what I need, and I eat it without complaint. I do what I'm told."

Ethan snorted. "I'll believe it when I see it."

Eric shoved him and turned to the carousel to grab his bags. Being home for a week, he had only brought minimal amounts because he had clothes at his home here, but it still filled one suitcase, especially with the gifts he'd brought.

The journey from the airport to home was informative.

"So, Max told Trent they were going to Zakynthos because they could blame Zak for it if the place was awful," Emily said, shaking her head. "He's such a menace."

Max and Trent had been together for a year, but they may as well have been together for life. When Trent had proposed last year, Max had jumped at the chance. Despite the quick wedding, no one batted an eyelid because they were so well matched.

"I can see the merit of the idea," Ethan mused, eyes trained through the windscreen on the road ahead of them.

As they chatted, Eric took the first deep breath he'd had in months. He didn't have to be anything other than a brother here. Not an actor, not a celebrity, not a pin-up, just Eric. It was something he was coming to wish for more and more often, confirming that his thoughts of leaving the spotlight might be the right ones. He rubbed a hand against his chest while a little voice inside reminded him of a big part of his life that he still hid from those he loved more than anything.

Being a Daddy was part of him, but he wasn't sure how his siblings would react to the idea; therefore, he'd kept it quiet. As more time passed from his realisation of what he needed in his life to the time when he should tell Ethan and Emily, it got harder and harder.

"Are you hiring a bodyguard for the ceremony?" Emily twisted in her seat to look back at him.

Eric scrunched up his nose. "I don't want to, but I need to speak with Max and Trent. If they can vouch for everyone, I might leave it. I don't want my presence to overshadow their wedding. I'd prefer to stay away."

"No, you can't do that. They want you there. I'm sure everyone will be on their best behaviour." Emily smiled, but it didn't reach her eyes. She was worried.

His heart sank. "I'll call Max later and have a chat. If he's happy for me to have a bodyguard, I'll sort one out."

Her shoulders lowered, and he was glad to have been able to stop some of her worries.

"Home, sweet, home," Ethan said, turning the wheel.

The car came to a stop outside his house, and Eric stared out the window at it, peace flowing through him.

"I've missed being here," he whispered to himself, his siblings having already exited the car. He followed suit and reached his arms to the sky, interlinking his fingers and rocking from one side to the other to stretch out his spine.

"I came by and checked it out before coming to fetch you. The fridge has been stocked, and everything has been cleaned within an inch of its life from what I can see." Ethan shuddered.

Eric chuckled. "You think blowing the dust from a shelf makes it clean, so I don't know if I trust you, but I do know those I employ. It will be perfect, but even if it wasn't, I'm home. I don't care how it looks."

He took the five steps up to his wraparound porch and unlocked the front door. His house was modest by celebrity standards. Sitting on the outskirts of Cambridge, surrounded by a large acreage of grass, his five-bedroom detached property was still far too big for him, but he'd wanted something he and Ethan and Emily could retreat to if the moment required it. With him being the famous actor that he was, life was unpredictable, and he'd ensured this property was as secure as it could be.

It looked like a farmhouse from an old black and white movie from the outside, but inside, every modern convenience you could wish for could be found. He refused to buy something he would never use, so extras like a TV that rose from behind a fireplace and built-in speakers throughout every room had been wiped off the plans at the beginning. Home comforts were all he wanted.

And someone to share it with.

The morning of the wedding dawned bright, and Eric found himself looking forward to seeing everyone. The previous day had been spent arranging a new suit because the one he'd left in the wardrobe and had planned on wearing had been too small for him. He'd obviously bulked up more since he'd last worn it.

After his brief conversation with Max, he'd decided against hiring a bodyguard, much to Emily's disapproval, but when he'd explained there would be at least four police officers, someone trained in evasive manoeuvres and several lawyers present, she had relented. They might not be able to assist much if something did happen, but it would certainly help.

The ceremony had been beautiful as was expected, and after, they all hustled to Crush, where Tom, the manager, had hired caterers to do a three-course meal for the reception. Ethan told him Max had insisted on mixing family and friends so each would get to know new people; therefore, Eric had been seated with several people he knew, but Samuel was new to him.

"You must be on Trent's side of the family because you bear a striking resemblance to him," Eric mused, leaning back in his chair and tilting his head at Samuel.

The man was handsome, to say the least, a lot older than he was but distinguished. He was probably in his forties, but Eric couldn't decide whether early or late. He had a rounded figure and face with short salt and pepper hair and beard. His eyes were hazel, although they seemed …empty.

Samuel nodded slowly. "Yes, I'm his older brother."

Eric held out his hand and twitched when a spark flew between them. He chuckled. "Must've brushed against something to make static, sorry." He rubbed his fingers against his thumb after they parted from the handshake, the tingle still noticeable.

Samuel gave a small smile and looked back at the glass he'd been rotating on the table. The corners of Eric's mouth quirked up as a slight flush stained the man's cheekbones. He hadn't expected such a confident-looking person to appear so timid in his demeanour. It was…endearing.

"Would you like some water," he asked, grasping the glass water jug and lifting it over to Samuel's glass, cupping a hand underneath it to catch any stray condensation drips.

Samuel cleared his throat. "Thank you." He stopped spinning the glass and held it steady.

"You're welcome." Eric filled his own glass and replaced the jug in the centre of the table again.

Seeing Samuel appearing uncertain, he decided to take his focus off the guy and catch up with Zak, who had been a friend for several years. "Zak, how's business?" He saw Samuel's shoulders lower from the corner of his eye.

"Yeah, good, thanks. I have a new partner in crime starting next month, hopefully. Colton is from New York and has recently moved over here." Zak pointed the guy out at a table two away from them. "Business is booming as they say. Can't wish for more than that."

Eric had been kept up to date with what had been happening around Cambridge, so he knew Zak had been given full custody of his son the previous month after a troublesome court hearing, but Eric wouldn't bring it up. The day was supposed to be a happy day.

"No, definitely a good thing. I'll have to get you booked in for some furniture for my house, or you'll be fully booked!" He chuckled and held up his glass.

"I always have time for friends."

They were interrupted by the first course being brought to their table and servers asking for drink orders. Once they were settled again, Analise said, "I could get used to being the one served instead of doing the serving." She grinned.

"Don't be silly, Analise. You would never give up working at the bar," Zak said.

Analise tilted her head from one side to the other as if thinking, then shook her head and scrunched her nose. "You're right. I'd never last a day."

The table's occupants laughed, and the comment even garnered a small smile from Samuel. Eric thought himself pretty good at discerning people's body language, and if he'd had to guess, he would've said Samuel was feeling like a fish out of water. He held the bread basket out to him.

"Would you like some bread?"

Samuel fumbled with his cutlery as he nodded and reached for one, but Eric beat him to it, choosing a nice crusty roll with the tongs and placing it on his side plate. Without showing anything amiss, he checked

Samuel's reaction surreptitiously. Eric didn't know why he felt the need to 'care' for the man, but he looked so lost and forlorn. He had a feeling Samuel was fresh out of a relationship.

"Thank you," came a soft voice.

Eric glanced over at Samuel and smiled. "You're welcome—" He inhaled rapidly and swallowed back the words that wanted to leave his mouth. The first time in a long time, he'd nearly slipped up. What was it about *this* guy? There was no way he'd be into the lifestyle. Shaking his head minutely, he changed course with the conversation, "What is it you do, Samuel?"

Samuel finished his mouthful, sipped his water and said, "I'm a lawyer. A family lawyer."

"And a damn good one," Zak said with a smile.

Eric flinched when Samuel spoke, eyes downcast to his plate, jaw tight. What the hell had they been thinking by putting him next to a goddamn lawyer? His gaze scanned the room until he found Emily, who was already staring in his direction with a look of apology on her face.

"I didn't know," she mouthed with a shake of her head. He assumed she meant that she didn't know he would be sat with Samuel.

Eric gave her a small smile in return and unclenched his white-knuckled grip from around his cutlery. Keeping his gaze lowered, he ate his food mechanically as conversation flowed around the table. Their plates were taken away, and their drinks refilled.

"I'm assuming you don't like lawyers from the scowl that has been on your face for the last few minutes." Samuel's lowered voice came as a surprise. Eric hadn't thought he'd been particularly obvious about his dislike, but if he was a lawyer, then he was good at body language, no doubt.

Eric tried to neutralise his expression as he'd been taught in acting lessons, though it was difficult. "I have my issues. Nothing personal."

Samuel chuckled softly, the sound vibrating through Eric. "Nothing personal, he says. It's only my life's work. Helping families to get the best result from their situation."

Eric scoffed. "Depends which side you're on, I suppose."

"What do you mean?"

"Who do you represent? The good side or the bad side? Or both depending on the situation?" Eric felt his lips pinch, his teeth clenching, and a headache brewing at his temples.

"I represent those I believe have been wronged. I believe I have enough experience to see the situation as a whole and decide whether to represent the people or not. I don't always win, I grant you that, but I try my damnedest."

"And what happens to those who are thwarted?

The good guys who are dragged through the mud and hedge and forest until they have nothing left?"

"I continue helping them until there are no other avenues left."

Eric stared at the man who was beginning to shake the foundations of his preconceived notions. The man who Eric had thought was meek and vulnerable was, in fact, strong and sure when it came to his work. Inhaling through his nose, Eric nodded.

"Eric! So, can you tell us any juicy tidbits about your work?" Analise asked, eyes sparkling as she leaned her elbows on the table. She winked in Eric's direction, so he assumed she had heard part of their conversation and was changing the subject.

He grinned his charming, media-appropriate smile and shook his head, wagging his finger in her direction. "You should know by now, missy, I don't spill anyone's secrets. No matter how hard you try to get them out of me." She was always—jokingly—trying to get him to tell her all about his colleagues and what they got up to behind closed doors. If she only looked a little closer, she would notice a secret being kept right under her nose. He pushed the thought aside.

As the second course arrived, conversation flowed smoothly again. Eric would have to remember to thank Analise for her diversion. Although he was still tense and annoyed at being sat next to a lawyer, he could play the part as if he were filming a movie. His whole career was based on whether he could fool the audience.

There was a short break after the second course, and Emily made her way over to him, dragging him to the bar stools. He ordered a beer for himself and a gin and tonic for Emily, then focused on her. "Go on, say it."

"He's not a bad guy, Eric. Not every lawyer is the same as the ones our parents used. That lawyer was an asshole, and I still believe he was chosen for that particular reason. Samuel is a nice guy. Don't tar him with the same brush; otherwise, parties and the like will become difficult." She rested her hand on his, squeezing gently.

He sighed, his shoulders lowering. Glancing over at his table, he saw Samuel staring at him before he quickly transferred his gaze to his lap. Eric lifted an eyebrow, unsure of how to interpret the look.

"Okay. I don't have to like it, but I hear what you're saying." He smiled. "Ever the peacekeeper."

"I have to be the peacekeeper, or else my two darling brothers would have killed each other by now." She laughed.

"True."

Eric kissed her cheek, and they weaved their way back to their respective tables, Eric sitting next to Samuel once more. He turned to him. "I apologise. I have…issues with lawyers from past experiences, as you probably know from the media being how it is. I shouldn't have taken it out on you, though. So, I'm sorry."

Samuel's mouth twitched in a cute move. "She gave you a spanking, did she?"

Eric choked on the drink he'd taken and grabbed a napkin to cover his mouth. "What?"

Samuel rolled his lips inwards and closed his eyes, his cheeks flushing with colour. "I meant…Emily…gave you a talking to." He refused to meet Eric's gaze.

Recovered, Eric grinned. "That she did. No spanking involved. I save that for non-family members."

Withholding a chuckle when Samuel's wide eyes met his finally, Eric teased his tongue at the corner of his mouth, watching as the man's gaze followed the motion, and his Adam's apple bobbed. Interesting.

The third course arrived—a vast array of desserts—and he watched as Samuel dallied over the choices. When he picked up the cheesecake, Eric chose a strawberry trifle and two bowls of fruit and placed one by the side of Samuel's plate.

He saw Samuel pause, then continue, moving from the cake to the fruit without complaint. Something inside Eric expanded at the sight of something he'd given the man next to him being eaten. The only thing better would be if he was feeding the boy…man. What was he thinking? Eric closed his eyes for a second, then refocused on his food. There was no way this guy would be interested in anything like what Eric needed. Although Samuel might be a fun distraction, there was no chance of it happening when he'd already insulted him.

By the time the food had been finished and the tables rearranged to give space for a dance floor, Eric had pushed his thoughts aside and watched and listened as the people who loved the married couple talked about their knowledge of them. Max's sisters had some great information that could be used as bribery if one were inclined.

"Earth to Eric?"

He snapped his gaze to his left and saw his brother staring at him with his eyebrows raised. "What?"

"If you stare at the guy anymore, you're going to end up with a restraining order." Ethan snorted.

"What are you talking about?"

Ethan cackled, holding onto Eric's shoulder as he bent at the waist. "Samuel. You're either glaring daggers at him, or your mouth is hung open catching flies."

Eric shoved Ethan away from him, earning him a couple of laughs from around him. "Shut up." He made sure to keep his gaze from tracking the man after that—mostly.

The music lowered as the night wore on, and although Eric was enjoying himself, he was also exhausted. His eyes were scratchy and undoubtedly bloodshot, and his vision was blurring. He needed sleep. Circling the room, he said goodbye to a few people, then the newlyweds and his siblings before heading out into the fresh air. He peeked out the door before fully emerging, making sure the street was fairly devoid of people so that if he was recognised, it wouldn't cause a mass swarm. His taxi waited by the kerb, and his hand was on the door handle when his name was called. Turning, he saw Samuel walking towards him.

"I know Trent was a bit inebriated when you said goodbye, but I know he also wanted to thank you for being here. He'd said to me more than once before today that you were worried about taking the light off them. Neither of them would've cared if you did. Thank you for making their day even better."

Eric stared at him, his heart beating erratically as Samuel drew closer. He leaned down to the taxi driver and told him to set the timer going before resting back against the vehicle, crossing his arms.

"I find you truly intriguing," he said. Samuel rubbed the back of his neck and darted his gaze anywhere but where Eric was. "Look at me," he said softly.

Samuel's focus came to rest on him, and Eric's body tingled, energy flowing through him. He was surprised to find himself wanting this guy even when he knew it was a bad idea, especially with who they both were. Eric reached a hand forward, running his finger down the collar of Samuel's suit jacket until he tugged on it and lifted it over the shirt collar, then smoothed his hand down the lapel.

"That's better," he whispered.

Samuel cleared his throat. "I'll let you go." He stepped back, and Eric immediately grabbed his arms as he stumbled over some loose stones behind him.

"Careful now, Sam. We don't want you to be injured." He kept his voice low and soothing, not wanting to freak the guy out, although he couldn't help the nickname that came out.

Roaming his gaze across the dimply cheeked man in front of him, he took in more details: arched, bushy eyebrows; a bulbous nose; straight, white teeth and full pink lips, all enticingly set within a slightly overweight but fascinating face. He couldn't help whatever this was between them—because he was sure Samuel felt something too—but he couldn't act on it. It would be too easy for his secret to be revealed, and Samuel was too close to home for that to happen.

Ensuring he had his balance, Eric squeezed his biceps and stepped back. "Thank you for the company tonight. I appreciate it. And once again, I'm sorry for how I acted."

Samuel inhaled and waved his hand, dismissing

Eric's words. "Don't worry. I've been called worse things."

Unable to help himself, Eric lifted a hand to Samuel's face and ran a finger underneath his eyes. "You look tired. Make sure you rest well this weekend. No working because no doubt you were planning to." He wagged the finger at him, giving Samuel a smirk when he flushed so beautifully. "Relax this weekend. For me. Enjoy the time to yourself."

He pulled back, and he saw Samuel's hand twitch as if to stop him from retreating. It was cold out there, though, and Samuel had no coat. "Go back inside and get warm. You don't want to get a cold or miss any shenanigans that might be going on."

They both laughed, breaking the tension, and Samuel nodded. "Nice to meet you, Eric."

"You, too."

He waited until Samuel had entered the bar after one more wave in Eric's direction before entering the taxi. "Thank you for waiting." He gave his address and watched the dimmed streetlights flickering as they passed. The traffic was non-existent that time of night.

Samuel was an enigma Eric didn't have time to figure out. But he wanted to, and that was a problem in and of itself. How could Eric look past what Samuel did as a career when those types of lawyers were the ones who had profited and helped his parents profit from Eric's childhood career? And on top of that, they tried to drag his name through the mud and take him for every penny he had. He believed himself to be an intelligent man, but the fluttering in his stomach had him feeling like a kid again.

It was both a nice sensation and a scary one.

CHAPTER FOUR

SAMUEL

The banging on his front door had him jumping with how loud and continuous it was. He scurried to it, flinging it open.

"What...?" He stopped, staring at Trent with a frown. "What are you doing here?"

Still tanned from their honeymoon in Greece despite having been home for five weeks, Trent barged past him into the apartment, followed by a smirking Max. The smirk didn't bode well for Samuel.

"We're taking you to a party," Trent declared.

"What?" Samuel shook his head, his forehead creased with confusion.

"You know, a party. The thing where you celebrate something amazing. The thing you never like to do." Trent quirked an eyebrow.

Samuel sighed, placing his hands on his hips. "I

know what a party is, Trent. And you know I hardly ever go to them."

"I know." Trent grinned. "But this one is special. It's a party and a Bank Holiday celebration. We're having music and a barbecue."

Max cut him off, "Basically, it's Noah's birthday, and they've invited you to come, and we are here to pick you up. So, go and get changed because we're here until you do it, and if we miss the party, Zak will be pissed because he has everything set up at his house."

Now the smirk made sense. Samuel flicked his gaze between them, seeing the stubbornness, then closed his eyes and shook his head, pivoting and striding to his bedroom. He knew there was no chance of him getting anything done if he didn't attend the party. Trent would be pissed at him, and they would both do as they'd said and annoy the hell out of him for the next few hours.

Besides, a short break would do him good. He could go, say hi, stay for a drink and head home again. Short but sweet.

When they arrived, the party was just beginning. There were already a few of the usual crew there, and while Samuel didn't interact with them much, they still asked after him and his work, which was nice of them.

Once a few more people had arrived, Emily gathered everyone together.

"So, to make sure everyone gets time to spend with everyone and no one is left looking after the kids all day, we've designated 'The Pit' to be covered by two adults on a rotating basis. The list is here, so check who you're with and what time, then have fun!"

'The Pit' was Zak's enclosed back garden that had been turned into a creche of sorts. Samuel was a bit worried about it as he was not good with children, but when he realised he'd been paired with Tom—who had two kids of his own—he relaxed a little. His decision to make this a quick visit had turned into longer than anticipated.

Several hours later, he was pushing Dane on the swing, glancing out of the corner of his eyes at the man who had dominated his thoughts for the past seven weeks. Eric Clarke.

"He's managing to get back here more and more often, which is great for Ethan and Emily," Tom said, and Samuel barely kept in his flinch. He hadn't realised Tom was so close to him.

"Yeah, it's good. They must miss each other."

"At least, he's happy doing what he's doing. We can't ask for more, can we?"

Samuel stopped the swing when Dane wanted to get out, glad for the chance to change the subject, then lifted the little guy from the seat, setting him on the ground. With a smile, Samuel watched as he toddled off as three-year-olds do to play with Janie, Asher's seven-year-old niece. Momentarily free, he picked up his water bottle and sat at the picnic table, leaning his forearms on the surface and listening to the laughter and hum of conversation around him. Considering he hadn't wanted to attend the party originally, he was content to be amongst those he thought of as friends, distant friends, nonetheless.

"Sammel!"

He glanced beside him and saw Dane scrambling into the chair next to him and helped him to get situated. Dane grabbed at the stack of colouring books, tipping them into an avalanche, which Samuel stopped with a laugh.

"Careful there. You'll be flattened under all that," he said.

Dane pulled a book towards him and picked up a crayon. "Boo," he said, holding up a red crayon.

"That's red, little guy, but good try." Samuel smoothed a hand down Dane's back, enjoying himself despite having been worried about not being capable of looking after the kids. Kids were kids, after all. It didn't matter. It had been slightly under twenty years since Trent's kids were young, nothing changed when it came down to the basic things.

"Hey, Dane. Can I do some colouring too?"

Eric's voice had a physical effect on Samuel. His stomach fluttered, his cheeks heated, and he blinked rapidly as the vision that covered many tabloids came into view. The movie star looked as at home in jeans and a polo shirt as he did in the tuxedo Samuel had seen him wearing in one of the articles he'd caught online the other week. His jet-black hair was short at the sides and longer on top, allowing him to style it differently—or so Samuel had seen from those photos —but that day, it was tousled and blowing gently in the breeze. His two-day facial hair growth was sexy as sin, but Samuel would not admit it no matter who asked.

When Eric sat opposite him, he instinctively clutched his hands around his bottle, the plastic arguing with a crackle until he softened his hold.

"Aren't you going to join us, Samuel?" Eric asked while opening a colouring book to a picture of a dog. "I love dogs. What colour shall I use?" Eric didn't seem to be asking anyone, in particular, so he kept quiet, watching the man's elegant fingers search through the different options.

"Blue," he found himself saying.

Eric lifted his eyebrows, glanced at him and selected a light blue. Samuel couldn't help himself and reached across to grab a darker blue, holding it out. His hand trembled. He had no idea what had come over him; he didn't usually care what colours people used. Swapping the colours with a small smile, Eric began slowly making short strokes with the crayon. Samuel was transfixed.

Janie came over to join them, taking a seat next to Eric. "That looks cool, Eric!"

"Thank you, sweetheart. Are you having fun?"

"Yes, thank you. Uncle Asher says I'm good at colouring because I stay inside the lines."

"I've never been good at staying inside the lines. There is one little bit that always goes over," Eric said, sending a twinkling-eyed smile over to Samuel. "But do you want to know what I do?"

Janie leaned closer and whispered, "What?"

"I get a different colour and colour on the other side of the line. It hides what I did, but don't tell anyone. It's my secret."

Janie's eyes were wide as she nodded.

Samuel felt his mouth twitch, and he firmed his lips to avoid it showing, though if the look he received from Eric was any indication, he hadn't succeeded.

A colouring book was put in front of him with a raised eyebrow from Eric, but Samuel ignored it and him. He tilted his head and studied the occupants of the table as they talked and coloured, barely taking their eyes off their pages as the conversation flowed between them. The book in front of him called his name, but he was forty-three, for god's sake. Why would he feel the need to colour like a child?

To keep his hands busy, he picked up the book, flicking through the pages until he saw a horse. A slow smile crept onto his face, but he carried on until he came to the end. Then he flicked through them again, the horse once more coming into view. When he did it for the third time, he stopped, resting the open book with the horse in view, his palm caressing the smooth paper.

Leaning forward, his elbows on the table, he stared at the vast array of colours within the box, but a light brown caught his eye. Biting his lip, he scanned his surroundings, seeing no one was paying any attention to him, and reached for the crayon. The wax felt warm to the touch, and he rolled it in his fingers for a short time, frowning down at it.

He had never been interested in colouring before, more of a board games or card games kind of person, especially solitaire and chess. However, he realized the monotony of the moves helped him to relax. Colouring could be the same thing.

Putting crayon to paper was harder than he imagined it would be. He found he didn't want to ruin the picture if he put the colours in the wrong places.

"It doesn't matter if you go wrong, Samuel. You can choose a different picture to colour if you do," Janie said.

The words made him self-conscious, but he realised Eric was helping Dane off the seat next to him, and Samuel hadn't even realised he'd moved.

"Thank you, Janie," he answered quietly.

Knowing Eric was no longer at the table made his

decision easier. He rested the crayon on the paper and lightly moved it back and forth, following the curve of the drawing. As he concentrated on the picture and choosing the colours he needed, he forgot about everything else. He needed yellow for the mane and tail, a dark brown for the hooves, and he was going to use a bright red for the saddle with blue tassels on it.

Becoming aware of his surroundings again once his picture was coloured in, he noticed there was only him and Eric left in the garden area. He glanced over at a bark of laughter and saw the kids enjoying being chased around the large grassy area by some of the other adults. Flicking his gaze to Eric, he immediately lowered his head, fiddling with the crayon, and felt his cheeks flush.

"Sorry. I got carried away."

Eric crossed his arms and leaned them on the table. "There's nothing to be sorry for. Everyone needs time to relax and regroup before continuing in the real world." The man wore a small smile and an open expression of being unruffled as if he didn't care that Samuel had spent however long it was colouring a horse.

"You have a good eye for colour," Eric said, his forefinger tracing the head of the horse. The touch felt tangible to Samuel.

He cleared his throat. "Thanks."

"So, tell me, Samuel, what do you do when you're

not working?" He rested his chin in his palm and pierced Samuel with his gaze.

Samuel linked his hands over the top of the picture and swallowed hard, his stomach churning with… something. "I, um, play chess with one of those automated opponents."

"Oh, yes! I know what you mean. I haven't played chess for years."

How Samuel knew Eric was smiling, he had no idea, but he could hear it in his voice. "I also like solitaire and reading."

"Solitary pursuits then?" Samuel didn't know what to say to the observation, so he kept quiet. "What book are you reading at the moment?"

"Well, I enjoy subjects that help me understand what other people are saying without them verbalising it. It helps with my job to know if they are hiding something." He winced when he finished talking and chanced a glance up at Eric's face, sure to see a grimace, but Eric smiled.

"You like investigating," Eric surmised.

Samuel thought about it. "Yes. Being a lawyer is all about figuring things out from bits of information you've been given. It's like the pieces of a puzzle that needs to be fitted together without any picture reference to use to guide you."

"You mentioned something about figuring out

what people are telling you. Do you mean like body language tells and things?"

Samuel nodded, smiling as he got more excited to share his knowledge. "Yes. The TV programme *Lie To Me* is a good example. I find it fascinating how information can be gleaned from how people react, small twitches, whether they sweat, their eye movements, their breathing—it all adds up when you put it together, and sometimes, the story tells a completely different one than what came out of their mouths."

"What does mine tell you about me?" Eric sat back.

Samuel rubbed the back of his neck. "You don't want me to—"

"Yeah, I don't mind. Go ahead."

"Well," he took a breath, "you have slightly bloodshot eyes, you're blinking more rapidly than when I last met you, and you've rubbed your eyes several times, which makes me think you're tired. You can keep yourself still when you want to, but your eyes are always vigilant, often scanning the area around you with a slight tightening to the outer edges of your eyes." He paused, lowering his voice, "You don't like being in the spotlight despite your job description."

Eric tilted his head, a small smile playing around his lips. "Not bad." He nodded slowly, his gaze never leaving Samuel's. "I am tired. Jet lag is a bitch when you're flying from the US, and the minute I get used to the time zone here, it will be time for me to leave again."

"How long are you here for?" Samuel didn't know if he wanted the answer to the question.

"I leave on Tuesday."

"Not a long visit then."

"It's never long enough." Eric smiled, though Samuel saw through his words. The man suddenly sat upright, reaching for the colouring book Samuel had been using. "Can I have this?"

Samuel laughed self-consciously. "Why would you want a picture I coloured?"

"To go on my fridge."

He said the words so matter-of-factly Samuel had to think twice before dismissing his words as joking. He waved his hand. "If you wish."

"Thanks."

Watching as he tore the paper from the book, then carefully folded it up and placed it in his jeans pocket, Samuel felt the heat creeping into his cheeks again and ducked his head, rubbing a hand along his neck, which felt warm to the touch. He should've put some suncream on.

"Are you getting burnt? I know the sun isn't too warm today, but you look a little overheated. Let's get you in the shade." Eric stood, holding out his hand and crooking his fingers. Samuel couldn't resist his lure and followed suit, though he didn't take his hand.

They moved over to the shade of the house and took a seat.

After a few minutes of silence, Samuel asked something he'd always wondered, "What is it like being a famous movie star?"

He heard Eric sigh heavily. "There is a long answer and a short answer to that question." He huffed a laugh. "I'll give you the short version for now. The hours are long, the mornings are early, the nights are late, the people are…an acquired taste. Everything is much bigger and faster and harder…" Eric snorted, a hand covering his mouth, and Samuel couldn't help the sheer joy that flowed through him at the sound. "That sounds like a bad porno intro."

Samuel snorted and rolled his lips inwards to stop any other undignified noises from escaping.

Samuel threw the papers onto the table and sat back with a sigh, rubbing a hand over his face. He was supposed to be in court in an hour, and his brain wasn't cooperating. All he could think about was the interactions he had with Eric three days prior, especially the colouring. He hadn't been so calm in years, and…he couldn't interpret what else he felt, and that was bugging him as well. Usually, he was in tune with his thoughts; even if they were self-deprecating at times, he still acknowledged them.

He swivelled in his chair, knocking his—thankfully empty—mug to the floor with a soft thud. It didn't break, so he picked it up and moved it further over, then stood at the window and stared out across the landscape.

Running his hands over his head, he tried to figure himself out, but there was too much information bouncing around. Giving up, he returned to his desk and gathered the papers he needed.

Three hours later, he sagged into his chair and lowered his chin to his chest. The hearing had gone on longer than he'd expected, but the result was in his favour, so he couldn't complain.

"Oh, Samuel? I forgot to mention. A package came for you earlier, so I left it in your tray."

"Thanks, Maggie. You head off for lunch now before you get collared by someone to do something."

"Okay. I'll let you know when I'm back."

Samuel picked up the brown envelope and flipped it over, only seeing his name and the firm on it, which meant it had been hand-delivered. He pulled at the gummed opening and shook out the contents, pausing when the items were only partway out of the envelope.

Not thinking any more about it, he shoved it back and closed the envelope before opening his drawer and putting it away. He couldn't consider the implications now; he had work to do. That proved harder than he thought. The image of the contents called to him as the afternoon wore on, and he flinched when there was a knock at the door.

"Come in!" he called.

"Hey. I thought I'd come and see how my big brother is." Luke entered, closing the door behind him.

Samuel stood with a smile and veered around his desk, bringing Luke in for a hug. "Hi. Everything okay?"

"These lawyer-types, always seeing problems where there are none." Luke grinned, and it brightened Samuel's soul. Luke had always seen himself as less than the rest of them, but he was so much more than he gave himself credit for. Luckily, Casey was helping with that. "I was concerned about you the other day. You were a little out of sorts."

Samuel guided him to the small armchairs and sat with a sigh. "Do you see me as the guy who goes to birthday parties?"

"Granted, but you seemed to be having fun with Eric."

He felt himself blushing again and cursed at his inability to hide his embarrassment. "It's strange. He's so much more than I was expecting him to be."

Luke tilted his head, and a small smile formed. "You like him."

Samuel laughed. "He's a movie star. What's not to like?"

"You know what I mean."

He stood, pacing to the window. "It doesn't matter. I won't ever go through a relationship again. I've had enough of expecting one thing and receiving another."

"That's no way to live, Samuel."

"It's my way, Luke." He stared at his brother, who nodded slowly and stood.

"Sorry I can't stay longer. I have a class to teach." He hesitated. "You don't know what you're missing." Luke stood, heading towards the door.

As it closed behind him, Samuel whispered, "Yes, I do."

When he finally got home that night, Samuel dropped the envelope on the table as he went for a shower. His brain had been well and truly fried that day, and he needed some time to decompress.

The soap suds and warm water were doing their job to relax him, but he needed more. He needed a release. He wrapped his hand around his cock and stroked, sending low tingles down his spine. Keeping his head under the spray, he closed his eyes against the water and stroked harder, flicking at his most sensitive nipple as he grazed his fingers under the head of his dick.

Switching to pulling at his nub, the fire streamed underneath his skin, his balls lifting as he thrust into his fist harder and faster. The words "harder and faster" circled in his mind, bringing Eric's comments to the forefront, and that was it. Once the movie star was there, Samuel couldn't wipe him away.

He imagined Eric winking at him, then leaning in for a kiss. The moment their lips touched, Samuel stiffened and cursed, his orgasm barrelling through him with the force of a judge's gavel.

After regaining his breath, he shook his head. One fantasy kiss was all it took for him to blow. Unfortunately, he wasn't a teenager anymore, and that was him done for the night. Until he remembered the envelope.

Drying off briskly, he wrapped the towel around his waist and padded down the hallway to the dining table. Staring at the brown packet, he reluctantly picked it up and emptied the contents onto the gleaming glass surface. There sat a colouring book and a packet of pencils and a smaller white envelope. He picked up the latter, his hand shaking, but for what reason, he didn't know. Opening it, his breath caught at the words.

Sam,

Don't overthink, though, I'm sure you'll ignore me. Just let yourself go. See what happens when you allow yourself time to be…you.

Eric

The note fluttered to the table, and Samuel sat, his legs no longer able to hold him up. He ran a hand over his mouth, his gaze not leaving the colouring book. The note caught his eye again, and he frowned, reaching for it. On the back of the note was more.

Whatever that might look like, don't be scared to let him free. I promise you won't regret it. X

CHAPTER FIVE

ERIC

"Cut!"

Eric blew out a breath and glanced towards the director, waiting for his input since he'd stopped them after several seconds.

"Elsbeth, please! A little more emotion wouldn't go amiss here! You're supposed to be in love with him, for Christ's sake." Don rubbed his hands over his face and threaded them through his thick, greasy hair. "Let's try again, people."

Eric returned to his original position for the start of this scene, leaning against a bar, nursing a drink and distractedly looking around. When Don called for action, his gaze snagged on Elsbeth, who was playing his love interest in this film. As much as he hated giving Don any credit, he had to agree with his sentiment towards Elsbeth. The reason she had been awarded the part was something only the casting directors knew.

She was beautiful, of course: roughly five-foot-eleven, slender with curves in all the right places, a larger than average bust size and an ass most men would die for. But her ability was a sticking point for Eric. She didn't seem to know how to act certain emotions. Did she not feel them, or was she unable to relate? He had no idea, but it was killing his muse.

By the time Don called for the day to end, Eric was exhausted. He trudged back to the makeup area and allowed the technician to remove what little makeup he had on before continuing on to his dressing room to change. He would've normally jumped in the shower, but he couldn't be bothered; he wanted to get home.

Collecting his things, he wandered towards the exit, hesitating when he heard a voice attempting to lay on the charm.

Eric paused and listened.

"Remember what I said, Elsbeth. I could do wonders for your career. I'll pick you up at eight, okay."

Eric rolled his eyes and sighed, knowing exactly how his evening was now going to be panning out, and he wasn't amused. He cockily strode around the corner, throwing his jacket over his shoulder.

"Ah, there you are, Elsbeth. Are you ready? Our table is booked."

Elsbeth looked like a deer in headlights, so he went easy on her, laying a hand on her lower back and encouraging her to follow his lead.

"See you tomorrow, Don."

"Hey, wait a minute. Aren't you gay?" Don's forehead wrinkled even more than usual when he frowned at them.

"Yeah. It doesn't stop me from eating. I promised Elsbeth dinner, so we could get to know one another and make playing our parts easier." At least that was what his plans *now* involved. Not his soothing, triple-headed shower and an evening of brain-teasing puzzles.

Don huffed, relenting, "Good idea. Get her up to speed. She's slowing us down." Don's parting shot had Elsbeth flinching.

"Ignore him. He's always this cranky. Come on." He led her out of the studio. "Do you have a car of your own?"

She shook her head, her long brown curls bouncing the way they do in commercials. "No, I usually get a ride from a friend."

"Are you happy with me taking you to the restaurant?" He stopped, seeing plenty of people still milling around, and waited for her answer before deciding on a direction to walk.

"You don't have to. I know you were trying to help—"

"I don't mind. We can do exactly what I told Don we'd do. Try and figure this onscreen romance out."

"Yeah, okay. Thanks."

He led the way to where his beloved Continental GT Convertible Bentley waited and held open the passenger door for her. Once she swung her legs in, he closed the door, slipped on his jacket to ward off the surprising chill of the summer evening and climbed into the driver's seat. They didn't say anything until they arrived at one of the less showy restaurants in New York, which, if Elsbeth's pinched mouth was any indication, she wasn't happy about.

Eric didn't care. They weren't on a date, so he wasn't going to show off by trying to get into one of the fancier ones on short notice, although he knew they would gladly accept him.

When they were seated with menus to peruse, the gentle conversation surrounding them, Eric quickly glanced around to see if there was anyone he knew. A few faces, here and there, but they should be fine for a while. It would be when they left that the vultures would descend. No doubt their faces would be splashed across the tabloids before the sun rose the next day.

"So, Elsbeth," he began once their orders had been taken. "How are you finding the role?"

She fiddled with the napkin on her lap, her gaze lowered to her hands. "It's interesting. There's a variety of emotions to portray, which makes it's a little tricky, but I'm enjoying it."

Mentally rolling his eyes, he smiled. "That's good. Wouldn't want you to feel like you hated the job when you've only just started it."

She giggled.

Eric studied their surroundings, wishing, yet again, he was home. "Is there anything you're struggling with? Anything you need help with?"

"Well," she said, gazing up at him from under her lashes, "a few lessons outside of hours might be beneficial, don't you think?"

Eric sighed quietly. Why did certain women believe they could turn him heterosexual? He had come out when he was fifteen. As soon as the emancipation had been legally confirmed, he had given an interview and told the world he was gay. His parents had insisted on him keeping that piece of information to himself to ensure he got more parts—apparently—but he didn't want that. He wanted to be able to live his life without having to hide anything.

Naturally, it didn't work out as his current lifestyle showed, but it was a different and more personal part of his life, which was no one's business except his own.

"I don't think you need them outside of hours. Just a gentle conversation between takes is all we need. We can deal with each thing as we come across it during filming."

Elsbeth's mouth pursed before it smoothed out again, her head nodding demurely.

The rest of the meal went according to his expectations, and as soon as she had declined dessert, he'd requested the bill. Elsbeth excused herself to the bathroom, and Eric checked his phone while he waited.

Hey, asshole! You up for a chat?

Sorry, no assholes here. Just kind gentlemen helping a lady out of a bad situation.

He replied to Ethan, a smile stretching his face while he pocketed his phone. Seeing Elsbeth crossing the room towards him, he stood, indicating for her to go first, the murmurs around them ebbing and flowing as they passed. Helping her into her jacket before pulling on his own, he eyed the entrance, seeing several people waiting.

"We have company," he muttered to his companion. "Have you dealt with this before?"

She shook her head, her lips turning up. Wonderful. Looked like she was going to enjoy the attention. "Okay, keep your head up, try not to answer any questions; otherwise, your agent will be on the phone with you within minutes, I assure you."

Without waiting for her reply, he rested his hand on her lower back and led her towards his car, which had been driven around. The valet opened the door for her while Eric rushed around to the other side, all the while ignoring the usual remarks about his 'playboy' status and finally settling down with a woman. He gritted his teeth, knowing he couldn't reply, though he truly wanted to.

Driving off from the hoards of journalists, he sighed and asked for Elsbeth's address, which she gave him with a pout that was even more pronounced when he stopped the car outside and kept the engine running.

"Would you like to come in?" she asked in a small voice.

He blew out a breath and prepared his usual speech. "You're a lovely woman, Elsbeth, but I'm gay. There's nothing anyone can do to change that. But thank you for your interest."

Elsbeth grimaced and huffed. "You could've said no instead of making some excuse." She grabbed the door handle to open it.

Eric clenched his jaw. "It's not an excuse."

"No one has ever seen you with someone, man or woman. What's wrong with you?"

Eric snorted and shook his head. "Wow. Seriously, Elsbeth, I think you belong in this world more than I do. Enjoy your evening."

The dismissal caused a frown to cross her face before she huffed again and exited the car. He *was* a gentleman; therefore, he waited until she was behind a closed door before driving home. The evening couldn't get any worse.

He threw his car keys with a clink into the glass bowl on the small table by the front door as he shut it behind him. Staring across the open-plan area to the large windows on the other side of the room and the city lights beyond, he wished things had been different. Most days, he loved the work, the media not so much, but other times, he would prefer to have a basic job where no one knew his name.

Exhaling heavily, he pushed away from the door, his footsteps clicking loudly on the highly polished wooden floors as he crossed to his bedroom, hidden behind a sliding door. The highly sought-after apartment had been purchased four years previously to give him a place he could retreat to whenever he was in the city. He hated living out of hotels, so a place of his own helped him stay sane.

Throwing his jacket onto an armchair at the end of his bed, he continued undressing, then hustled through to the bathroom—or wet room as he called it. The shiny black tiles from ceiling to floor allowed him to have space to shower in comfort instead of be enclosed behind glass doors or fabric curtains, which annoyed the crap out of him.

He walked over to the shower area and, the moment he did, the water started automatically. It had been a luxury he hadn't known he needed, but when he'd seen it, he'd fallen in love. So much so, he'd had them installed in his other houses as well.

Eric wasn't one for spending vast amounts of money, but some things were bought as a necessity—the apartment being one—and some things were bought because he believed he'd earned them. What he spent on himself wasn't half as much as what he peppered Ethan and Emily with, though they hated him doing it.

Showering for much longer than necessary, he finally dried off, dressed in joggers and wandered out into the main area. As he did, his phone began to ring. He jogged back to where he'd left his jacket and retrieved his phone, smiling when he saw it was Ethan.

"Hey, asshole," Ethan greeted.

"Is that any way to greet your brother?" Eric grinned as he crossed to the fridge, grabbing a bottle of water and dropping onto the pristine white sofa, which was surprisingly comfortable despite how it looked.

"How else do you suggest I greet you, Oh Wise and Wonderful One?"

"That will do nicely." He laughed.

"In your dreams. Anyway, what have you been up to tonight?"

Eric rested the phone between his ear and his shoulder, clicking open the bottle before answering, "I took a lady out for dinner."

"Say what?"

The shock in Ethan's voice made him chuckle again, and he sipped his drink. "The director was sleazy, so I gave her an out. Ended up taking her to a restaurant and being hounded after we left as usual. I'm sure there will be photos tomorrow morning at the latest."

Ethan blew a distinct raspberry sound. "There are probably photos now. Hold on."

He could hear Ethan clicking in the background and could envisage him sitting at his desk in his house, checking the news sites.

"Any luck?"

"I'm an architect student, not a bloody computer whiz. Give me a minute."

Eric chuckled at his response, the stress of the evening reducing more with every minute he spoke to one of the two people who meant everything to him. At the thought, another face flew through his mind. Samuel. Sam. The Samuel whom he was convinced would be perfect as his Sam. That was a thought he could contemplate until the end of time, but there needed to be some serious interest coming from the guy before he approached that conversation.

"Ah, I have one. Ooh, she's pretty. Who's she?"

"Elsbeth Grainger. A newbie picked up for some reason that escapes me. She's nice enough, but she didn't like me brushing off her invitation when I dropped her home. She accused me of using being gay as an excuse." Ethan howled down the phone, and Eric allowed him his moment of mirth. "I can put in a good word for you if you like?"

"Nah, I'm good. As much as I'm sure I would enjoy the spotlight, I don't think I could live in it continually. I don't know how you do it."

"You get used to it. And anyway, you get some attention by being my brother."

Eric twisted on his seat and lifted his feet to the sofa cushions, settling himself further down and getting comfortable.

"It's not so much the attention; it's the rumours that would piss me off," Ethan said.

"What are they saying?"

"Let's say wedding bells are ringing."

"Fucking hell!" Eric said with a laugh. "That was quick. How long until she's knocked up?"

"Day after tomorrow if you're lucky."

Eric grinned, staring at the lights in the distance, the continual flicker of light and dark as cars drove between buildings. He would love to get married one day; not so sure about the kids because who would want them to be shoved into the limelight like he was, but marriage was definitely on his bucket list.

Once more, Samuel's face entered his mind. He'd not heard from him since Eric's last visit home, and he wanted to know what the man's reaction had been to his gift. Knowing what he did of Samuel, Eric would guess he'd thrown it aside and not thought about it again. It would be a shame if he had, but it was his choice. Remembering the look of pure serenity on Samuel's face while he had been colouring the horse was endearing.

Eric was certain Samuel didn't have enough peacefulness in his life.

"Okay, that was the only picture I could find so far. I'm sure Emily will be on the phone tomorrow when all hell breaks loose!"

"Thanks for the heads up," he joked.

"You know what she's like. She needs to make sure you're okay."

"I know. Anyway, how's work?"

Ethan groaned. "Busy. I'm working alongside studying, but, fuck, I can't wait until I can do it for real. It seems like so far away before it will become a reality."

"It seems like far away now, but it will fly by. You watch. Before you know it, there will be a fully-fledged architect in the family to go with the accountant and the actor."

"I know. Some days, it's harder to see over the hurdles."

"I get that. I'm so proud of you, Ethan. You've worked and are working so hard for what you want, and I'm impressed with your dedication. You deserve this."

Ethan cleared his throat and said, "Thanks."

"Right. I need to sleep. I have another achingly boring day tomorrow, so I need my beauty sleep."

"Damn right you do."

"Asshole."

"Weirdo."

They laughed. "Night, Ethan."

"Night, little bro."

Eric exited the lift into the foyer the following morning and was called over by the security guard.

"Mr Clarke, we wanted to let you know there is a large media reception waiting outside today. If you wish to use the back exit, we can arrange to have your car moved."

He blew out a breath and shook his head. "Thank you for letting me know, but I may as well face the music. I've been in the business long enough to know the longer you avoid them, the more tenacious they are. Have a good day." He tapped the top of the desk, smiling at the man.

"Good luck."

Eric brushed down the front of his clothes and trudged to the doors. The moment he stepped outside, bright bulbs flashed in his eyes, blinding him for a second at a time. The voices rose as each person tried to get their questions heard.

"Eric! Eric! How long have you been seeing Miss Grainger? Was this your first date? Eric! Why didn't you take her to a classier restaurant? Is it true love? Why have you been telling everyone you're gay?"

He couldn't tell who asked what questions, but the final one got his attention. Having no agent himself—he refused to hand over so much control to someone; therefore, did most of the work himself—he had the choice of when to speak and when not to. He decided to speak.

Stopping near his car, he spun back around to face the men and women who worked hard to get the stories they needed to earn their wages. He didn't hate the people as individuals, but as a collective, they were animals.

Holding up a hand, they settled into semi-quiet. "Firstly, I will say, I am *not* seeing Miss Grainger. We are co-workers, and that is all. Secondly, I *am* gay. It's not a story I'm telling to hide something else. I am gay. I have been for as long as I can remember, as you are all aware from the speech I made when I was fifteen years old. In response, I ask you this: why would a fifteen-year-old boy admit to being gay if he wasn't?

Why would he put himself through the stigma involved with such an announcement if he didn't truly believe it?" He paused. "Finally, I'm allowed to have dinner with whomever I choose. That's not against the law. Also, it does not mean I am in a relationship with each of those people. Have a good day."

The shouting began again, but he ignored them, climbed into his car and started the engine. He pulled out of his parking space carefully, in case anyone thought to jump in front of him to stop him leaving—he'd had that happen before.

Once he was on the road, his phone rang. He answered it through his car speakers.

"Good morning, my darling sister. Or should I say, good afternoon?" He automatically worked out the time difference whenever he spoke to one of his siblings.

"Wow, good speech," she said.

"How the hell did you hear that so fast? It happened like ten minutes ago."

Emily's light titter of laughter had him grinning. "That's the joy of social media. With these people, it's like the first person to get it out there is the winner. Plus, I have your name tagged. It pings me whenever your name is mentioned. I've been pinged multiple times since yesterday. You've been busy."

Eric huffed, "Yeah, so it seems."

"What's the story, morning glory?"

Chuckling, he said, "I haven't heard that in years! You're showing your age."

"Oi! Be kind."

"Sorry. Elsbeth was being harassed by the director—"

"—and you were her knight in shining armour. All right, I get it."

"I won't tolerate it happening under my nose, Emily. It's not fair that anyone should have to put up with it."

Emily sighed. "I know, Eric. Watch your back, okay. You ruffle too many feathers, and your career goes up in flames. No one will touch you."

Eric was surprisingly okay with the thought, which made him frown. "I know, but I won't let it go if I'm there to stop it."

"I know, Eric. I know. I'm asking you to be careful. You're too far away from us to help if you need it."

"I'll be fine."

"I'd feel better if you had some friends nearby."

"Well, funny you should say that, actually. Vaughn is here for the next few days. I'm going to catch up with him if I can."

"Aww, how is his little jellybean?"

"Carlie is doing well from what I saw last time he sent me a picture. She's getting big now, though. I can't believe she's seven already. Where did all the time go?"

"Who'd have thought one of the first people to

help you in the business would be the one to stay around the longest?"

"I know, right? I'm glad for it, though." Eric wasn't the only one keeping secrets, but that wasn't for him to tell. He pulled into his designated parking space at the studio and said goodbye to his sister, promising to video call her later so she could speak to Vaughn. Why she didn't call him, he never knew.

Vaughn Hayes had been in the business for far longer than Eric had been. He'd been in the prime of his time when Eric had been starting as a child actor at age four. Now, at forty-seven, Vaughn was still going strong and was one—if not the only one—of Eric's friends. Vaughn also knew *everything* about Eric. Absolutely everything.

He climbed out of his car, locking it behind him, and sauntered his way to his dressing room, greeting people as he went.

"Eric! Wait up a minute."

Withholding a grimace, he twisted around and smiled at Don. "Morning. How're things?"

"Looking good so far. I think we could get through a good amount today if everyone does what they're told."

Asshole. "I'm sure we'll be on our best behaviour for you."

"Like you were last night?" Don smirked. "I hear you went home alone."

"I did. As had been the plan all along. What's your point?" He gritted his teeth in a semblance of a smile for several people as they passed.

"My point is…you can't keep all the good ones to yourself, Eric. It's not kind." Don's eyes narrowed on him, and his mouth firmed.

Eric stepped closer, his blood boiling. "And my point is…I will keep anyone safe that is within my power to. From the likes of *anyone* who would do them more harm than good."

The thinly veiled threat was received if Don's furious expression was anything to go by.

"Be careful who you piss off, Eric. Be very, *very* careful."

Eric watched Don stormed off, yelling at his assistant, who happened to be in his way. His voice echoed off the studio walls, making several people flinch along the way. Why some directors had more power than others was beyond him, but he wouldn't ignore Don's words. He would watch his back.

What he would not do was stop fighting for those who couldn't fight for themselves. His whole life had been one fight after another until he took all the control upon himself. Finally free from his parents' rule, he had promised himself he wouldn't look the other way if he saw other people in a similar situation —or even anyone who was in a bad situation. It wasn't fair for anyone to be taken advantage of when they believed they didn't have any other choices, when, in fact, they had plenty; they couldn't see what they were.

His body vibrated, his knees wobbled, and his fists clenched harder. Emily's words bounced around his head, and he realised he didn't care what happened to his career. He was becoming tired of the limelight. There was plenty of money in his various bank accounts, many assets, many investments; he didn't need to worry even if he never found another job. But one thing he would do: he would make sure those who deserved it were taken down with him.

CHAPTER SIX

SAMUEL

"I need you to take me to my parents' house."

Samuel jerked his head up as the words were screeched from his office doorway. He raised his eyebrows and stared at his ex-husband. "No." Returning his gaze to his paperwork, he could perfectly imagine what Milton's face looked like: his brow would be creased, his eyes narrowed, his lips pursed, and his cheeks flushed. There was no need to witness it first-hand.

"What do you mean, no? I need to see my parents, so I need you to drive me there."

"It's not happening, Milton. You have Gregory to take care of you now; therefore, go and ask him to figure it out." Milton didn't drive and had never wanted to. It was no longer Samuel's problem.

Milton stomped closer to his desk. "But Gregory can't get away from work. He says he's too busy."

"Not my problem." He sighed inwardly. He was fed up with pandering to the man.

"Why are you being like this, pumpkin? You always used to help me out when I needed it." Milton perched his hip against the desk, and Samuel kept his gaze on the files, ensuring there was nothing Milton wasn't allowed to see.

"That was then. Things changed." Why was Milton unable to see what the problem was? Samuel's head began to ache, the stress of dealing with what used to be his daily life now too much for him to take.

"But Samuel…" Milton whined.

He focused on the pitiful man beside him. "My answer is no. Now leave."

"Mr Walker, your appointment is here." Maggie's voice was a welcome reprieve from the undoubtedly high-pitched argument Milton was about to start. It stopped as soon as Maggie had spoken.

"Time to go, Milton. Go ask your new boyfriend to hire you a car or something." It was more information than he should've given Milton, but he needed him out of the office. Though, thinking about it…he glanced at Maggie. He didn't think he had any appointments. Her face was neutral and stern as always, giving nothing away. She would've made a fantastic lawyer with a poker face like hers.

"Samuel…"

He pointed to the door, evicting Milton with no other words. Milton huffed, sashayed himself to the entrance and glanced over his shoulder at Samuel before exiting.

"That man…" Maggie muttered, closing the door behind her and moving closer to the desk. "You need to get rid of him."

"I try. Every single bloody time. He's tenacious and too used to the attention. Short of getting a restraining order—which I would *love* to do to see the look on his face—nothing is likely to keep him away." He rubbed at his temples, massaging away the tension pounding away at the edges of his eyes. "Anyway, what can I do for you?"

"Nothing at all, except have a break. You have been staring at paperwork for as long as you've been here, which is now going on six hours, and that's not counting the hours you were here before I arrived. You haven't eaten any lunch, haven't had any kind of breaks that I know of and have been living on caffeine. This ends now."

A knock sounded. Samuel hesitated and quietly asked Maggie, "Do I have an appointment?"

Maggie shook her head. "No more today, except for a short call with Mr Raines about a meeting next week, but that's not for another hour."

"Come in," he called with a sigh.

"Ah, Samuel. You're still here. That's good."

Gregory waltzed in like he owned the place and sat on one of the leather armchairs, crossing his legs in a posture of immense ease.

"What can I do for you?"

"Maggie, you may leave us." He dismissed her as if she was *his* assistant, but Samuel had hit his limit.

"Maggie, stay, please. We still have things to discuss." He gave her a look which he hoped conveyed how much he needed her to stay before refocusing on Gregory. "What do you need? I'm inundated at the moment, as you can see." He waved to his desk.

"Yes, well…" Gregory stood, smoothing down the front of his charcoal suit and refastening the buttons he'd undone when he'd sat. "Milton is—"

Samuel snorted. "If the next words out of your mouth are asking me to do something for him, the answer is no." He dropped into his office chair, harder than he probably should have, the sound of it creaking worrying him that he'd end up flat on his ass if he kept doing it. He needed to lose some weight. It wasn't good for him or his chair.

An undignified noise came from Gregory's direction, but Samuel slid his chair under the desk, picking up some papers and pretending to know what he was doing.

"Well, I think as he was your husband, you might—"

"Nope. I have nothing to do with him now. He's your problem."

"Well, I never."

Maggie moved closer to the other lawyer, resting a hand on his arm. "I think Samuel is stressed today, Gregory. Maybe you can figure out what Milton needs this time."

Samuel kept his smirk to himself as he heard his soon-to-be-higher-paid assistant sweet-talking the lawyer into figuring out what his new boyfriend needed. When the door closed behind them, Samuel buried his face in his hands, withholding the need to burst into tears. He was at his wit's end. There was no way he would get anything else done today.

Packing away the papers into the relevant files, he placed them neatly where he could find them the next day, then sorted his briefcase. Once he was ready to go, he exited his office, finding Maggie back at her desk outside.

"Maggie, could you please rearrange the phone call with Mr Raines? Apologise profoundly for me that a family matter has cropped up."

"No problem." She leaned closer. "Are you okay?"

Samuel nodded, then shook his head. "Not really. I'm going out for the evening. I need to breathe."

Giving him a small smile of understanding, she patted him on the arm and returned to her computer. "Try to have a good evening, Samuel."

"You, too. See you tomorrow."

He walked out of his workplace two hours earlier than he should have, and probably five hours earlier than he usually would have and went home. Not the home where he lived, but the home he and his siblings all claimed as being the one with their souls. His parents' house.

As he parked on the driveway of his childhood home, he turned the engine off and listened to it while it ticked and cooled. Even though he had not set foot outside of his car, he could feel the tension releasing in him. There was something about this place that made everything easier. Despite the differences in their relationship during the past few months, he still needed to feel the comforts of his childhood home.

He leaned his head back against his headrest and blew out a breath, closing his eyes against the sun that was still shining high in the sky. The sun that he never usually saw from anywhere other than his office window.

The simple act of breathing in and out slowly calmed him enough to click open the car door and step onto the gravel. He removed his suit jacket and threw it back into the car, checking that his phone was in his trouser pocket first, then pivoted and aimed towards the two people who would, despite their disagreement, welcome him with open arms, which his mother did as soon as he let himself into the house and called out a greeting.

"Well, I never expected to see you, but what a fantastic surprise. I've put some shepherd's pie in the oven. Are you staying for dinner?"

"If that's okay?"

"Of course it is. You know that." His mother wrapped him up again as if she knew how much he needed her strength at that moment. "You're welcome whenever you want to be here." She held him and rubbed a hand up and down his back. Despite the height difference and the fact Samuel had to bend at an awkward angle to receive the hug, he refused to end it before she did because it felt so good.

When she released him, she cupped his face, her forehead creased and worry clouded her eyes. "Relax, sweetheart," she whispered. "We've got you tonight." She gently patted his cheek and retreated to the kitchen, the central hub of the household.

As expected, his father was sitting on a wooden chair, reading the paper when Samuel entered.

"Hi, Dad. What's the score?" he joked, knowing his father was checking his investments, not the sports results.

"Good evening to you. Everything all right at work?" Charles Walker had retired several months ago after spending more than fifty years working, and he was enjoying his free hours, or at least, Samuel's mother said he was.

"Yeah. I'm swamped as usual. I needed…"

He didn't have to say anymore. His father nodded his head in understanding and asked him if he wanted a hot drink. When his tea was brewed and warming his hands, Samuel sighed and released his hold on his tension. He lowered his head, focusing on the swirls spinning around the top of the liquid. The simple act of letting his mind wander and allow thoughts to come and go as they pleased helped him settle. It was a meditation of some kind, probably. He didn't care. He allowed himself to be, watching the little bubbles spin and pop and move around the top of the drink.

His parents didn't force conversation as most parents would. Samuel had grown up expecting them to prod and push their way into his life, but they never had. It made it easier for him to open up to them. For this reason, he found himself beginning to talk through the issues he had with finding out about his brother he'd never known about. Both of his parents spoke to him about why they kept it a secret—not because they were trying to hurt him, but because they wanted their children to have a full life, not knowing about the sadness that once permeated the house. They wanted their children to have a happy childhood without the darkness of knowing someone wasn't there who should be.

Once they had talked it through, Samuel could see their side of it. "You still need to tell everyone. We're older; we can handle it now. Just make sure you tell it how you told me. I understand why you did it, although I will say I would've loved to know I had an older brother despite him not being here."

And like that, the disagreement that had been hovering over their relationship for the last few months was settled. He turned the subject to something else, explaining his issues with Milton and that he was still floating around, distracting him and getting on Samuel's last nerve despite them having been divorced for several years.

"He's realised he lost a good thing, Samuel. That's all. He's been trying to get you back from the moment you told him it was the end. The moment he realised his mistake, he backpedalled. But you can only take him back if you truly forgive him." His father glanced at his mother, who smiled at him.

"He doesn't deserve anything from me. How can someone cheat on another person? It's not as if he couldn't have said, 'Samuel, I don't want to be with you anymore, and I want to see other people.' I would've let him go. It's a ridiculous excuse."

"You're right. Words are better than actions in

some cases, but not all. Milton should've spoken to you first."

After spending some time talking through it, he went to the bathroom, all the caffeine finally making its way through his system. As he washed his hands, he studied himself in the mirror. He looked at least ten years older than he was. Life was not wearing well on him, and he needed to get his act together and work through it.

Eric's face floated through his mind, and he immediately brushed it away. His life had no room for a celebrity in it, especially one who was never home.

He spent another hour with his parents before bidding them goodnight and vowing to see them on Sunday as usual and with less of an attitude.

Letting himself into the apartment, he threw the keys on the kitchen counter. He couldn't get his mind to settle, and his thoughts reverberated through his mind, bouncing off the walls and circling back again and again. After wandering around his house for however long, he shuffled for the cupboard, dragging out a large bottle of whiskey he'd been given as a birthday present several years ago. He had never been in the mood to drink it because it wasn't his drink of choice, but if he needed it at any time, now was it. He would drink the night away and deal with it in the morning.

Grabbing a glass tumbler, he sauntered past the

table to the sofa, hesitating when his gaze snagged on the colourful cover of the book Eric had sent him. He stared at the book, his bottom lip caught between his teeth, then focused on the whiskey. Returning his gaze to the colouring book once more, the smile on Eric's face as they talked over the colouring Samuel had done at the party appeared front and centre in his mind.

"Why did he look at me like that?" he whispered out loud.

His brain reminded him of the peacefulness of his emotions when he was colouring, the feeling of light-ness. That was what he needed. Not the obliteration of his emotions through drinking.

The clink of the bottle resting on the glass table made his mind up. He left the bottle where it was, placed the tumbler beside it and picked up the book and pencils. The sofa called his name, but he needed something else. His gaze roamed around his room, finally settling on the rug in front of the fake fireplace.

Ignoring the little voice in the back of his head, telling him he was unmanly for wanting to *colour*, he dropped the items to the rug and lay on his stomach. It wasn't the most comfortable position, to begin with, because his oversized tummy got in the way, but once he was settled, it was nice to be off his ass for once.

He chuckled to himself and reached for the book, gasping when he saw what was inside. Every single page—and he flicked through them all—was full of horses. Different stances, different pictures, different people with them, different landscapes—it was fantastic. No one knew he had a fascination with horses, not even his parents. Although everyone knew he was deathly afraid of them. He would've loved to be able to ride one, but he was too scared.

The idea that Eric had figured out his small secret had his eyes widening, worry coursing through his veins until he realised Eric wouldn't know. He guessed because Samuel had chosen that picture at the party.

Relaxing into his position on the rug, Samuel opened the book to the first page, smiling when he saw a cowboy sitting on top of the horse, hat and all. He tipped out the pencils and chose a dark brown. The horse would be the same colour as the cowboy's hat.

Time ceased to exist for Samuel. He concentrated on choosing the right colours for his picture and nothing else. Nothing else mattered at that moment. When he finally coloured the last blade of grass, he sighed, smiling at the result.

Eric's voice floated through the air, "That looks amazing. Well done, Sam."

He stayed within his little bubble for a while longer, looking through the pages and deciding which one he would do next. His phone's peeling ringtone brought him back to reality with a bump, and he felt his cheeks flush as he gathered up the book and pencils rapidly. Refusing to answer the call when he had the items in his hands, he struggled to his feet before glancing around his room to find somewhere to put them. His heart raced when he shoved them haphazardly into a drawer in the unit beside the TV.

Blowing out a breath, he pulled his phone from his pocket and checked to see who had rung. It was Trent. The phone vibrated in his hand and began ringing again, Trent's name flashing once more. He inhaled, then answered, hoping his voice was as calm as wanted it to be.

"Hi."

"Hey, you. As you have been more inclined to come out and socialise with us lately, I wanted to let you know we've all been invited to Eric's birthday party this weekend. I was supposed to have called you several days ago, but I'm an idiot and forgot. We will pick you up and drop you back home afterwards, like a date. How's that sound?"

Samuel raised his eyebrows. "That was like diarrhoea of the mouth, Trent."

Trent howled down the line, making Samuel smile despite his newly remembered inner turmoil. "Do you know what? Yeah, let's do it."

"Really?" Trent sounded shocked, which he supposed he should when Samuel usually kicked up a fuss about going out.

"Yes, sure. I could do with a breather, especially as Milton is hounding me again."

"That fucker. What does he want this time?"

"He wanted me to drive him to his parents' house."

"That's five fucking hours away! What is wrong with the guy? Jesus, Sammy, you are well shot of the guy, thank god."

"Yeah, well, I should be. Unfortunately, he doesn't seem to have received the message."

"Want me to knock him out?"

"Thanks, but I think we'll put that idea on the back burner for the moment. How about that?"

"All right, but know it's on the table should you want it."

"I do, thanks." He paused. "What does Eric like? I need to get him a gift. I keep turning up without anything for anyone because you don't give me enough notice."

Trent laughed. "No idea. I'll get Max to text you some thoughts."

"Perfect."

"Anyway, I best go. Max is waving madly at me for some reason."

"All right, see you in a few days."

The dial tone sounded in his ear.

The lure of finding out what Eric was doing proved too much for him and Samuel settled himself on the sofa with a glass of cold milk and brought up his internet. He felt a frisson of excitement when he typed in Eric's name, and when the first images came up, his eyes devoured him as if he hadn't seen him in months when, in fact, he'd searched for him the previous week. It was like a drug he couldn't resist.

Zooming in on several images to get a close-up of his face, Samuel imagined what it would be like to have your life splashed across the internet without a care in the world to those that looked at them. He wondered what Eric thought about it. The guy didn't seem bothered by the scrutiny, but he hid things well. Samuel knew about his family history and the fact he'd filed for emancipation at age fifteen because his parents had stolen and spent all the money he'd earned as a child.

The case had nothing to do with Samuel, but he knew of the lawyer who handled the case, and the man wasn't a nice guy. The now-retired lawyer had been set on getting everything from Eric for his parents, and in the end, Eric had made himself bankrupt to get them off his back. Luckily, he was a big enough star that he bounced back and made his first independent million within a year.

Since then, his career had blown up.

Samuel's gaze caught on a picture of Eric lying on a beach towel, surrounded by sand. His knees were bent, his feet sole to sole. One hand was behind his head; the other was over his groin as if cupping his package through his shorts. The sheer sexiness of the posture had Samuel tenting his trousers immediately.

He switched off his phone, eyes widening as images

flew through his head. No, he couldn't. His gaze flicked over to his bedroom door while he licked his lips. No.

His brain had other ideas, though, and Samuel found himself on his bed naked before the movement even registered with him. Squirting some lube into his hand, he encircled his dick before stroking slowly, allowing his eyes to flutter closed. When it wasn't enough, his free hand scrabbled across the bed, searching for his phone before bringing it to his face and opening it on the same picture.

His gasp echoed off the walls as Eric's sensual face stared through the phone to him. Samuel followed the curve of his jaw, the bump of his Adam's apple, the line of his collarbone, the valleys of his abdomen, the waistband of his shorts, the curve of his hand, the length of his fingers, the…shape of his cock.

Samuel focused on that, occasionally flicking his gaze to Eric's face as his hand moved faster and faster, the slick sounds loud in the silence.

"Fuck," he whispered, licking his lips and swallowing hard. His focus returned to the outline of his shaft, cupped so lovingly in his hand and ran a finger over the top of his cock, causing the unmistakable feeling of his climax rushing down his spine. He grazed his nails across the sensitive underside of the head and came, loud and cursing and long. Rope after rope of white fluid covered his stomach and chest as his vision greyed around the edges, still focused on Eric's face.

CHAPTER SEVEN

ERIC

"Good morning. Could I make an appointment to see Mr Walker today, please?" he asked the person on the other end of the phone.

"I'm afraid I don't have any appointments for him today. Can I ask what it's regarding?"

The voice sounded pleasant enough but with a hard edge that showed she would put her foot down if she needed to. "Can I be frank with you…?"

"Maggie."

"Can I be frank with you, Maggie?"

"Go right ahead."

"I'm a friend of his, but I'd like to ask him out for dinner. To do that, I need to get in to see him because, if you know him as I do, you know he's also stubborn and won't accept unless I'm right there in front of him to persuade him."

"I don't know you from Adam, sir. How do I know you're telling the truth?"

Eric grinned. "At least my voice is not recognisable. That's a bonus."

"Can I take your name, please?"

"If I give it to you, you need to keep this confidential. It's more than your job is worth." He lowered his voice to get his point across, but all he heard was a laugh on the other end of the line.

"If I couldn't keep confidentiality, I wouldn't be working here in the first place. Now, if that is all…?"

"Okay, my name is Eric Clarke."

There was a pause, then she cleared her throat. "Okay, Mr Clarke, I can fit you in at two. Is that all right?"

Eric was impressed. His name had thrown her, but she hadn't contradicted him. "Two would be great. May I ask…is there a quieter entrance I can use? I would prefer to remain as anonymous as possible."

"If you ring on this number when you arrive, I will personally collect you and bring you in the back route. No guarantees, but it will be quieter."

"That would be great, thank you."

"Mr Clarke?"

"Yes, Maggie."

When she started talking again, her voice was lower, as if she didn't want others to hear. "Please only do this if you're serious about him. He's been through enough shit over the past few years. He doesn't need to be the butt of a celebrity's social media joke."

"I assure you, I know how it feels and would never do that to him."

"Good."

"Thank *you* for looking out for him."

Several hours later, dressed in jeans and a polo shirt with a baseball cap and sunglasses, he called up for Maggie, who collected him as agreed and took him through the maze of the hallways and into a lift at the back of the building.

"Not many people use this because it's such a walk from the front of the building as you saw."

"Thanks for this, Maggie."

"You're welcome. Although, it's a bit surreal." She chuckled.

"I can imagine. I was born and bred here, and when I walk the streets, it still feels weird to have people staring at me when I'm feeling like a teenager again."

Maggie gave a small smile. "I'm sorry about what happened. I know it was before my time, but you didn't deserve that."

Eric's throat closed up, and he stared up at the numbers of the lift. When he could speak again, he said, "Thank you."

They didn't say any more until they came to a door

where Maggie stopped. "This is his. If I lose my job for this, you're hiring me."

Eric grinned. "Deal."

"Give me one sec."

Maggie knocked and opened the door a little way. "Your two o'clock appointment is here. Are you ready?"

"Yes, send them in." It had been far too long since Eric had heard his voice, and he closed his eyes at the deep baritone.

When he opened his eyes again, Maggie was smiling knowingly at him. "You can go in." She leaned in closer and lowered her voice, "If by any chance someone enters his office, there is a bathroom through the door behind his desk."

Eric nodded and entered. Samuel was sitting behind a desk piled high with folders, files, paper and a laptop, plus a mug, teetering precariously on the edge of the table.

"Good afternoon, please, have a—"

Eric watched as Samuel lifted his head and smiled in greeting until the realisation of who he was had sunk in, then his face flamed—interestingly—and he stopped talking.

"We meet again. How have you been, Samuel?"

Samuel briefly closed his eyes, then reopened them, indicating for Eric to sit. "I've been better." His eyes widened at his words, and Eric wondered if he had not meant to say them. He felt a rush of happiness at the thought Samuel was opening up to him, even if he didn't understand why.

He sat, crossing his ankle on the opposite knee. "That's not good. What's keeping you awake at night?"

"Forget I said anything. What can I do for you?" Samuel asked, sitting back in his chair and picking up a pen, running his fingers along it and twisting it around and around.

Eric smiled. "I'd like to cook you dinner."

Samuel's eyebrows rose. "Dinner?"

"Yeah, you know, the meal after lunch but before bedtime." He knew he was being sarcastic, but he wanted to get back to the funny, unself-conscious Samuel he'd met at the parties.

Rolling his eyes, the corners of his mouth twitching, Samuel avoided Eric's gaze. "Funny."

"I try." Eric studied the man in front of him. He looked exhausted and gaunt. The lacklustre expression on his face and in his eyes caused Eric some concern, and his confidence that this was the right course of action stumbled a little. Dropping his foot to the floor, he leaned his elbows on his knees. "What's happened, Sam?" Throwing out the nickname was a bold move, but he hoped it would bring results.

"I've had a lot going on lately, and things…have become…difficult. I don't…" He blew out a breath, rubbing a hand over his head.

"When was the last time you had someone cook for you except your parents?" Eric asked.

Samuel's forehead creased, and his gaze flicked to Eric's and away again. "Um, Trent, maybe—"

"Except family?" Eric amended.

Samuel rolled his lips inwards. "Never," he whispered.

He couldn't believe no one had been given a chance to cook for this guy. Although he had been married, he assumed Samuel had been the cook as well as a lot of other things. It was time to take care of him, even if it was only for a short time. "Then let me. Please."

"You don't have to cook. We could go out?"

"That's a nice idea, but I don't think you're ready to be given the media treatment it would bring. If I cook at home, we can have some peace and quiet, however, if you'd prefer not to be alone with me, then we can try to find a small place somewhere. No guarantees, though."

Samuel shook his head. "Sorry. I forget."

"And that is one of the biggest compliments you could have given me. Thank you."

The older man tilted his head. "Why?"

Eric sighed and stood, wandering over to the large windows, hoping no one would recognise him, or if they did, that they wouldn't believe their eyes. "Because it means I haven't become what Hollywood usually makes of actors, and I have retained some of my humanity."

"You're not like what I read and watched." Samuel's voice was solid and certain, giving Eric the impression it was a subject he had thought about previously. He'd thought about him?

Brushing aside those thoughts, he whirled around, hands in his pockets and asked, "Will you come to dinner?"

There was a beat of silence, each man studying the other. When Eric saw Samuel's mouth open to give his answer, someone knocked, then opened the door without waiting for a response.

"He's in a meeting! You can't—"

"I'm going to use the bathroom." Eric turned away from the newcomer and dashed through the door, softly clicking it behind him but not engaging the lock. He didn't wait to see if Samuel agreed to it, but Eric did not want to bring any problems to Samuel's work. That had never been his intention.

Leaning back against the door and tilting his ear towards it, he could hear voices from the other side, but only the odd word until the voices rose in anger.

"Clients have a right to confidentiality, Milton! It is none of your concern who is in my bathroom. All you need to know is that I've asked you to leave. If I have to ask you again, I *will* call security regardless of who your new boyfriend is! You have no right to barge in here whenever you wish, but especially when I'm with a client."

"But—"

"But nothing. Out!"

The voices lowered again, leaving Eric in his little bathroom bubble with an unfortunate erection. The authority in Samuel's voice was heady, but the visions that flashed through Eric's head were of that voice being used as a bratty little and Eric needing to punish him. He pressed his hand against his groin and bit his lip, swallowing a groan and closing his eyes. Which didn't help. Seeing Samuel in a pair of shorts and a t-shirt with an argumentative expression on his face was doing nothing to calm him down.

He turned his thoughts to Elsbeth, and immediately his blood cooled, so when a knock came at the door, he was audience-friendly once more.

Opening the wooden barrier a short distance, he saw Samuel and pulled it wider. This Samuel was back to the person he'd seen when he'd first entered the room, and Eric was not happy with the change.

"I'm so sorry. He doesn't get the picture. He's always letting himself in here whenever he wants and won't—"

Eric took hold of Samuel's hands and dragged him to the sofa, sitting himself down and pulling Samuel right next to him. He gathered the man in his arms and tucked his head underneath his chin.

Despite Samuel being tall, Eric was taller, so he fit nicely.

At first, Samuel's body remained tense, holding himself stiff and unyielding, but as Eric mumbled nonsense to him and rubbed a hand up and down his back, he slowly relaxed until he sank into Eric's embrace. When a hand gripped Eric's shirt, holding on for dear life, something inside Eric eased.

He had not been able to bring himself to visit Infinity since the beginning of the year. Something had happened to him, and he hadn't been able to figure it out until now. He hadn't wanted to be *anyone's* Daddy —he wanted to be *Samuel's* Daddy. The discovery shouldn't have shocked him, but it had. He had seen many age gap Daddy and boy or Daddy and little relationships, but hardly anywhere the Daddy was the younger of the couple. It hadn't even crossed his mind until this moment with Samuel tucked so completely against him, with him so relaxed.

What the hell was he going to do about that now?

After several long minutes, a quiet knock sounded, and Eric braced himself for the need to hide, but no one entered. Unfortunately, the disruption caused Samuel to tense and pull away, eyes wide, cheeks blazing.

Samuel stood, cleared his throat and walked to the door, only opening it a crack.

"Your three o'clock appointment is here. I'm

sorry, but I need to figure out a way of getting Mr Clarke out of here without anyone seeing him. I can distract Mr Houghton with a coffee, but not for long."

"It's okay, Maggie. You distract Mr Houghton, and I will help Eric to the lift."

"Use the back ones, Samuel. I checked with security, and there doesn't seem to be anyone loitering outside, but no guarantees."

"Thanks." The door closed again, and Samuel rested back against it, pinning Eric with his stare, his lawyer demeanour firmly back in place. "You need to leave."

"Not without an answer."

Samuel frowned. "To what?"

"Dinner."

Eric stood, wandering over to Samuel's desk and picking up the baseball cap and glasses. Sliding the cap in place, he held onto the glasses, fixing his gaze on Samuel while he stepped closer.

"That doesn't disguise you well, you know," Samuel muttered when Eric stopped toe to toe with him.

"It does what I need it to do, which is make people think they are seeing things. That's the only distraction I need. Now, dinner. I will pick you up at seven from your apartment. Please wear something comfortable. You do not need to wear a suit. Joggers and a t-shirt are fine, or even shorts and a t-shirt." His groin tightened at the thought, so he quickly went on, "Whatever you feel most comfortable in."

"But…I don't…" Samuel dropped his head back on the door, exposing the column of his neck, which Eric wanted nothing more than to lick the length of.

He licked his lips before he could help himself but stopped short of completing the act. Instead, he focused back on Samuel. "It's just dinner. Tonight." He couldn't help tagging on the final word, making Samuel's eyes widen again.

He watched the storm rolling through Samuel's expressive eyes and waited while he figured out his course of action and was mightily surprised when Samuel nodded his assent jerkily.

He leaned forward. "Good. Bring your appetite." Eric grinned.

Samuel's Adam's apple bobbed hard, but he stayed silent. Eric stepped back, dropping his gaze to the man's groin and seeing a bulge there.

He hid his smile and slid on his glasses. "After you, Mr Walker."

Samuel cleared his throat, exhaled deeply, then turned and opened the door, checking outside before indicating for them to leave. Several people stared at them, so Eric had no doubt his visit wasn't as incognito as he had wanted it to be. It was to be expected, though. He was an A-list celebrity, after all.

Before he left Samuel's care, he reminded him to

be ready for seven, then cupped his jaw and lifted his face towards his. While he wanted nothing more than to kiss him, he tilted his face to the left and pressed a kiss on his cheek. Then he walked away.

Eric couldn't resist getting himself through the entrance to the building and up to Samuel's front door when the opportunity presented itself. And when Samuel opened the door wearing some loose khaki shorts and a plain light blue t-shirt with a hoodie over the top, Eric's pulse skyrocketed. Samuel appeared younger and fresher than he had earlier in the day, and Eric was glad for it. The man also looked perfect for their evening plans, which would go one way or another depending on Samuel's reaction to their dinner conversation.

"How did…Never mind, I'm ready."

"Good evening to you too, Samuel." Eric grinned as red splotches darkened Samuel's cheeks.

"Sorry. Good evening, Eric."

His name spoken in Samuel's deep voice had his heart racing, and he gave himself a little pep-talk. He was a confident, experienced Daddy; he didn't act like a teenager on a first date. The first date thing was correct if you excluded the other times they had been together and spoken, but he was certainly not inexperienced.

"Shall we go?" he asked, holding out his elbow and daring Samuel to take it.

"Sure." Samuel closed his door and hesitated before slipping his hand around Eric's bicep. "How do you get around with hardly anyone recognising you?"

Eric laughed, causing Samuel to grip him tighter. "Cambridge is my hometown. Nearly everyone knows me here. Most of them are used to it and understand I want to be left alone, and they will abide by that. Some ignore it, but mainly people either leave me alone or treat me like anyone else."

"I would've thought everyone would be all over you, wanting a piece of the fame."

"Sometimes, yes, but most don't care. With all the drama from years ago, they're happy to leave it all behind."

He couldn't help the bitterness that tinted his words, and therefore, he stopped talking, guiding Samuel out of the lift and through the foyer to his car.

"Wow, nice car."

"Thank you." Eric opened the passenger door, closing it behind Samuel when he was seated. He jogged around the front and climbed in beside the man he wanted to know so much more about. Hopefully, tonight would prove to be enlightening.

He pointed the car in the direction of home and watched Samuel stare out of the window. "What has you looking so pensive?" he asked quietly.

He saw Samuel turn to him out of the corner of his eye. "I'm wondering what this is all about."

"What what is about?"

"This dinner? This…" His hand waved between them.

"Tell you what? Let's have a nice dinner, getting to know one another. I will answer any questions you have. Some I may leave until after dinner is finished, but most, I will answer directly. I won't keep secrets from you, Samuel. That I promise you, and if you are as good at body language as I believe you are, you will be able to tell."

"Not always," came the muttered reply.

"What do you mean?" Eric turned onto the long road that eventually led them to his house.

"I seem to have a blind spot when it comes to things relating to me, or at least, I think I do. I can never figure out what my behaviour is telling me, and as for Milton…well…"

His words trailed off, and he returned to staring out of the window. Eric cursed mentally at the asshole who had hurt this man beside him, but he made a promise to himself to help him heal, to help him become the best version of himself he could.

"Here we are."

Samuel leaned forward, getting his face closer to the windows. "Wow, this is amazing. I expected…" He stopped and flushed.

"You expected a mansion? Yeah, most people do. Don't get me wrong, it's bigger than I need, but I don't see the point in having something so large you go for days without seeing anyone who lived in it. It never made sense to me." He clicked open the door. "Let me give you a tour."

He walked around the car to Samuel's side, pleased to note he hadn't climbed out. When he opened the door for him, Samuel's cheeks were flushed. "Sorry, I didn't know if you wanted to make this a proper date or not, so I wasn't sure how to react, then when I'd decided to get myself out, you had already opened it."

Eric shut the door and backed Samuel into the car, resting his hands on either side of Samuel's body on the top of the car. "Don't be sorry. I'm happy you stayed because I love being able to take care of my dates. Relax, Sam. This is a place for both of us to relax, be happy, be…free."

He knew what he meant by the last word, and hopefully, by the time the evening had ended, so would Samuel.

Running a hand down Samuel's arm to his hand, he linked their fingers and tugged, turning towards his home. Biting his bottom lip, he tried to see the house as a newcomer would and prayed Samuel would like it.

Unlocking the door and stepping inside to turn off the alarm, Eric retained hold of Samuel while he dragged him through the ground floor layout, answering questions and pre-empting some.

As they climbed the stairs, Eric could feel Samuel's hand trembling in his—or was it his trembling in Samuel's? He didn't know. He started with the bedroom furthest away and slowly brought them closer to his bedroom. He purposefully bypassed one door, ignoring Samuel's questioning gaze, and entered the place he spent his nights.

The deep blue carpet, he knew from experience, was soft and thick; the wood furniture dark against the white walls was lovingly made by Zak for him; the four-poster bed dominated the room.

"This door leads to an en-suite, which I will admit to paying a ridiculous amount of money on when I found a shower I liked." He laughed.

"What's through there?"

Samuel pointed in the direction of a door that led to the same room he had bypassed earlier. The man was not ready for that reveal, so Eric said, "It's something for later. And no, it's not full of sex toys or torture equipment, I promise."

"Why can't I see it now?"

"Because there are some things I need to explain before you will understand what the room is. Just seeing it won't make any sense. You need the background to it. I promise I will explain it all to you, and you will be allowed to see the room should you wish. Give me some time to do this the right way."

Samuel studied him, and Eric stayed still, attempting to show him how truthful and open he was trying to be. When he nodded, Eric relaxed.

"Let's get some dinner." They headed back downstairs. "I had planned on cooking salmon fillets with broccoli, cauliflower and asparagus, along with a jacket potato if that sounds okay to you?"

"Perfect, thank you. Is that what I can smell?"

Eric chuckled. "It's the jackets. I put them in before I left to collect you. That way, they'd be perfect by the time everything else was ready."

"I love the smell of them."

"Yes. They're so versatile too. You can have any filling with them you can think up if you suspend your beliefs of what is right or wrong."

Samuel laughed. "So, in other words, leave all reasoning behind and go with the flow?" He raised an eyebrow.

"Pretty much. The same thing goes for life, I think. Have a seat."

"Can I help?"

Eric smiled. "Sure. You can do the salad. I'll bring it over in a moment."

He went to the fridge and gathered the milk, two glasses and took them over to the table. Without saying anything, he poured two glasses of milk, sliding one across the table to Samuel and keeping one for himself. It was a test of sorts, although Samuel didn't know it. Eric felt a bit mean, but he wanted to see how well Samuel reacted to what Eric placed in front of him and what he asked him to do.

"Thanks." Samuel didn't flinch at the liquid, which Eric was pleased about. He lifted it to his mouth and took a healthy gulp. A milky moustache was left behind before Samuel licked it off. Eric hid his smile in his glass, taking a few small sips.

Returning to the fridge once more, he grabbed the salad ingredients, a chopping board, a knife and a bowl and took them to Samuel. "Here you go. The knife is super sharp, so be careful. Throw everything in the bowl, please."

Samuel grinned at him. "Sure."

Eric returned the smile, then strode back to the fridge, pulling out the salmon fillets and preparing them for the oven. Once they were safely on their shelf, he turned to the vegetables, bringing them to the table next to Samuel.

"How are you doing?"

"Good. It's so peaceful here. I can't remember ever being somewhere that doesn't have some kind of noise around."

"Do you like it?"

"I love it. I don't realise how noisy everything is

until I don't hear it anymore. It's strange, but in a good way."

"Yeah, I know what you're trying to say. The silence is a necessity for me, especially as I'm hounded often. This is a retreat, basically. As I said before, most people leave me alone, even the reporters, so I can usually keep my peace and quiet while I'm here."

They continued in silence, Eric enjoying the presence of someone else in his home. Their conversation was pleasant and enlightening through the meal but still only scratching the surface of what he needed to discuss with Samuel.

"What did you want to talk about?" Samuel asked when the food had been eaten, and they had both placed their cutlery on their plates.

Eric had wondered how long he would last before he asked about what he'd hinted at upstairs.

"Shall we go into the living room with a drink, and I will try and explain?"

CHAPTER EIGHT

SAMUEL

Samuel followed Eric into the spacious but cosy living area and settled himself in the corner of the beige sofa, sinking into the surprisingly soft cushions while being careful not to spill his refilled milk glass. Eric sat in the opposite corner and twisted to the side to face him.

"Okay, so what I'm going to tell you is a lot of personal information about me, and I will be honest with you; I have no idea what you're going to think about it."

For once, Eric appeared unsure and nervous, a far cry from his usual confident exterior. "Everything you tell me will remain confidential. You have my word."

"I'm not worried about that. In fact, I would suggest you speak to someone about it, without my name attached."

Samuel lowered his brows. "You have me both confused and nervous now."

Eric chuckled and leaned to rest his glass on a coaster on the coffee table. "Sorry." He sat back, laying one arm along the back of the sofa. "What do you know about Daddy and boy or little relationships?"

Running through the information in his head, he realised it wasn't a great deal, which is what he told Eric.

"That's fine. It makes it a little easier, in all honesty. All right, Daddies and Mummies are people who have a need to care for someone else's wants and needs. They wish to provide everything for that person—that boy or girl or little. Sometimes, these relationships are part-time, so they only happen, for example, in an evening after work a couple of times a week or on the weekend. Other times, they are full-time, so twenty-four-seven. The type will depend on the people within that relationship. There is no one size fits all."

Samuel's heart raced. Is that what Eric needed? Why was he explaining this? "What kind of things do they do?"

"Every relationship wants different things. The same happens here. Some Daddies want more control over a boy or little, while others want less control. Some boys or littles want everything to be done for them, and others only want a few things. It's a case of whatever you want from it."

"But what in particular? What do the Daddies want to do, and what do the boys want to have done for them?"

Eric inhaled. "Daddies like taking control of when the boy or little eats and drinks, and what they eat or drink. They want to help them to relax, so they might help them change their clothes, give them a bath or shower, or tuck them into bed for a nap. A boy or little might want to play with some toys or watch TV. There are so many variables with the lifestyle, it's difficult to list them all."

Samuel had been watching Eric closely during his speech, and he surmised Eric was in the lifestyle and enjoyed it if his smile was any indication.

"Okay. What does this have to do with me?"

Leaning forward to place his elbows on his knees, Eric gazed at Samuel for a moment. "I think you would do well within the same lifestyle."

He snorted and held out his hands. "I'm not Daddy material, Eric. I can barely keep myself organised without having to think about another person."

"No. I mean, you would benefit from being a boy or little."

Samuel stared at him, unable to say anything to that announcement. Why would Eric think that? He was forty-three years old. Bringing his gaze to his hands, he tried to make sense of the information Eric was providing. He rubbed at the back of his neck, swallowing hard. It didn't make sense. Why would he be a good candidate for a boy or little? He was too busy to take time to do what someone else told him to. Stomach fluttering, he shook his head.

"I can see your mind going a mile a minute, Samuel. Talk to me. Tell me what you're thinking or ask me questions."

"I don't know how you think that. I don't understand."

"Okay. Let's start with this. When we were colouring at the party the other week, how did you feel?"

Samuel felt his cheeks heat but promised himself he'd be honest. "I felt at peace. Like nothing was bothering me."

"Exactly. Sometimes, the…aim, if you like, is to be free of responsibility, free of stress, free of anything but that peaceful feeling. The idea you can go to work and become stressed out as fuck, then go home to someone who will strip everything away and allow you to be free."

"The idea sounds nice, but how would it work? There's no one around?"

"There's me."

The words had Samuel refocusing on the man beside him. "Aren't you a boy or little?"

Eric shook his head, the corners of his mouth curling up. "I'm a Daddy."

Holy fuck! "But aren't Daddies older than their boys?"

"Most of the time, yes, but I would be out of the running of having a relationship if I relied on finding someone younger than me. Plus, it's not about age. What matters is how you feel on the inside. The outside can be changed to reflect how you feel inside if you want it to, but even then, nothing needs to outwardly show. Relationships like these can be contained within the walls of a house. Everyone is different."

"Have you looked after a boy or little?"

Eric scrunched up his mouth a bit. "Kind of. I haven't found anything long-term, but I help out at one of the clubs, either here or wherever I may be staying. I'm a surrogate Daddy of sorts, one night only type for those who don't have one."

"Do you mean like one-night stands?"

"It's not always about sex either. Some of my littles want to be looked after, fed, changed, read a book and allowed the time to relax under the careful eye of someone who will make sure they are taken care of. Other littles or boys want to be spanked or given a time-out, and some want sex as well. Again, it's a personal preference."

Samuel blew out a breath. "That is a lot of infor-mation. I don't know…"

"You don't have to do anything with it." Eric sat

back. "I wanted to let you know what I saw in you and to help you if you wanted me to."

"Why?"

"Because you're a friend. Because I can see how stressed you are. Because I think you'll benefit from it."

He remembered something from earlier. "What has this to do with the room upstairs?"

Eric chuckled. "I wondered whether you'd get back around to that. Would you like to go and see?"

Now that Eric had said it, Samuel wasn't sure whether he was ready for what was behind that door, but he nodded and stood, following Eric up the stairs. He still couldn't understand why Eric thought he would be good as a boy or little, although he could certainly see the lure of it, especially when he thought back to the several evenings he'd spent colouring that book of horses.

Heart racing with his palms sweating, he inhaled deeply as Eric entered his bedroom and walked them over to the door.

"You ready?"

No. He nodded.

Eric opened the door, flicking the light on now that it was becoming darker. As Samuel stepped through the door, he gasped. The walls were painted a pale yellow with farm animals dancing around a border. There were shelves full of books and boxes and toys and games around the whole room. Under the window was a single bed covered with a patchwork quilt, which looked truly inviting. In one corner, there was a mound of pillows waiting to be jumped into. Next to them were some larger boxes with labels on them. On the opposite side of the room was a small table and four chairs with a cuddly toy sat in each place and a tea set ready to use. The final item held his gaze for a while: a changing table complete with nappies, wipes, cream, talcum powder and other things he couldn't identify but remembered from when his nieces were little.

He stepped forward, his thumb and forefingers rubbing at his bottom lip as the cushion mound called his name.

"You can sit," came a whispered voice from behind him.

Samuel glanced over his shoulder, seeing Eric leaning against the doorframe with his hands in his pockets and a small smile on his face. He wasn't sure what he was feeling, but he peered at the cushions again and decided to do as invited to do, sinking into the huge pile and laughing when they tumbled down around him.

He smiled when he saw a large cuddly monkey sitting on the shelf next to where he was. He reached for it before hesitating, and again, Eric prompted him to go for it. The monkey felt as soft as it looked and had the same texture as his duvet covers at home.

His gaze wandered around the room slowly as his

fingers played with the fluffy ears of the monkey in his arms. When he reached Eric, he paused, staring at the man who seemed to know him better than he knew himself.

"You don't have to figure it all out now, Sam. Do what feels right."

What *feels* right? *What* feels right? Then he knew. He carefully placed the monkey back in his perch and stood from the cushion mountain, making a note to go back and tidy it up once he'd done what felt right.

He crossed the room to Eric, stood on tiptoes and pressed their lips together. It *felt* right. It felt perfect.

The scent of something masculine invaded Samuel's nostrils as he felt Eric slip his hands behind his back while Samuel grasped his biceps to stop himself from overbalancing. The softness of the material beneath his fingers made him slide them slowly up over Eric's shoulders and around his neck as their lips pressed and released in a chaste kiss.

It wasn't enough. A spark began in Samuel, and he whimpered against Eric's mouth until Eric's tongue licked at his lips. Samuel opened, wanting more. His eyes closed against the sight of Eric, and he abandoned himself to the kiss as Eric sank his tongue deeper, exploring every inch of the mouth before him, making Samuel dizzy.

Eric pulled him closer, his hands firm against Samuel's back, and their cocks aligned nicely with how Samuel was standing on his toes. Not knowing what to concentrate on most, he gave up and let himself feel instead. The silkiness of Eric's hair beneath his fingertips, the firmness of Eric's hands on his spine, the strength of Eric's body against his, it was intoxicating.

Eric pulled back slowly, nipping Samuel's lips with his own before resting their foreheads together and breathing as one. Samuel didn't open his eyes, but he lowered to his feet, not wanting to let Eric go.

"Open your eyes, little one," Eric whispered, his fingers brushing along Samuel's jawline.

The gentle command had him blinking open until he was staring into the eyes of a man who was beginning to mean more to Samuel than he'd ever expected him to. He focused on him, laying everything on the line, although knowing Eric would be leaving again soon. This was nothing more than Eric helping Samuel to understand what—or who—he was, and that was fine with Samuel. It had to be.

"Do you want this?" Eric asked.

"More than you know," Samuel answered in the same low voice.

Eric appeared to understand the underlying meaning of his reply and gave a small smile before pulling back and dragging Samuel with him into his bedroom. Once again, Samuel was in awe of the size of the bed and the detail in which the wood was designed, but knowing it was likely the work of Zak, he wasn't unduly surprised.

The dark wooden posts at each corner of the bed reached to the ceiling and connected to the frame from which sheer white curtains hung, allowing the occupants of the bed to be hidden behind a veil of privacy. It was a decadent addition to a more masculine feel of the room. Samuel loved it.

When Eric stopped them by the bottom of the bed and squeezed his hands, Samuel moved his focus back to him.

"Are you sure?"

Samuel smiled at the care Eric was already taking of him, making sure Samuel was with him the whole way. "I'm good."

A hand cupped his jaw. "I'm sure you are." Eric's mouth quirked.

Samuel snorted and covered Eric's hand with his own, pressing it firmly against his cheek. "I'm sure."

"This isn't the end of our discussion, you know."

"I know."

"Let me take care of you, little one."

Hearing Eric talk like that sent a frisson of delight through him, a little kindle of fire flowing through his veins.

Eric's hand slid to the zipper of Samuel's hoodie, which had been strange to put on, but now was glad he had. He had always felt comfortable in those clothes, but they had seemed to be too young for him. He hadn't wanted to look like a fool, so he refrained from wearing them where other people could see. But something about Eric's request earlier that day had him doing it regardless. Something inside him knew Eric wasn't going to make fun of him.

When the hoodie was pushed off his shoulders and slid to the floor, Eric's hands retraced their path back up his arms, over his shoulders and down his chest until they reached the hem of his t-shirt. By this point, Samuel's hands were shaking with the need to touch, to feel, to taste, but he had to be patient.

"Shh, it's okay, little one. Do what feels right, Sam. Touch me if you want. I won't break."

Samuel glanced up at him with those words and saw the corners of his mouth curling up. Feeling himself flush, he closed his eyes and shook his head at his foolishness. He needed to get out of his head.

"Sorry, my mind is a jumble."

"That's why we're taking this slow."

Samuel lifted his arms when Eric tugged at the hem of his t-shirt, then yanked it over his head, throwing it somewhere to the side. Samuel's hands automatically went to Eric's shirt, following the same motions as Eric had done with him and removing it. When he'd dropped the material, his fingers traced along Eric's collarbone and down his sculpted chest to the eight-pack he sported. Feeling suddenly shy and uncomfortable, he withdrew, stepping back.

"What's wrong?"

Samuel kept his gaze on the floor, wrapping his arms around his waist, trying to hide the excess weight he'd put on when Milton had left him. Eric's body put his to shame, and he felt so…

Eric's hands pulled at Samuel's arms until they uncovered his body, and Samuel closed his eyes, holding back the tears of shame.

Hot air touched his skin seconds before lips did, and his eyes flew open, seeing Eric on his knees in front of him.

"This is nothing to be ashamed of, Sam. This is life being too stressful for you. This is your body's way of telling you that you need to rest and relax and recuperate from everything that has been going on. It's not a bad thing. It's something that can be sorted if you allow someone to help."

His lips kissed a path around his rounded stomach and up to his pecs that were definitely not as defined as the man in front of him. Eric's hands followed his lips, and soon Samuel was tingling all over.

"I hate it," he whispered when Eric stood in front of him once more.

"Then we will sort it. You're not alone now, little one. You have me." Eric cupped his face and pressed his lips to Samuel's, requesting entry once more and deepening the kiss until Samuel gripped at his waist to steady himself.

Something was suddenly against his lower legs, and he opened his eyes to see they were by the bed. Samuel hadn't even realised they'd been moving.

"Lie back for…me."

Samuel could see Eric had changed his wording, but he didn't want him to censor himself. "Tell me," he whispered.

Eric's eyes brightened, and he said, "Lay back for Daddy."

The word sounded strange, but something about it made sense, so Samuel followed the instruction, climbing onto the bed and lying on his back. Eric climbed on, nudging Samuel's legs wider so he could rest between them. Samuel felt his cheeks flush again at the position but smiled when Eric gazed at him. Eric braced his hands on either side of Samuel's head and leaned down to kiss him, sliding his lower body across Samuel's in small movements, making their cocks catch on each other's clothing and sending sparks to his nerves.

Samuel pulled away from the kiss. "That feels good."

Eric kissed and licked his way down Samuel's chest, sending goosebumps along his skin in a wave of pleasure. When hot breath blew along his waistband, Samuel glanced down, watching as Eric's gaze flicked to his and waited until Samuel's minute nod gave him permission to continue. Eric lifted the band and revealed the briefs below, and Samuel closed his eyes when Eric mouthed at the head of his covered cock. The heat had him shivering as need raced through him.

"Please, Eric."

Eric answered by pulling the joggers under his ass and running a finger along the waistband of the briefs.

"What do you want, Sam? Do you want me to taste you? Because I'd love that."

"Oh, god, yes! Please!"

"Or do you want me to slide my cock along yours while my hand is wrapped tightly around us both?"

"Oh, hell!" Samuel felt his dick pulse at the imagery shining behind his closed eyelids with Eric's words.

"Or do you want me to slide my cock between your thighs while you thrust into my hand?"

"Please!"

"So many things I could do to you. Hmm."

"Whatever you want," Samuel panted, feeling lightheaded at all the amazing thoughts of what could be done to him.

Eric lifted the waistband of his briefs and pulled them down to the same place as his joggers, freeing his dick to the cooler air. Samuel let out a shaky breath, which was inhaled again when Eric's tongue lapped at the head of his shaft.

Samuel gripped the sheets below him, his head pressing back into the mattress as pleasure streamed through him. That arousal increased when Eric took the tip into his mouth and wrapped a hand around the base. Samuel had no choice but to blink open his eyes and watch as Eric sank down onto his cock, his gaze on Samuel's face as he did. The sight of his dick disappearing and reappearing was something he doubted he'd ever forget, and the wet, sucking sound was surprisingly sexy.

It had a climax rushing closer to the surface, but he didn't want to come yet.

"Wait!"

Immediately, Eric pulled off, concern in his expression. "Is everything okay?"

"No. I mean, yes. I don't want to come like that." His cheeks heated. "I want to come with you."

"All right, little one." Eric sat up, undoing his jeans and pulling his cock free. It was gorgeous, like the man himself. "I want us both to come over your stomach. How does that sound?"

"Yes, please," he croaked.

Eric positioned himself so their cocks were touching, then encircled them both with his hand. "Move your hips a little, Sam. Make yourself feel good. Use my hand and my cock to get you there," he whispered in Samuel's ear.

Samuel gazed down at their dicks peeking through Eric's hand with every thrust. His mouth watered, and he glanced up at Eric, realising the man had been watching him.

"Kiss me, please?"

"Any time, little one."

Their mouths joined gently but soon became a frenzy as their bodies reached for their orgasm. Samuel began panting into Eric's mouth instead of kissing, and his hands found purchase on Eric's back the closer his climax came.

"Oh, god!"

"I'm going to come all over you, Sam," Eric gasped. "Are you ready?"

"Fuck! Yes, please, Eric. Please!"

Their movements became frantic, and Samuel groaned as his orgasm washed over him in wave after wave. All he could hear was a rushing sound until his body calmed enough to make sense of his surroundings again. It had been a long time since he'd come that hard and even longer since he'd come with someone else.

He blinked up at Eric, who had sweat beading along his smiling face.

"Thank you, Sam." He leaned down and licked into his mouth, claiming an air-stealing kiss.

When Eric pulled back, Samuel realised their come covered his stomach, and although the sight was as arousing as hell, it was becoming uncomfortable. At his grimace, Eric laughed.

"Come on, little one. Let's get you cleaned up." They both undressed fully, Samuel turning back into his shy self again.

Samuel wasn't sure what that entailed but followed him into the bathroom, gaping at the sight of the large, fully tiled, open-plan room.

"Nice, isn't it?" Eric grinned. "This was what I meant when I said earlier that I paid extra for a decent bathroom. You wait until you feel the shower. It's like standing out in a rainstorm."

Samuel watched as Eric walked underneath three slightly protruding metal shapes in the ceiling, then the water started. Eric waved at Samuel to join him. Moving slowly so that he didn't slip, he stepped underneath the water and closed his eyes. It truly felt like being caught in a storm, but it also felt cleansing in more than the cleaning way.

Arms came around him, and he startled before settling again.

"What do you think?"

"It's amazing."

Eric pressed a kiss to his neck and pulled back. "As much as I'd love to be a caveman and have you covered in me, I think I better clean you up." He reached for some shower gel and spread it over Samuel's body, washing every inch of him before washing himself. Samuel would've loved to have done that but didn't know if he was allowed, and instead, he enjoyed the shower experience.

When they moved out of the water, it automatically stopped, and Eric reached for a towel from the radiator. As he wrapped the large fabric around Samuel's shoulders, the heat seeped into him, making him smile.

"There we go. Nice and cosy." Samuel stayed wrapped in the towel while Eric dried himself, then Eric pulled him into the bedroom. "Let's cuddle up on the bed for a little while."

Samuel went to take the towel back to the bathroom, but Eric draped it over a chair instead. He hesitantly climbed back onto the bed and into Eric's arms, which enclosed him in a hug once the covers were over the top of them. Samuel slid a hand around Eric's waist and rested his head on his shoulder. It was comforting.

"What's going through your mind, Samuel?"

He said the first thing he thought of, "Why do you sometimes call me Samuel, sometimes Sam, and sometimes little one?"

"Some relationships require the people to have clear differences for when they are in Daddy and boy or little mode and when they aren't. For me, I like to have a name to show the difference. For you, it's Sam or little one. I swap and change between those. As for Samuel, I use that when we need to discuss things or other times when I'm not being a Daddy."

That made sense. It made it easier for Samuel to navigate when he was supposed to be… "What do you call it when I am a boy or little?"

"Well, I don't have a certain word for it. Some people call it age play; some call it caregiving. I call it being 'little' or being 'a boy.'"

"How do we know which one I am?"

CHAPTER NINE

ERIC

Eric exhaled, the air blowing across the top of Samuel's head, ruffling his hair. "It all depends on you and what you enjoy doing. I gave you examples earlier of different aspects of the role, but I also said that each relationship defines it differently, too. Therefore, what happens between us, may not happen between you and someone else, or me and someone else." He didn't like the thought of them being with other people and shoved it from his mind, concentrating on the here and now.

"Is it me doing something and seeing if I like it then?"

"Yeah, basically. I can give you ideas of things I think you'd like as I did with the colouring…oh, did you use the book I sent?"

Samuel hesitated, and Eric wondered if he would

be honest. "Not to begin with. I only started a couple of days ago when things got…"

Eric waited, but when Samuel didn't continue, he asked, "Got what?"

"Bad."

Eric frowned, his protective instincts coming to the forefront. "Bad, how?"

Samuel began drawing with his finger on Eric's stomach, and he wasn't sure whether he would talk to him. "My ex turned up, being an entitled asshole as usual. Stressed me out, then I had a huge discussion with my parents…"

Eric didn't prompt him. He knew how difficult it was to impart information to anyone, let alone someone you knew; therefore, he allowed Samuel the time he needed to gather his thoughts.

"I found out my parents had another baby before I was born. He didn't survive. They never told any of us. I was…" He blew out a breath.

Pain spiked through Eric at the sadness in his voice. "I think I get it. We all think our parents are invincible, but they aren't. They're human."

"But it's wrong! How could they not tell us? Well, they explained that, but it's still difficult for me to understand."

"Everyone has different reasons for why they do or don't do something. Even if someone explained something, it might not be what our own reaction would be, making it difficult to see their side of things."

"Can't you be on my side?" Samuel chuckled, and Eric let out a silent breath of relief.

"I am on your side, Samuel. Taking care of you is my priority."

They stayed silent for a few moments, Eric giving Samuel the reprieve of the quiet. After several minutes, Eric said, "You have a choice now, Samuel."

"Do I?"

"You always do. You choose, but then you receive the consequences of whatever you have chosen. Be that good consequences or bad."

"Okay."

"You can stay here, and I will cook you breakfast in the morning, then take you home to get ready for work, or I can take you home now. Whichever you choose is fine, Samuel. Don't think you will be punished for choosing the right path for *you*."

Eric's heart thumped, and no doubt Samuel could feel it. He knew what he wanted the answer to be, but he also knew what he thought Samuel would choose. The silence was deafening, but Samuel's finger never stilled on Eric's skin.

"Please, could you take me home?" Samuel whispered finally.

"Of course." Eric pressed a kiss to the top of

Samuel's head, then slowly untangled them, pressing another kiss to Samuel's lips. "Let's get you dressed."

He helped Samuel, giving him a taste of what it would be like if Eric were to care for him properly, then dressed himself before linking their fingers as they descended the stairs. He didn't want Samuel to feel like he was being cast aside now their time had ended, which was why he tried to always keep a hand on his body.

"Do you have everything you came with?" Samuel nodded. "Come on then." Eric smiled, holding out his hand again.

He helped Samuel into the car and jogged around to the driver's side. The journey was quiet but not silent, with Eric trying to keep up the narrative and questions about Samuel's work. When they arrived, Eric asked, "Can I walk you up?"

"It's probably better if you don't. You are a movie star, after all." Samuel gave a small smile.

"Okay, let me rephrase…would you like me to walk you to your door?"

Samuel hesitated. "No, it's okay, thank you."

Eric reached for Samuel's hand, giving it a squeeze. "If you have any questions at all, ring me. Day or night."

"I will."

"Are you coming to the party on Friday?" Samuel nodded again. "Great. Shall I pick you up?"

Samuel cleared his throat. "Trent and Max are picking me up, but thanks. I'll see you there."

Eric wasn't happy with that, but it was Samuel's choice. It always would be. "All right. Have a good night and get some rest."

"You, too." Samuel pulled his hand away as he climbed out, closing the door softly behind him.

Watching until Samuel entered the building, Eric bit his lip, wishing this part of the process would get easier, but it never did. Letting someone go who was new to the lifestyle came with its repercussions. Samuel may decide it was not for him, or Eric was not for him. Either way, Eric would stand by Samuel's choice, though he knew the man would be so much happier as a little. Despite what he'd told him earlier, Samuel was a little, no doubt about it.

All he could do was wait and see what happened.

The evening of his party arrived, and Eric had heard nothing from Samuel. He hadn't wanted to check up on him outright, so he'd been sneaky and rang Maggie, checking in with her. She wouldn't give him any information until he'd explained that he liked the guy and they'd been on a date. As soon as he'd said that, she was a fountain of information; however, she always kept it within certain limits. There was no way Maggie would be called a gossip.

He'd invited her to his birthday party, to which she'd declined, much to his surprise.

Ethan rapped on his doorframe. "Wow, don't you look sparkly and dapper!"

"Shut up!"

He hadn't wanted to get too dressed up as it was only a small gathering, but he also wanted to make an effort because people were coming to spend time with him. It was the least he could do. The black shirt had sequins lining the button panel and around the cuffs and collar. His black jeans were fitted but not the skinny type—he hated those, though wore them for the cameras on many occasion—and his boots were plain black.

"I wouldn't say I was dapper," he mumbled, brushing the front of his hair back just so.

"Come on; otherwise, you'll turn into a pumpkin before we get to see anyone."

"God, you are impatient."

They wandered down the stairs to where Emily was waiting for them. Eric slipped on a light jacket because although it was the end of September, it could turn cold when the sun went down. As they went to Emily's car—she was driving so he and Ethan could drink if they wanted to—he wondered whether Samuel *would* attend the party.

He had seemed interested in what Eric had explained, and he hadn't thrown anything back in his face, which was a good sign. Unfortunately, not wanting to stay the night didn't bode well. Then again, Samuel was a lawyer and would probably turn the situation upside down and around and around until he had figured it all out before he made a decision. It wasn't a bad way to be, but it had Eric more impatient than was usual for him. He had the patience of a saint under normal circumstances, but for some reason, Samuel made him lose every bit of it.

By the time they entered Crush, Charlie had sorted everything out, as usual, insisting on closing the place like he had last year so that Eric wasn't bothered by the public. All they had to do was sit and enjoy themselves. Easier said than done.

Amazingly enough, Samuel was one of the first people there, no doubt because of Trent and Max's eagerness. He could see Samuel lingering behind them as they stepped closer, and Eric wished Samuel could be more certain of himself.

"Happy birthday!" Trent declared, throwing his arms in the air.

Eric laughed, clapping Trent on the shoulder. "Have you hit the bottle already?"

Trent mock frowned. "No! Though not from want

of trying." He side-eyed Max, resulting in another laugh from them all.

"Happy birthday, Eric," Max said, giving him a hug. "We're both drinking tonight. That should be fun." He smirked.

"Thanks." He took the gift he'd been presented with and turned his gaze to Samuel. "Thanks for coming."

Samuel's cheeks darkened a little but not as much as they had two nights ago. "Thanks for inviting me. Here." He handed over a small gold box decorated with a bow. "It's not much, but…"

"I'm sure it's perfect. Thanks." Checking where the others were, he indicated with his head. "Can we talk outside for a few minutes?"

Samuel rubbed the back of his neck but nodded. Eric led the way, placing both gifts on the small table, which had been set aside for that particular role. He veered to the left, stopping beside one of the heaters that were currently switched off.

"I don't want things to be uncomfortable between us," he said when Samuel was standing in front of him. "If you don't want to say anything to anyone about our date, then don't. It's up to you." He lowered his voice. "No one knows about my…role as I said before; there- fore, if we did tell anyone, it would be a normal date we went on where I cooked for you, and we watched a movie. But like I said, it's your choice. I will keep my hands to myself if that's what you'd prefer."

Samuel inhaled deeply, then exhaled slowly. "I don't want it to cause issues between our friends. I don't know how to categorise our relationship when there is still so much we need to talk about, especially as you work thousands of miles away more often than not."

Eric grimaced, his stomach churning with nausea and fluttering with a spark at the same time. "I know. I'll do my best to keep myself to myself then."

"It's not that I want to keep it a secret—"

"I know. You're right. I'm getting ahead of us, which is unusual for me." He frowned and shook his head, wondering what it was about this man that changed how he behaved.

"I do have more questions, though."

"I expect you have plenty. Would you…like to come over again tonight? Stay this time and see how it works out?" Eric couldn't believe he was acting… needy. Was he that lonely, or was it this man who made him like it?

Samuel grated his teeth against his upper lip, then nodded. "Yeah, okay. I'll need to head home first to get some clothes, but yes, I'll drive to yours if that's okay?"

"Definitely."

Eric couldn't resist and reached a hand forward to

squeeze Samuel's arm, then let go again. "I better go and make another appearance."

Samuel smiled, and they both entered the bar, a frisson of energy running through Eric. He could show Samuel a few more things about how he would take care of him.

When he stepped back inside, Zak collared him, bouncing with excitement about something. He was handed a gift and tore the wrapper off, eyes widening when he saw a replica of an award statue but with significant differences. It looked like him. Kind of. The whole bar cracked up at the sight of the gift, and he sneaked a glance at Samuel to see him grinning and looking ten years younger. His eyes caught and held onto the man before Samuel cleared his throat and turned away.

Eric shook his head from acting so out of character. Refocusing his attention on some of the people surrounding the table he was sitting at, he listened and joined in with their conversations as the drink flowed and the food came and went.

"You seem like you're enjoying yourself."

Eric leaned his head to the side, resting it on his sister's shoulder. "I am." Even to him, he sounded surprised by the fact. It wasn't that he never enjoyed himself when he was around the people in Cambridge, on the contrary, but he seemed more…invested.

"I've never seen you so relaxed and open as you

have been today. What's caused the change in behaviour, oh wonderful brother?"

"Do not mock those who love thee, sister," Eric growled in fake anger.

Emily giggled. "I love it when you go all Shakespearean."

Shaking his head, he grinned. "I don't know, to answer your question. I love acting, but…" He lowered his voice, tilting his head since his words were for her ears only. "I think I'm getting fed up with it all, Em. I'm beginning to believe enough is enough."

Emily pulled her head away, staring at him, her gaze roaming his face until a small smile graced her lips. "I truly believe you mean that. It would be wonderful to have you home." She wrapped her arm around his shoulders and squeezed him tight. "Despite what you've always thought, these people…" She gestured around the room. "These people aren't here because you're famous. They're here because they're your friends. There has not been a time I can remember when they haven't been there for us when we've needed something or had our backs when we needed them to. It's no different from us doing it for them. That's what friends do." She held up a hand. "I know there are people out there who have proven to you that some people are assholes. I know that. You know that. Hell, everyone knows that. But you need to realise these people here…they're not like that.

These people are as much your family as Ethan and I are."

Eric sighed, trying to see what Emily was getting at. He was beginning to realise her point, but it was difficult. After having their parents reduce him to bankruptcy so he and his siblings could get away from them, trust was hard to give to others. And after living in the Hollywood bubble for too long, many, many people had proven they were the same as his parents were: only after his money or what he could do to make them shine or make them succeed.

No one wanted him because he was Eric. They wanted him because he was famous.

Until Samuel.

If anything, Eric's fame seemed to be a downside to their relationship, if he could call it that. It was another reason why he was leaning more towards leaving the spotlight—at least as much as he could, anyway. He would always be famous and would always have his picture taken, but it would happen less and less the further away from it he became.

It was a difficult decision to make, and one he couldn't take lightly, not with everyone who was relying on him for certain things. It was something he could discuss with Samuel as well. Samuel wouldn't be able to be his lawyer, but he would be able to give him advice if nothing else. Eric was beginning to realise he trusted Samuel to be truthful with him. The same kind of trust he would give someone he spent an evening with in one of the clubs.

"Hey, man. Sorry, I'm late."

Eric stood, embracing Joey and slapping him on the back. "Hey! How are you? I've not seen you for a while. What's been happening?"

"Same old, same old, unfortunately. Still hidden?" he whispered, leaning closer.

Eric nodded. "For the moment."

"Yeah, me too."

"Let's go find a quiet corner and catch up. What drink do you want?"

He held up the beer Eric hadn't seen him holding by his side. "I'm sorted. What? Did you think I would come to see you first?" Joey chuckled.

"Asshole."

Eric laughed and pushed Joey in the direction of one of the vacant tables a bit further away from prying ears. Despite his newfound realisation, he was still paranoid to some extent.

When they were seated, Joey raised his eyebrows. "So, what's got you all twisted up?"

"What do you mean?"

Joey leaned forward, resting his forearms on the table. "You seem a little more…outgoing tonight. Not your usual aloof self."

Eric rubbed a hand over his mouth and sighed. "I

think I've found someone who might be a longer-term prospect."

"That's great news! Or not," he added after studying Eric's face.

"He's completely new to the lifestyle as in I only told him about it a couple of days ago."

"And he's not run screaming?"

"Ha, ha, very funny."

"I wasn't joking, Eric. If he didn't run, what are you so worried about?"

Eric blew out a breath again, trying to figure that information out himself. "I don't know. I don't want to seem like I'm pushing him towards something he might not want. He's older than me, which is not a problem as far as I'm concerned. He's been hurt before, and I don't want to do it again. He's here, and I'm not most of the time. What's not to worry about, Joey? This isn't an easy life for anyone."

Joey nodded slowly. "No, it's not easy until you find someone to spend your life with, then everything else fades into the background, or so I'm told."

Eric huffed a laugh. "That would be nice." He paused. "I'm realising I feel more for him than I expected to. When I first started down this road, it was because I'd seen something in him, and I wanted to help him to figure it out and live his life relaxed, settled and free. I hadn't expected for me to want to be part of his life in a permanent way. Now…"

"Your feelings are changing. You can see him as being part of your life as you've never seen someone else fit in the empty jigsaw space."

Eric's gaze wandered around the room, seeing laughter, joy and happiness flowing from everybody. He wished for that. To be so…free.

The realisation was disarming, and he sat upright. Joey said something, but he held up a hand, trying to grasp the end of that thought and follow it through. He wanted to be free. He was as locked away as all these other people who hid themselves away from friends and family and who were stuck doing things they didn't want to do. He needed to free himself before he could be of use to someone else. To Samuel.

He glanced at Joey. "I need to be free."

Regardless of whether he understood what Eric meant or not, Joey nodded and stood. "Then get to it."

"What if I hurt him?"

"What if you don't?"

The rest of the evening passed by in a blur of laughter and stories—good and bad—about Eric's younger years and the roles he'd played. There were plenty of characters he'd wished he'd never portrayed, which would forever haunt his past, but not one of those people who surrounded him mentioned his parents. It had never been an explicit demand that they were never to be spoken of, but his friends must've understood where to draw the line.

Eric refused to leave before the final person had bid goodbye, including Samuel, who had nodded in silent agreement to their plans. Eric was exhausted, but he'd wanted to make sure everyone had realised how grateful he was to have them there celebrating with him.

The many realisations he'd come to that night had been astounding and would take some figuring out properly, but he looked forward to the idea that he had more waiting in Cambridge for him than he'd thought he had.

"Thank you, Charlie. I appreciate you doing this for me. Again."

Charlie brought him in for a hug. "It's not a problem. I do this for other friends, and you are one of us, so why wouldn't I?"

Eric ducked his head, feeling suddenly exposed and fragile, which made him uncomfortable. "Thanks."

Grabbing his jacket from the edge of the bar where he'd left it when people started to leave, he slipped it on and strode over to where Emily and Ethan were waiting to drive him home. He'd not had much to drink because he'd been too overwhelmed by a lot of things, so he could've driven himself, but he hadn't known that at the time.

The journey was less than silent, with Ethan and Emily chattering between themselves and occasionally asking Eric for his opinion on something, but he was too wrapped up in his head to answer properly.

When they started up the driveway at his house, Ethan asked Emily to stop the car.

"What's the matter?" Eric asked.

"There's a car there I don't recognise."

Eric stared out of the window and smiled. "It's okay. I know who it is."

Ethan peered over his shoulder from the front seat and waggled his eyebrows up and down. "You have a hook-up waiting for you? Go you, birthday boy!"

"He's not a hook-up," Eric stated before he realised what he'd said. "Fuck."

"Would you like me to stay here, so we don't make him uncomfortable?" Emily asked softly.

"Yes, please." He paused. "Look, I didn't mean… He's not…Fucking hell. I don't know what we are. Okay. We're trying to figure it out. Please don't read more into this for the moment." He opened the car door, hesitating again. "And if you know who it is, please pretend you don't. At least for now."

"Have a good night, Eric," Ethan said with a small smile.

"Happy birthday, little brother," Emily said.

Eric closed the car door and moved out of the way as Emily reversed and drove off. The crunching of the tires disappeared into the background as he stepped closer and closer to the visitor's car. When he stood to the side, he realised the car was empty and glanced over at his porch, seeing a dark shadow sitting in his rocker. Drifting closer, more of Samuel's features became recognisable, and Eric's stomach fluttered.

This man meant something to him.

"Hey," he whispered through the lump in his throat.

"Hi. Sorry, I thought you'd be back earlier than this. I can leave if you want. I'm sure you're tired." Samuel stood, moving towards the steps instead of towards the door where Eric wanted him.

"No! No. Please, stay. I want you here."

Eric dared not step closer with how flighty Samuel seemed. Instead, he unlocked the front door and held it open, waiting for Samuel to enter. The moonlight splashed across the man's face as he moved from within the shadows, and his eyes glistened.

"Come on, little one. Let's get ready for bed." Eric smiled and placed a hand on Samuel's lower back, guiding him into the house.

He helped Samuel take his jacket off, resting the bag he'd brought with him on the floor while he hung the coat up. He crouched next to him and tapped his leg, indicating for Samuel to lift his foot where Eric slid off the shoe and repeated with the other side. Standing once more, he slipped off his own, pushing them to the side, and lifted the overnight bag. Linking his fingers with Samuel's, they slowly climbed the stairs, their steps quiet, but their breathing was loud.

They entered his bedroom, and Eric closed the door before putting Samuel's bag next to the chest of drawers and pivoting to the man who was standing uncertain at the end of the bed.

"Sam?" He waited for Samuel to look at him. "Time for a shower." He held out his hand.

Samuel hesitated, then walked forward, slipping his hand into Eric's again. Eric swallowed hard. Although there weren't many words being said between them, there were also a *lot* of things being said. He hoped everything he had to show Samuel tonight—the basics of the caring Eric would love to be part of their relationship—would help him decide if this lifestyle was the right one for him.

CHAPTER TEN

SAMUEL

Before they entered the bathroom, Eric stopped and faced him, his hand unlinking from Samuel's and going to the hem of his t-shirt. He moved slowly as if expecting Samuel to stop him, but he didn't want him to stop. He wanted whatever Eric wanted him to have.

Having overheard some of what Eric had said to Joey earlier in the evening, he knew a bit about how Eric felt, which had gone a long way to easing his mind about what they were doing. Neither of them was with other people, and although Samuel was a little hesitant about starting something with someone who was so much younger than him, he realised he was beginning to feel something more for the man, too. A tether he couldn't stop himself from following to see where it led despite the fear that coursed through him.

"We're going to get cleaned up now."

Samuel hadn't realised Eric had undressed him completely or that Eric had undressed too, but he followed Eric's directions, walking under the rainstorm and lifting his head to the flow with a smile. If this was what it felt like to shower in a thunderstorm, he might have to do it when it next rained.

"What is that happy smile for, little one?" Eric stepped closer, grinning at him, and reached for a washcloth and soap from a nearby shelf.

"I want to stand outside when it rains next," he answered honestly.

Eric chuckled. "That sounds like fun, but wouldn't it be a little cold?"

"I could wear my clothes. They'd keep me warm."

"And how would you get back up to your apartment? You'd be leaving splashy puddles everywhere."

"Hmm. I could do it at my parents' house."

Eric laughed, the sound echoing off the tiles. "I'm sure they'd love to clean up the puddles."

Samuel frowned. "There must be a way."

"Why not use this shower and pretend you're outside in the rain? If you close your eyes, you can believe you are."

Samuel closed his eyes and held his arms out wide, turning in a circle as the water covered him. "Can you see?" he shouted. "It's raining!"

"That it is, little one. That it is." Samuel wobbled a

bit, and Eric's firm hand steadied him until Samuel opened his eyes. "I need to get you clean. Look what flannel I have for you." Eric held up a blue washcloth with lots of fish on it.

"Fish!" Samuel tilted his head. "There wouldn't be fish in a rainstorm, though."

"No, but there can be fish in the shower." Eric rubbed the soap onto the washcloth, making little bubbles pop on the surface, then stepped closer to him. "Wash time."

He stood still as Eric ran the fabric over his skin, transferring the bubbles to him. The sensation was soothing, and he felt himself relaxing as he watched the movements of the washcloth and the bubbles as they ran down his body.

"Rinse off, Sam, while I wash myself."

Samuel stepped under the spray again, moving from one side to the other and lifting his arms. It did feel like he'd been caught in a downpour.

"Come on then, little one. Time to get you dry."

Samuel pouted, there was no other word for it, but he did as asked. The silence that followed the ceasing of the water was deafening. Then Samuel heard a gurgling sound and laughed.

"That sounded like your tummy, Sam. Was it?"

"No!"

"Are you sure?" Eric asked with a smile as he returned with a warm towel and began to dry Samuel.

"It was the water."

"Hmm." Eric moved around him until he was completely dry, then dried off his own body. "Time for sleep now. We've had a busy day, haven't we?"

As soon as Eric had spoken the words as if they were magic, Samuel yawned, hiding it behind his hands. "Okay."

Eric pulled him towards the bed, lifting the covers for Samuel to climb in, then getting in the other side.

"They're cold," Samuel said.

"Come here. Let me help you get warmer." Eric tucked Samuel's head under his chin and wrapped his arms and the covers around them.

Samuel snuggled deeper into the embrace, and unbidden, tears formed. He couldn't remember the last time someone had held him like this. Like he was fragile. Like he was special. Like he meant something.

Eric had given him so much in the few days they'd begun to get to know one another. He didn't know how he could repay him for it because he was beginning to understand Eric was right. Samuel needed to let go, to relax, and letting someone else think about all the minor details was freeing in a way he hadn't understood until he was standing under the shower.

Then he realised. He knew how to thank Eric.

"Goodnight, Daddy."

Samuel woke in the warm embrace of another man and willed his body to stay still, content as he was. He smiled when he felt the faint brush of air against his neck and kept his eyes closed against the bright morning sun. The time of day was inconsequential as he lie there surrounded and cared for.

Eric's words from the previous evening floated into his mind, and his mouth curled. He was beginning to have feelings for this man, too. There was no telling where they would end up because of Eric's career in Hollywood and Samuel's career in Cambridge, but he knew they could work something out if they both wanted to. That was the conversation they would need to have. Did they both want to try something real? Even though it would be long distance.

Samuel had many hang-ups from his relationship with Milton, but he was willing to try with Eric. He didn't know how their relationship would look, especially with the long hours Samuel usually worked and with this new dynamic to add into everything, but he hoped Eric would have some of the answers.

"That tickles." The voice rumbled through his spine, and Samuel frowned until he realised he had been playing with Eric's fingers while the musings had been running through his head.

"Sorry," he whispered.

Eric pressed a kiss to the back of his neck. "It's okay. Did you sleep well?"

"Very. I feel more relaxed than ever."

"That's great news. Well, how about I make us some pancakes for breakfast?"

Samuel scooted around until he was facing Eric, a huge smile on his face. "Pancakes? Do you have syrup?"

Eric chuckled. "Yes, and strawberries and bananas. I think I should make my berry-banoffee pancakes. What do you think?"

"Yes, please!"

"All right, then. Let's get our teeth cleaned, and if you want, you can play while I cook. How does that sound?"

Samuel paused before he stood, checking in with himself and recognizing he was happy with that scenario. His gaze went to the attached nursery, remembering what he'd seen in there that had caught his eye a few days ago.

"Would you like to take something down with you?" Eric asked quietly. Samuel nodded. Eric moved closer, bringing a pair of pyjama pants with him. "I got these from your bag. I hope that was okay."

Samuel lifted each of his feet, allowing Eric to pull

them up over him, ignoring the morning wood they were both sporting. Eric grabbed his hand and tugged him towards the nursery. Samuel's gaze immediately went to the monkey he'd cuddled, but he glanced at Eric first.

Eric smiled. "Go on. Grab whatever you'd like to play with while I cook."

Samuel picked up the monkey and box of playing cards he'd seen on the shelf. It wasn't a normal set of cards, but ones with pictures on instead. He could make a castle with them. Or a bridge.

"All set, Sam?"

Samuel jumped and chuckled. "Yep."

He got set up on the table, the monkey sat beside him while he emptied the cards onto the table. Looking at some of them, he saw they were different characters dressed up in different uniforms, although some were identical. It looked like a game of snap. Picking up two cards, he leaned the tips together in a steeple shape, carefully balancing them until they stayed. He continued for a few more, then placed some flat on the top, making sure not to drop them too heavily, or the ones below would collapse. Then he started on the second row. He needed three floors for his castle. It needed to hide Monkey.

After he had finished the third row, Eric called his name softly, so he glanced up at him, eyes wide, barely daring to breathe.

"That is a fantastic job, Sam. It looks great." He didn't move closer. "Shall we sit at the dining room table, so we don't knock your tower down?" he asked.

Samuel stared at his castle, then shook his head. "Ready, monkey?" He lifted the monkey and exhaled, blowing the castle down. "Timber!"

Eric laughed, and Samuel joined in. "Okay, then. Tidy up time, then you need to wash your hands before breakfast."

"Yes, Daddy." Samuel froze. The words had come out automatically. The previous night he had said them with intent as a thank you. That morning, it was different. He liked the sound of the word.

"Don't overthink it, Samuel. Let it happen if you want it to."

He listened to Eric and brushed it aside. Once he'd tidied up and washed his hands, he sat back in his seat and waited, watching as Eric—his Daddy—put pancakes onto plates. When his was placed in front of him, they had been cut up into triangles made into the shape of a star with a small circle pot of syrup in the middle. Around the star were pieces of banana and strawberries. Samuel grinned when he saw it and lifted his fork.

"Thank you!"

Eric hesitated, then lifted his fork. "You're welcome, little one. Enjoy."

Breakfast was finished in record time, and Samuel licked his fork clean.

Laughing, Eric took his plate. "There will be nothing left of the fork if you keep doing that."

"They were delicious."

"Good." Eric returned to the table. "Now, we have to make a decision. We need to talk a little, don't we?" He waited while Samuel nodded. "Would you like to play for a little while first or do the talking first?"

Samuel was enjoying the freedom of not having to think for himself as much; therefore, it took him a few minutes to get back into the headspace of making decisions. "Play first, please?"

"All right. Up to the nursery with you. I don't have any toys down here, so you'll need to choose some from upstairs."

"I like the nursery."

"I thought you might."

They climbed the stairs, Samuel clutching the monkey, unsure whether his easy acceptance of the lifestyle Eric had described was a good thing or not. When they entered, he discarded his thoughts and wandered around the space, looking at the different things that were in there. He checked out the boxes on the floor and found some Legos.

"I've not played with Lego for years."

"Come on then. Let's tip some out, and we can see what we can build."

Samuel started sitting on the floor but soon moved to his stomach. Eric passed him a small cushion. "Put it under your chest; it might make you a bit more comfortable."

Between them, they built a house with a garden and a swing. He tried to find the correct bricks to make a bench but couldn't see which ones would fit together as he wanted and sighed.

"What's up, buddy?"

"I want to make something for them to sit on."

"How about these? You could put some of the bricks along the bottom and use these fence pieces as the back?"

Samuel grinned. "Perfect." He fitted them together, narrowing his eyes when his fingers fumbled, then brandished his success.

"Well done! Looks great! How about you keep going while I grab us some drinks?"

"Okay."

Samuel distantly noted Eric had left the room but found himself humming a tune as he finished the fence around the garden and put some flowers in the patch. He jumped when Eric sat next to him again.

"Sorry. Sit up for me and have a drink. Building is thirsty work."

Samuel rose to his knees, grimacing as an ache shot through his back. It pulled him from his peacefulness. "Oh, god. I can't lay like that for too long." Rubbing at his side once he'd sat back against the bed, he reminded himself he wasn't a kid anymore, even if he was pretending to be.

"Let me help. Turn sideways and rest against the bed that way, then I can rub your back a bit and soothe away the aches. Nothing should stop you from having fun."

Samuel did as Eric said, leaning his elbow on the bed covers and his head in his hand while he drank his water from a plastic cup, he realised. The purple plastic caught his eye, and he raised it to look at it, smiling when he saw boats floating around the outside of it. When Eric pressed against a sore spot, he yelled.

"Sorry. Let me work on the area for a bit. It will ache, but it should ease after a few minutes."

"Thank you," he said a while later.

Eric pressed a kiss to the exposed side of his neck. "You're welcome." He slid his arms around Samuel's waist and rested his chin on his shoulder. "How are you feeling?"

"You've done a great job. It barely hurts now."

"I'm glad, but I meant about what we've been doing."

Samuel tilted his head, staring at a spot in front of him as he ran through the memories of what had happened so far that day. He was surprised at how easy he'd found letting everything go. Inhaling, he said the same to Eric.

"I must admit, you sank into the little frame of mind far quicker than I expected you to. That's not a bad thing," he added. "I was expecting some resistance, which still may happen depending on what you like or dislike about other aspects of it, but so far, you seem content and less stressed."

"You're right. Nothing matters when I'm…playing or having fun. I know you will stop me if you need to, and, like with the drink, you will provide me with what I need, even if I don't know I need it."

"That's right. And that is the basis of the whole dynamic. I will look after and care for your basic needs, and you get to relax, release the tension and stress, and know I will catch you."

"It sounds too good to be true. It doesn't seem… right that I pretend to play."

"There's no pretending about this, Samuel. You're not pretending to be someone you're not. You're allowing yourself to be who you are."

They stayed in that position for the time it took for Samuel to drink all his water. Eric took the cup from him.

"Now it's time to tidy up." Eric laughed, and Samuel assumed he must've seen his scowl. "Not a fan of tidying up?"

"Not more than I have to," he admitted, his mouth curling slightly.

"Ah, I'll keep that in mind. If you misbehave, you'll

end up with a punishment of some sort." Eric raised his eyebrows, spearing Samuel with his gaze.

"Punishment?"

"Let's tidy up, then we can have that conversation."

Working together, they tidied away all the Lego and replaced the lid on the box. Eric put the box back, then they went downstairs and into the kitchen, and Eric asked if he wanted coffee.

"Could I have some milk, please? I only usually drink coffee when I'm working or out with people."

"Sure, but why is that?"

"I need it at work because it helps me to focus. As for when I'm out..." He shrugged. "It's the done thing, isn't it?"

"Do you even like coffee?" Samuel ducked and shook his head. "We can find you something else to drink that you'd like instead of putting up with something you hate? I'll have a think."

Eric placed the milk in front of him, and Samuel stared. "Remember..." He waited until Samuel glanced up at him. "If there is anything you don't like, say so. This is about finding out what works and what doesn't."

His gaze was drawn back to the bright blue beaker that had two handles and a lid with holes in the top. Samuel picked it up and studied it as he chewed on his bottom lip. Why was this something he liked the idea of? He was too old for this, wasn't he? Tears filled his eyes, and the beaker wobbled in front of him. Why did he need this? Because he did need it. He felt it deep inside him. Eric had somehow found the thing Samuel had been missing from his life, and he hadn't even discerned it.

What would've happened if Eric hadn't approached him? What would've happened if he'd carried on as he had been and not had this chance to discover the missing piece of *his* jigsaw?

"Hey, come on, little one." Eric wrapped his arms around Samuel's shoulder, pulling him closer until Eric's scent surrounded him. Samuel turned and gripped the back of his t-shirt, burrowing his face into his neck as Eric leaned down and whispered nonsensical words into his ear.

The breeze brushing across his naked torso from somewhere had Samuel coming back to himself some time later, still in the same position, which couldn't have been comfortable for Eric.

"Sorry," he croaked.

"Nothing to be sorry for. The beaker was too much. I apologise. I wanted to see if it was something you'd like."

"I do like it. It made me realise how right everything has been feeling. How content I am. That turned into wondering what life would've been like if you hadn't taken this chance on showing me what I was missing."

"Oh, sweetheart. I'm so happy I was able to give you this. I wish I had recognized earlier, but we hadn't seen each other often before Max and Trent's wedding. I'm glad I've helped you."

Samuel cleared his throat. "Where do we go from here? You go back to work soon, don't you?"

Eric sighed and briefly let go of Samuel to sit on the seat next to him, then slid his arm around his shoulders again. "I'm here for another week and a bit, then, yes, I will be going back to New York."

"For how long?"

"Until the end of filming, which actually shouldn't be long. We've run over a little, but the director assured me it would be finished within two months. I won't be back during that time, though. I've used all my allotted time off." Eric grimaced.

Two months is a long time without seeing someone who was becoming more to Samuel than he ever expected to find.

"Is this…" Samuel stopped himself from asking. It wasn't his business. Eric couldn't have meant that he wanted to stay with Samuel. Did he? How could Samuel ask?

"Is this, what?"

"Where do we go from here? I mean…us?" he repeated his earlier question.

Eric stood, heading over to the kettle to finish making his coffee, and brought it back to the table.

"Honestly, Sam. I don't know." He inhaled. "I'd like to think this is more than you experimenting with me. I know it's a large change for you and a lot to get your head around, but I'd like to continue helping you if you want."

"I do," he breathed, barely getting the words out loud enough to be heard. "How do we do this when you're not here?"

"Do you know Joey Kirkland?"

"Isn't he one of Logan's friends?" Samuel refused to admit he knew the guy only because it might show he'd been eavesdropping at the party the previous night.

"He's in the same lifestyle, though on the BDSM side of things not the Daddy side. If you'd allow it, I can talk to him and see if he can be your tether if you like."

"Tether?"

"Someone who helps you keep grounded when I'm not here."

Samuel chewed his lip, trying to understand how he felt about others knowing what he wanted. He supposed the only way would be to try it and find out. "I don't know."

Eric smiled. "Okay. We can decide later. Would you like to try your beaker now?" Staring at the plastic cup, he rolled his lips inwards to withhold his smile. Eric chuckled to the side of him. "Go on, give it a sip."

Samuel lifted the cup to his mouth, fitting the hard plastic between his lips and sucking gently. Some of the cool liquid squirted into his mouth and over his tongue, and he closed his eyes, the sucking motion soothing. When nothing more came from the beaker, he opened his eyes again and pulled it away with a frown.

"Good boy, Sam. That deserves a reward, I think."

With no idea what reward Eric was talking about, Samuel followed him back up the stairs once more.

"Take those off for me, then get on the bed."

Once more feeling shy because of his body, he kept his head down so he couldn't see Eric's expression. He climbed onto the bed and laid on his back. Eric followed a few seconds later.

"Have you ever been rimmed?" Samuel scrunched up his face but shook his head, and Eric laughed. "Don't like the idea?"

His brows drew together. "I don't know. It seems, kind of, unhygienic?"

"It can be if you don't take care to clean yourself properly. Although some people don't care either way."

Samuel had no idea who would enjoy something like that but to each their own.

"Onto your hands and knees, please." Eric pulled Samuel's hips back when he was in position, using his hands to open his ass cheeks.

Samuel's face flamed, and he buried it in his hands. To be so open, so exposed to someone he both barely knew and knew better than some others, left him feeling vulnerable. He wanted to close his legs, but Eric's body was between them, so he couldn't.

Warm, soft hands soothed up Samuel's spine, tingles following in their wake. "Shh, calm down. Nothing will happen if you don't want it to. I think you might enjoy this, though."

Samuel inhaled deeply and exhaled shakily, trying to calm his racing pulse. His stomach fluttered as he said, "I want to try."

"At any point, if you're not enjoying it, tell me, and we'll stop, okay? This is supposed to be a reward, not a punishment."

The word reminded Samuel they had veered off topic earlier when they were supposed to discuss punishments, not their future, but both discussions had to happen. He was sure the punishment one would come up again.

Eric's lips zigzagged a soft path down his spine, closer and closer to his destination. Samuel tried not to tense, but the unknown had his breath increasing again. Eric's hands were busy, touching him all over and sending waves of pleasure through him. When he reached his ass, Eric squeezed Samuel's ass cheeks, taking small, sharp bites from the globes before licking at the top of his crease.

Without speaking, Samuel knew Eric was waiting for his agreement, and Samuel, unable to voice anything, pressed back a little, and Eric licked lower and lower but bypassed his hole. Eric's tongue pressed against his sensitive skin behind his balls, then back up again, this time skimming over the entrance before retracing his steps. After doing this several times, Samuel was more than ready to feel Eric press harder.

When Eric pushed his tongue against Samuel's pucker, he wailed in response.

CHAPTER ELEVEN

ERIC

Eric grinned as much as he could against Samuel's ass. He'd had a feeling Samuel would enjoy being rimmed, but the shout confirmed it. With that, Eric went to town, licking, biting, pressing, spearing, constantly keeping his hands and mouth on Samuel to increase his arousal. Some men could come from this; he'd have to wait and see if Samuel was one of them. Eric couldn't, but he preferred topping anyway.

On the other hand, giving this to someone was something Eric loved.

The thought that they were on the same page with their new relationship had adrenaline and warmth radiating through his body. He had never wanted to be so close to someone before, and for them to want the same thing—which had nothing to do with him being famous—was…intoxicating.

Sliding his hands up Samuel's spine once more, his touch was gentle and teasing not hard and dominating. He wanted all of Samuel's senses firing as a reward for being so receptive to this new lifestyle Eric had thrown at him.

As his tongue worked Samuel open, his hand finally found Samuel's cock.

"Fuck!"

Sweat beaded on Samuel's skin, and amidst curses, the man fell to his elbows, baring himself further to Eric's ministrations, which Eric took full advantage of. He pressed against Samuel's entrance with his tongue, pushing harder against the pucker until his tongue speared inside.

"Holy fuck!" Samuel's voice was muffled, but he was pushing back against Eric's mouth, demanding more without saying the words.

Eric's hand continued to stroke the man's dick, the leaking fluid easing his movements. When he felt the trembling begin within Samuel's body, he removed his hand to the annoyed huff of his partner.

Pulling back, Eric asked, "Do you want to come like this?"

"Fuck, yes. Please!"

Eric's cock was hard as steel, but he refused to bury

himself inside what he knew would be a tight ass. He wanted to save it for a later time.

"Shout as loud as you want, sweetheart. No one can hear you," he whispered with a grin, then lowered his mouth once more.

He didn't go easy that time; his sole purpose was to drive Samuel to the edge of climax as many times as he could before tipping him over. If the curses were any indication, he was doing a good job. His hand resumed the stroking of Samuel's cock, the man bucking into his hold.

"I'm there. Oh, please, let me come! Please!"

Eric thought he needed one last thing. "Come for Daddy."

"Shit!"

Samuel came. His hole tightened rhythmically against his tongue, his cock thrust through Eric's hand, and Eric was overwhelmed. His other hand encircled his own dick and stroked while his tongue lapped at Samuel and brought him down from the high. When Eric's climax approached, he pulled back and released over Samuel's heaving back with a loud shout.

Riding the euphoria for a few seconds, Eric kept a hand on Samuel, then carefully helped him down onto his side. Standing, Eric smiled as he wandered to the bathroom to grab a washcloth and cleaned the exhausted man. Samuel's release coated the cover, so Eric pulled it from beneath Samuel and threw it in a corner, pulling a new one from the cupboard and covering Samuel's sated but exhausted body.

As soon as Eric climbed into bed, Samuel snuggled up against him. "I like rewards," he mumbled.

Despite it being lunchtime, Eric decided to allow a nap for them both. They deserved it.

"Even though I've talked about the situation with my parents, I don't know how to face my siblings today," Samuel admitted into the early morning light.

Eric couldn't see his features well enough to decipher the expression, but the pain in his voice was unmistakable.

They would be separating for a few hours later that day because Samuel had a family dinner, and Emily was complaining they hadn't seen enough of Eric. But once they had taken care of business, so to speak, Samuel was returning to Eric's house for the night and would go to work from there the following morning.

"You'll need to play it by ear, I think. Think about it as one of your cases where evidence is thrown at you at the last minute. What do you do?" He paused. "You adapt."

"It would break my brothers and sister's hearts to

find out, but I think they need to know. However, it can't be me that tells them."

"I agree you shouldn't tell them, but why should you suffer alone. You need someone, who is close to the situation, to talk things through. Someone who understands where you're coming from. You know my history—the whole world does—and I can only give you advice, but to share the burden with someone who is going through it as well will help you both heal. I'd suggest asking your parents to tell your family. It's not fair on you to carry the burden alone."

Samuel was quiet, and Eric kept his hand movements slow and easy on his back and side, keeping him calm and centred. His lover—his little—had so many things thrown at him lately, he needed as much relief and relaxation as he could get. Tomorrow, he would be back at work, and Eric was worried about how it would change their dynamic. He hoped Samuel would come back to Eric's house after he'd finished so Eric could take care of him and release the stress of his day, but it was something he wanted to discuss with Samuel after he'd been through the strain of the weekly family dinner.

"What drives people to cheat?" Eric wasn't fazed by the change in the subject but knew it was a rhetorical question. "I've seen it so many times within my career, and Milton was the icing on the cake, so to speak. It doesn't make sense to me."

"I don't understand it either, but that's what makes us who we are. If we understood, we might be capable of it ourselves."

"I couldn't do that to someone. The pain of feeling worthless and unwanted is too much."

Eric hated the way Samuel's voice cracked. He tightened his arms around the man, pressing a kiss to his forehead. "You have to know you are neither. I know you felt it then, but you are so much more than that…person."

Samuel chuckled, the heat of the exhale blowing across the skin of Eric's neck. "He's an asshole. You can say it."

"Thank god! He *is* an asshole. Even more so because of what he's put you through after you separated." Eric's lips pursed, and his eyes narrowed as he thought about the man who had treated Samuel so badly. He had no idea how to get that mouse of a man to leave Samuel alone. It was as if he didn't want Samuel, yet he wanted to make sure no one else had him either. "What has he been doing to you at work?"

Samuel sighed. "He drives me mad because he turns up whenever he wants to, swanning around like he owns the place. His new boyfriend is not even a partner or someone hugely important within the firm, so I have no idea why he gets the impression he can do what he wants. I'm surprised no one has mentioned anything to him before now, come to think of it."

Eric had his suspicions Milton had not *one* boyfriend within the firm, which was why he was allowed such freedom. It wasn't good for Samuel, though, and Eric planned to think of some ideas that might be able to help.

"I think you are amazing for putting up with him and not losing your temper." Eric chuckled. "Although I heard you close to it when I was hiding in your bathroom."

Samuel snorted. "Yes. I think that might have been the sharpest I've ever been with him."

Eric calmed. "If you need anything today, anything at all, call me, okay. If you need me to be there, I'll be there within minutes, no matter who sees us." He increased his hold for a few seconds, hoping to pass on his strength to Samuel.

The soft touch of Samuel's lips to Eric's nipple startled him, but he withheld his response. He circled the nub, nudging the hard peak between the seam of his lips, firming them around it. The motion had Eric wondering if nursing or a dummy was something Samuel might enjoy, especially with how he'd reacted to the beaker, and this was another step in the same direction. He'd find a way to bring it into their time for him to try.

As it was, he held the back of Samuel's head as he played, the occasional flick of his tongue sparking a flint within him, but not in a sexual way. When Samuel found suction and pulled the nub rhythmically, Eric felt Samuel's muscles relax, and he smiled serenely. He would find a dummy for him after the difficulties were over with later that day. He was sure Samuel would react positively to it.

After several more minutes, the suction released when Samuel's body went lax with sleep. Eric held him tightly, staring through the chiffon curtains into the room that was slowly lightening with the dawn. He would find a way to help Samuel with his work, with his parents and with his little side. He refused to allow his little to deal with everything on his own anymore.

"Are you going to give us any more information about the guy you're seeing?" Ethan asked, prying as ever.

Eric's mouthed curled one side. "Not at the moment. We're still taking things one day at a time. It's not easy for him, so I'm trying to give him some time to…" he almost gave away his secret, "get used to being with me."

"Yeah, I suppose being with a famous dude will get him more attention than with someone else."

"Thanks for the vote of confidence," he joked.

"You're welcome." Ethan smirked in his direction, buffing his nails against his chest in pride.

Eric returned his gaze to the landscape outside the window of his sister's house. While Samuel was busy with his family, Eric was catching up with his. He had missed the hell out of them—he always did—but this time seemed worse than usual.

"How's uni?" Eric focused on his brother, waiting for Emily's return from the takeaway place.

Ethan was looking more grown-up every time he saw him. Despite being the youngest of them, Eric acted more like an adult, whereas Ethan was still a kid in some respects. He assumed it had something to do with still being at school and Eric having to grow up a lot quicker. Not that Ethan didn't deserve to have this freedom. He did. They all did. Unfortunately, their parents had made life difficult for them all.

"It's good. I'm enjoying working with Thompson Architect Company. It helps that Sean is there too. He keeps me in line and doing what I should be doing when I have no idea *what* I should be doing." Ethan laughed self-deprecatingly. "I love everything about the job, but sometimes, I look at something and go 'What?' You know?"

Eric nodded. "I know exactly what you mean. It's similar when I look at some of the scripts I'm sent. Everyone thinks I'll be great for these roles, and I look at them and wonder what planet they were on when they thought I could play a historical, sword-wielding Scot."

They laughed, joking back and forth about the different things Eric would have to learn before he would be able to fit that role. The first one being the accent, which was one Eric had never been able to master no matter how hard he'd tried.

"What's so funny?" Emily asked as she entered carrying three bags full of food.

"Eric playing a Scot," Ethan quipped, setting them both off again.

It was damn good to be around his siblings again. He'd needed this break, but he'd not understood how much. Between them and Samuel, this was going to be the best vacation he'd ever had.

"Yeah, not seeing it. Sorry, bro." Emily grinned and placed the bags on the table, pulling out the containers. "You could get away with it in looks, but that's about it."

"Hey, I'd make a convincing Scot, I think," he said in the worst Scottish accent.

None of them stopped laughing for some time, helped by the fact that they reminisced about some of his worst roles. Eventually, those talks turned to a topic they didn't broach often.

"Have you heard from them?" Emily asked.

Eric put his cutlery down and crossed his arms on the table edge, finishing what was in his mouth before he spoke, "No. I've heard nothing. I still have the private investigator keeping tabs on them every couple of months to be on the safe side, but so far, they've kept to the agreement we made."

He could see by the clenching of his brother's jaw and fists that he was angry. Ethan had thought the best of their parents, defending them to the end. When he'd found out the truth, he was distraught. More so than Eric even. Emily, on the other hand, had seen it coming and had begun to work her magic behind the scenes. Nobody had known what she'd been doing until the court case.

Those eight months had been torturous, but when the judge ruled in Eric's favour after Eric had provided his new conditions, it had been over.

Emily, the wonderful accountant-to-be at the time, had been requesting money from their parents for years and investing it in places where their parents couldn't touch because it was all in her name. When she had explained, she'd revealed she had enough to buy a small three-bedroom terrace house for them, pay the bills for a year and pay for the other bits and pieces needed to look after the three of them. She got a student loan so she could finish her degree and did the same for Ethan when he wanted to start college and uni.

It was only when Eric had been cast in numerous starring roles that he could pay her back for everything she had done for them. The first thing he did was pay off her and Ethan's student loans. After that, he'd bought them each a decent car and a house. He had been determined not to let their parents destroy his relationship with his siblings. None of them deserved that.

To this day, he still paid for things, regardless of their arguments about it. It wasn't about him having more money than them; he saw it as his turn to look after them when they had been looking after him for years.

"It doesn't matter. We don't need them. Look at us," Ethan voiced, spreading his hands wide. "We're amazing. An accountant, an architect and an actor… Whoa, that sounds like the start of a bad joke."

"And I've realised, our jobs all start with A like our names start with E. Crazy how things work out." Emily chuckled.

"What are we watching tonight, anyway?" Eric changed the subject.

"*Coercion.*"

"Seriously," Eric grumbled. "Why the hell do you put me through this every time I come home. I think I'm going to stay far away from now on."

Emily shoved his shoulder. "Stop complaining. Even you admit it was your best performance."

Eric rolled his eyes. "Yes, but not enough to watch

it over and over again. You know I hate seeing myself on screen."

"Only because you quibble at everything you do. If you relaxed and pretended it wasn't you, it would be great."

"How can I pretend it's not me? I see the same face in the mirror every time I stare into it!"

"You love it," Ethan said.

"Oh? Well," Eric stood, heading over to the cabinet that held the videos and DVDs of their childhood activities, "I think it might be time to revisit Year 9, don't you? If I remember rightly, there was a wonderful performance from you in the school fashion show. Ah, here it is!" He pulled a DVD from the shelf.

"Don't you dare!" Ethan stood, his leg knocking the table with a thunk.

"What?" Eric asked, all innocent, waving the case in the air. "Don't you want to relax and pretend it's not you?" He tilted his head, a small smirk resting on his lips.

"Fine." Ethan pouted and dropped back into his seat, arms crossing his chest.

Eric snorted. "See. It's not so easy, is it?" Eric rolled his eyes. "But we can watch it if you like. Just don't grumble if I nit-pick."

"Deal."

"Do I get a say in this?" Emily asked, her head

resting firmly on her fist as she stared at the two of them in turn with raised eyebrows.

"Uh, oh," Ethan and Eric said in unison.

"Sit down and finish your food," she said, her no-nonsense voice settling them down like nothing else.

After several minutes of comfortable silence, Emily said, "But I agree. A night focused on a fashion show would be highly entertaining for a change."

"Emily!" Ethan whined, then promptly shut his mouth when she gave him that look.

By the time he left Emily's house for his own home, he was centred, settled and content with only a Samuel-shaped hole left to fill, and when he parked in his driveway, a smile lit his face to see himself fully complete for the first time in years.

He stepped from the car and found himself with his arms full of little Sam. Burrowing his face into Eric's neck, Samuel didn't say a word, just held onto him as tight as his arms would allow. Eric returned the embrace, gently rocking him side to side and cradling the back of his head. Inhaling, he smelled the lingering scent of food, and underneath that, the scent of Samuel.

"Come on, little one. Time to play," he whispered in his ear.

He walked them forward, stumbling a little as Sam wouldn't let him go, but with a chuckle and the occasional muffled curse, they managed to get into the house. The moment he closed the door behind them, Eric felt Sam's shoulders drop, the whole-body release of tension evident in his sudden…relief?

"Hey, now. What's wrong, Sam?"

Sam breathed in deeply. "Nothing now."

"Let's go and sit down for a moment and talk, and then we can get comfortable and play before bed."

"No! Please. Can we talk while I play?" Sam lifted his head, his eyes shiny but clear.

Eric studied him for a moment, then nodded. "All right. Let's go wash up first."

"Yeah! Rainstorm!"

Laughing, Eric watched as Sam turned and ran for the stairs. He followed at a more sedate pace and found Sam under the shower already.

"Come on, Daddy!"

The word warmed his heart, more so when Eric realised Sam didn't flinch or hesitate in using it as he had done before. "I'll be there in a moment, Sam. Make sure you wash yourself. Don't stand under there and drink the water." The silence that followed made him snicker because he knew if he looked, he'd find Sam with his face to the ceiling and his mouth open wide.

Undressing quickly, he threw the clothes in the basket and joined Sam, ensuring they were both ready for the night ahead. After drying his little one, he dressed him in some loose shorts and a t-shirt, dressed himself in similar clothes, then linked their fingers and strolled to the nursery.

"We're going to rest in here for a while. You can choose whatever you want to play with."

Sam immediately scurried over to the Lego, yanking the lid off.

"Don't tip them all out; remember, you have to tidy up after yourself."

"I will," he promised, then proceeded to tip the majority out of the box.

"Sam," Eric warned. "You have a lot of tidying up to do before bed."

"I will, Daddy. I want to see the different bricks."

Eric raised his eyebrows. He set his watch to vibrate in half an hour and settled himself on a comfortable fabric armchair in the corner by the bed, lifting the puzzle book and pen he kept there for specifically this reason. It allowed him the chance to watch his little boy play but also relax his mind through the puzzles he did.

When his watch notified him of the time, he put his book and pen away, then gave Sam a five-minute warning.

"But I've only just started! Look at what I've built!"

"It looks good, Sam, but it's nearly time for bed. We need to get ready, so you have five more minutes, then you need to tidy it all away."

Eric had a feeling he would be punishing his little

boy tonight. There was a whining tone in his voice that had not been present in their past exchanges, and he put it down to the stress of the family dinner and being tired. A long, good sleep would do wonders for them both.

"Okay, Sam. Time to tidy it all away."

"No! I'm not finished!" Sam continued to click bricks together, adding to his design.

Under normal circumstances, he would've allowed Sam to keep his building out and only put the other bricks away so he could finish it the following day; however, the next day was Monday, and Samuel would be back at work.

"You can build it again another day. Put them away now, please." Eric firmed his voice as he leaned forward from his seat and rested his elbows on his knees.

"No!" Sam brought his hand down on top of his bricks with a crash, then pushed it away from him. He stood and bolted towards the door.

"Stop!"

Sam froze in the doorway, his back rigid, his breathing loud in the silence that followed. Eric stood, wandering over to him, giving him time to calm and think about what was happening. When he stopped close to him, Sam shivered.

"I would like you to go and sit on the bed and face the headboard with your legs crossed. I want you to look at the design on the headboard while you think about what you've done." His voice, although firm, was not loud or angry. He stated what he expected Sam to do without there being any mistake. They had not spoken about punishment, which in hindsight, they should have done before now, but Eric knew this would be a learning curve for Sam. Eric would be with him the whole time for this first one because he needed to ensure Sam was all right. "Go now."

Sam sniffed, and with his shoulders and head lowered, he climbed onto the bed and assumed the position Eric had requested. When Eric had the headboard made, he'd asked for a large maze design to be featured in the centre of it. It was a unique twist that provided a bit of information about Eric— that he liked puzzles—but he'd also planned ahead for this reason. By staring at the maze, someone could get lost in their mind, trying to find their way around it without realising it. It helped some people to relax, and he hoped the same thing would happen to Sam.

The poor boy was exhausted and needed time to settle; otherwise, he wouldn't sleep.

He gave Sam twenty minutes of silence, then climbed on the bed behind him and wrapped his arms around Sam's waist, both facing the maze.

"Time's up, little one," he whispered.

"I'm so sorry, Daddy. I'm tired and worried about

tomorrow, and I don't want to go, but I know I can't stay here forever and hide away from the world."

"Sam. You are welcome to stay here as long as you want to, but you're right. You do have to venture out into the world tomorrow and do your job. Think about all those people you help. They need you." And before meeting Samuel, Eric never would've thought he'd say those words about a lawyer. "And then, when you have finished helping them, you can come back here and let *me* help *you*. How does that sound?"

Sam twisted until he was facing Eric. "Wonderful!"

Eric pressed his lips to Sam's, cupping his face gently and wiping the tears from his cheeks.

"All right. Go and tidy up your toys, please. I'm going to the kitchen, then I'll come back with a snack before bed, all right?"

"Yes, Daddy."

Sam jumped off the bed and raced into the nursery. By the time Eric had returned with a beaker of milk, a banana and a surprise, Sam had finished and was waiting on the bed, holding onto the monkey he'd taken a shine to.

"Does he have a name?" Eric asked.

"Cheeky-Boo." Sam grinned.

"Lovely name." He passed over the snack and drink. "Be careful not to spill any, please," he said as he rested the tray on Samuel's legs.

They ate in silence, then Eric placed the empty tray

on the table by the door and helped Sam to get changed into some pyjamas—special train pyjamas he'd ordered the other day. Sam's eyes lit up, and his hands caressed the front. They climbed into bed, and Sam wrapped himself around Eric as usual. When Sam's lips found Eric's nipple, the man smiled and reached for the surprise he'd brought. He didn't mind Sam using him as a soother, but something easier for him to hold onto would be better.

Placing the dummy next to Sam's mouth, Eric felt him falter. A few seconds of hesitant silence, then Sam took it into between his lips. A sucking sound started, and Sam relaxed against him again.

His little boy was home.

CHAPTER TWELVE

SAMUEL

Samuel woke with a jerk, unsure whether it was from a dream or something else. He lay on the edge of the large bed, the sheer curtains caressing his arms as he rolled onto his back and stared up at the ceiling, listening to Eric's deep breathing. He felt overheated and jittery, and his thoughts immediately went to his office. He sighed when it dawned on him that he had to go back to reality tomorrow, and his life was no longer suspended in the dream that had been this weekend.

It was inevitable but had come around a lot quicker than he'd wanted it to.

He rolled to his side again, plumping the pillow to cushion his head and slid his hands underneath it. Swallowing hard, he tried to clear his mind of what was to come, but every time he closed his eyes, he tensed and tried to find another comfortable position.

"What's wrong, Samuel?"

Eric's sleep-hoarse voice filled him with joy and sadness in equal measure. He had been good to him, knowledgeable and giving throughout this whole weekend, but what was Samuel giving him? Not a lot, he didn't think.

"Sorry for waking you. I'm all right. Go back to sleep," he mumbled, trying to keep his voice calm and neutral.

"You're not all right." Eric pressed his body against Samuel's and slid his arm around his waist. "You're sweating. Are you ill? Let me help."

Samuel sighed, knowing it was impossible to keep it from him. Eric had a way of finding out, even if Samuel never said a word. And he thought *he* was good at body language and invisible signs. "I have to go back to work tomorrow, and it's…I don't want to. That's the short version."

"Can't you take the day off?"

He cleared his throat. "Even if I did, the work would still be there the day after or the day after that."

"When we first met, you said you enjoyed the work. What's changed in the last six months?" Eric rubbed his lips against Samuel's shoulder, his hand resting over Samuel's stomach.

"I do love it. I love helping people get what they

deserve. I love making others pay for what they should be paying for instead of trying to get out of it. I love helping children figure out which parent they would like to live with or which they wouldn't. Everything about the actual job, I do enjoy."

"Then what has you not wanting to return…Ah, your ex and the lawyer."

"Yeah. They make it so that I dread going into the office because I never know whether they're going to pop through my door and make my life ten times worse."

Eric tightened his grip for a few seconds. "I think you need to face them both and tell them that things need to change. You can't go through your day dreading being there. You're there for hours at a time."

"I've tried telling them. Milton won't listen, saying he has every right to be there, which is bullshit in a lot of ways, but correct in others, and Gregory tells me to get on with my job, even though I'm probably doing part of his job, too."

Eric scooted away and rolled Samuel to his back. "Have you considered finding a new firm?"

"I did a while ago, but when I realised what hassle it would be. I found it easier to stay. Better the devil you know and all that."

Eric ran his fingers over Samuel's cheek and across his lips, and he found his eyelids flickering. He needed sleep but knew he wouldn't get anymore, no matter how early in the morning it was.

"You are so good to people, even those who don't deserve it. Ever since my parents…Anyway, ever since, I've fought for those who couldn't fight for themselves. I've helped people who didn't have anyone else in their corner. It was why I was hesitant when I found out you were a family lawyer. One, because my parents had found the nastiest lawyer known to man to represent them and bleed me dry, and two because I've seen other lawyers do similar things. It's hard to overcome those experiences, but I have with you, and now you are in a situation where I want to help, where I need to make sure you're okay. But I can't because you're able to fight your own battles, and as much as I want to do it for you, I know you won't let me."

Samuel reached for Eric, pressing their lips together. "Who am I if I get someone else to fight for me?"

"Someone who knows how to let others help?" The light-hearted response made Samuel chuckle until it was swallowed by Eric's mouth covering his.

He clasped Eric's head, needing him close as Eric's tongue slipped into his mouth and explored. Eric's hand smoothed along his biceps, his forearm and his hand until he linked their fingers together and pulled one of Samuel's hands away, then he lifted his head.

"You're going to be a good boy for Daddy, aren't you, Sam?" he whispered.

Samuel swallowed hard, and the heaviness in his chest lifting with being relieved of making choices, of making decisions. "Yes, Daddy."

"Put both hands under the pillow above your head and keep them there until I say otherwise, all right?"

"Mmmhmm." Sam's eyes fluttered closed as he followed the instructions.

"Sam?" He opened them again and focused on Eric. "I need your words, sweetheart, not just your gorgeous sounds."

"Okay."

Eric's lips touched his with a barely-there, chaste kiss before moving his mouth along his jaw, nipping at the skin beneath his ear, then brushing the full mounds down the column of his neck. When he reached Sam's collarbone, he licked along to the other side and continued down his chest.

Sam arched his back after a lick across his nipple had pleasure firing down to his groin, and he wanted nothing more than to grip Eric's head and keep him there for more. He didn't, though. His Daddy had asked him to keep his hands where they were, and he needed to listen. Breathing became more difficult while Eric played with both his nubs, alternating which had his mouth and which his fingers, but either way, Sam felt the tingling in his body's reactions.

He loved cataloguing all the different feelings Eric brought out in him because it was so different from what he'd ever had with Milton. As soon as the man's name crossed his mind, he wiped it clean, his ex-husband having no business there.

Sam lifted his hips, wishing for friction of some kind, but there was nothing. Not even his clothing gave any kind of resistance against which he could reach for release.

"Such a good boy, letting your Daddy love you like this." Eric's mouth prolonged Sam's torture and lapped at his skin as he lowered to his stomach. Instinctively, Sam sucked it in, but under the sensual ministrations he was receiving, he soon forgot about his worries.

Soft fingertips caressed the waistband of the pyjama bottoms Eric had dressed him in before bed, and his breath hitched and held as Samuel waited for his Daddy to decide what he would do next.

"Daddy," he whispered urgently.

"I know, sweet boy. Soon."

Sam held his bottom lip between his teeth, and his eyelids flickered, wanting to see what Eric was doing but wanting to feel the warm pleasure flowing through him as well.

"Let's get these off you," Eric mumbled, sliding his fingers underneath the waistband and lifting it over Sam's cock. Sam moved enough, Eric could slide the trousers from underneath him, then slid them down his legs and off somewhere into the room. "Look at you," Eric crooned, shifting into the bracket of Sam's legs.

Sam smiled at Eric, their gazes meeting and holding while Eric caressed his stomach and legs. Underneath Eric's hands, he felt loved and cherished, even if he knew it was only in this moment. He felt worthy of being with this amazing man and being allowed to call him Daddy.

Eric rose to his knees, sliding off his pyjamas, then crawled above Sam until they were face to face with Eric braced over him.

No words were said, but everything was understood, regardless. They were both there, both wanting, both needing what the other could give.

"Please, Daddy," Sam breathed, thrusting his hips upwards and being rewarded with a hint of friction against Eric's body. He broke eye contact and pressed his head into the pillow, exposing his neck.

"Mine," Eric declared before sliding a hand under Sam's neck and fastening his mouth against the thick column, drawing against the skin of his throat. Then he progressed down, faster this time, until he was in line with Sam's weeping cock.

Eric opened his mouth and enclosed the head of Sam's dick in his mouth, sucking the fluids from him and making Sam whimper. He needed more, but Eric pulled off.

"I was going to take my time and taste your ass again, but I need to be inside you, little one."

"Yes, please! Oh, please, Daddy!"

Eric kneeled up and forward, reaching for the bedside table and withdrawing a small bottle and a condom.

Sam bit his lip. "Daddy?"

The man paused and gazed at him. "Yes, sweetheart."

"Can we do it without a condom?" he muttered, ducking his head to his chest and closing his eyes as his cheeks heated.

"Look at me, Sam. We need to make sure we're on the same page before we do this." Sam inhaled and opened his eyes, his gaze caught on the lust-filled one before him. "I'm negative. I have a test every month without fail, and I haven't been with anyone in seven months."

The news surprised Sam, and his eyebrows rose. "I was tested after Milton left and haven't been with anyone in years but haven't been tested since then."

"If you're happy to take my word for it, we can go without. I wouldn't hurt you, but if you're unsure, we'll use one today, then get new tests. The choice is yours."

"What about you?"

Eric's forehead creased. "What do you mean?"

"Why are you taking my word for it?"

Eric smiled. "I know you wouldn't hurt anyone on purpose. You're too honourable for that."

Sam's eyes filled, but the tears didn't overflow. "Please, Daddy. Let me feel you."

"Okay, little one." He leaned down and kissed Sam, who returned the kiss with everything he was feeling.

A cool, wet presence slid along his taint, and he jumped in surprise, having not heard the bottle, being distracted as he was.

"Sorry, I should've warned you it would be cold."

Sam didn't reply. He widened his legs, uncaring of the picture he presented. He wanted to feel everything, and he wasn't denied.

Eric prepared him well, starting with one finger until Sam was taking three without any discomfort and sobbing with the need to be filled.

"Are you ready, my sweet boy?"

"Yes, Daddy, please!" Sam's breath hitched, his heart rate and breathing fast and hard.

A long, loud moan erupted from his throat as Eric pressed his lubed cock into his channel. It had been far too long since he'd had a dick in there, and he'd missed it. He loved every burning inch, and when Eric bottomed out, they were both panting.

"Please, Daddy! Can I move my hands, please?"

"Hold onto me, Sam. Hold me tight."

No sooner had the words been spoken and Sam

wrapped his arms around Eric's neck and burrowed his face than Eric withdrew and rammed back into him, hitting his prostate immediately. Despite their position, Eric moved and hooked Sam's legs over his forearms, opening him further to his thrusts.

"You feel amazing, Sam. So tight and hot. Are you going to come for me, little one? Are you going to come for your Daddy?"

Each word sent Sam higher until a keening cry left his mouth. Eric drove into him until Sam tipped over the edge, coating their bodies with his release.

"Give me your lips, Sam," Eric demanded.

Sam dropped his head back and fused their mouths as Eric's orgasm coated his insides with warmth. He had never let anyone go bare inside him before, and the feeling was foreign, but he loved it. Eric lifted his head as his hips slowed to a stop, his chest heaving and sweat dripping down his face and body.

"Fuck, Sam," he gasped. He shook his head. "Did you enjoy that, little one?"

"God, yes, Daddy. It was amazing."

"You're amazing." Eric tenderly kissed him, sipping from each lip alternately as he carefully withdrew. "We need to have a shower. Are you up for an early morning rainstorm?" He winked at Sam, who beamed in return. "Yeah, I thought so. As soon as we're clean, though, it's back to bed. We need some more sleep."

"Yes, Daddy."

His week had been nothing short of hell on earth, and he was at the end of his tether. Despite spending every evening with Eric, decompressing and relaxing as a little, Samuel reversed all that hard work the minute he stepped inside the office each morning.

That day was no different, except he was facing an even bigger opponent—his ex-husband.

"Milton, why are you coming to me about this when you have a boyfriend who is supposedly now taking care of you?"

"Because he doesn't understand why I need to do this. He says it's pointless."

It was pointless, but it was also Milton's choice. Samuel sighed and rubbed a hand over his face. "No, Milton. Go see Gregory. I'm not getting in the middle of this."

"But you have to! Can't you explain it to him?" Milton whined.

"No."

"Why?"

"Because you need to grow up and explain to your boyfriend why you feel the need to spend that much money on a ticket to a convention in America every year. It's not my problem anymore."

"Samuel!"

"No, Milton. I've had enough. Get out. I have to get back to work."

He turned his gaze to the papers on his desk, ignoring the noises coming from the man he was beginning to detest the sight of. When he realised Milton wasn't moving, he pressed a button on the phone, and Maggie entered the office.

"Maggie, could you please see Milton out? Thank you."

"Of course, sir." She indicated for Milton to precede her, then shut the door behind them.

Samuel sagged back into his chair, slumping and blowing out a long exhale. He'd spent the morning in court, fighting a custody battle for a thirteen-year-old who wanted to live with his aunt instead of his parents. The case was a pro-bono one he'd insisted on taking because the girl reminded him of a younger version of his sister Ava—strong, capable and sure. It had been the initial hearing today, but he didn't think there would be many more. From the evidence the child and the aunt had provided, the parents were emotionally and verbally abusive towards the girl, so he was certain of a positive outcome.

That night, all he had to look forward to was a lonely night in his apartment. Eric was meeting up with everyone at Crush as usual, but Samuel didn't want to go. He still felt out of sorts and uneasy around them—not because they were unkind, but because he wasn't able to relax and relate to them easily.

Samuel had begged off, saying he'd be exhausted, which he was, and that Eric should go and enjoy himself. Besides, Eric left in four days, and Samuel needed to remember what it was like to be alone because come Tuesday, he would back to where he had been before Eric had turned his world upside down.

He worked for several hours past finishing time, trying to catch up with anything he predicted he would need ready for the following week, then gathered up his briefcase and traipsed home. After being away for so long, it was strange entering the cold space he owned instead of the warm, cosy house Eric had bought. He'd been back a few times to pick up things he needed, but for the most part, he'd remained absent, and the slightly stale air reminded him of that.

His phone beeped as he slid his shoes off, and he retrieved it from his pocket as he pottered down the hallway to his bedroom, intent on a shower then a late dinner.

I hope you're already home because if not, I'll be sending you instructions for you to obey as punishment.

The thrill of receiving a message from Eric was muted by the threat. He hated time-outs, and he'd had several throughout the week when his emotions had boiled over. The worst one had been sitting in the corner of the living room, staring at nothing but a blank wall. At least the bedroom had something for him to stare at.

Another beep startled him from his musings.

Sam…?

He quickly typed a reply.

I'm home. I'm heading for a shower, then possibly an early night.

He tossed his phone to his bed, stripping off his clothes and throwing them in the washing basket by the door. Being at home was a different experience from being at Eric's. The shower, for one thing, was going to be something he missed, but he'd get over it. As soon as he was back to his routine, he would be fine.

If he kept telling himself that, he would eventually believe it, he hoped.

Standing under the spray, he tried to reconcile how different his life was from a week ago. Last week, he was in his own apartment, his own life, his own quiet living arrangements. Last week, he felt dead inside.

That morning, he'd felt alive, wanted, cherished, needed. Now, he felt the emptiness in his life, and Eric hadn't even left yet.

Blowing out a breath, he cleaned himself, then dried off, heading back to his room with a towel around his waist, the silence deafening. Throwing on some joggers and a t-shirt, he wandered back to the living room and pulled out the chess set he used. Although the game he played was against the computer on his laptop, he always set up the glass chess set to view it easier. There was something in his brain which made the physical set easier for him to plan with than seeing it on a computer screen. And besides, the set had been a gift from his siblings one birthday.

Before starting a new game, he made himself a glass of milk, wishing he had a beaker to use, and hesitated before grabbing a pack of biscuits. He'd eaten better than he had in years while he'd been with Eric, but he didn't have the energy to cook anything now.

He sat at the table, ripped open the packet and set the computer to start the game. As he stared at the pieces, his mind threw pictures at him of the time he'd spent with Eric. Trying to brush them away, he refocused, but it was as if the game was in a foreign language. His shoulders slumped, and he felt tears stinging at his eyes.

Dropping his head into his hands, he pressed his fingers against his eyes, breathing deeply. He rubbed at his face and over his head before pushing away from the table.

What he wanted wasn't there. He went to bed,

tears silently soaking into the pillow while he shivered under the cool sheets—nothing like being at Eric's surrounded by warmth in more ways than one.

The following morning, he woke, groggy from a restless sleep. He had no idea what had woken him because it was Saturday, and he had nowhere to be.

His whole body jerked when a pounding began on his front door. Yawning, he shoved the tangled sheets away from his body and stumbled to the entrance. Blinking blearily, he opened the door, hiding another yawn behind his hand, and almost burst into tears when he saw Eric standing there.

"It was too quiet without you there," the man muttered.

Samuel yawned once more, his eyes leaking those happy and sad tears while Eric wrapped him in his arms. "It's going to be hell without you, Eric. I don't know what to do with myself when you're not with me anymore. How can you have changed so much in my life in such a short time?"

"I know. I'm sorry. I didn't think we'd get this close. I honestly thought I would help you into the lifestyle, then help you find someone, but I can't do that now. I'm in too deep."

Samuel tucked his face into Eric's neck, tightening his grip around his waist for a brief second before pulling away and stepping back. "If we can't manage one night without each other, how the hell can we manage two months?"

Coffee called his name despite his hatred of the taste, and he drifted to the kitchen area to switch on the older-style machine. Bracing his hands on the counter, he lowered his head, tears continuing to drip down his face while the pressure in his chest increased. His whole body felt too heavy. With some effort, he managed to lift his head and wipe his face as the machine gurgled the contents into the glass jug.

There were no words that could be said to express the shittiness of the situation they were in. Instead, he kept silent, though he felt the all too familiar presence behind him.

Filling two mugs when the coffee was ready, Samuel doctored them and held one out to Eric, who took it without a word. It didn't stop the tingling that sparked from where they touched.

Samuel trudged to the sofa, sinking into the soft cushions and resting his elbow on the arm of it while cradling his mug.

"I don't know what to say to make this better, Samuel." Eric laughed without humour. "I'm usually the one with all the answers, but this has got me feeling guilty for bringing you into this and not thinking of the consequences."

Samuel flicked his gaze up to Eric. "You don't need to feel guilty. You don't know what you've given me. Yes, it's going to be difficult going back to what life was like before you'd opened my eyes, but I'll manage somehow." He inhaled and let it out slowly. "I think I might need to speak with someone and explain the situation so I have someone I can talk to."

"That would be a great idea." Eric finally sat next to him, placing his coffee on the table. "I don't want this to be the end of us, Samuel. You say I've given you something? Well, you've done the same for me. Not only have you changed my mind about lawyers," he winked, "but you've also made me realise how hollow my life was before I found you. I've been going through the motions for years."

"I think we all have." Samuel rubbed a hand over his mouth, eyes on his coffee. "We have three days before you leave. Let's enjoy it, but let's also prepare ourselves for when you leave."

"And how do you recommend doing that?"

He grimaced. "Reducing the amount of time we spend together. We can spend some time with others in between our time with each other. I don't usually socialise much, but if we're certain we want to try this, we need to let others know."

"Is it a good idea right before I leave? Won't it make things more difficult for you in the short term?"

"That you're leaving is going to make things difficult." Samuel closed his eyes. "Sorry. I don't mean it like that."

"I know," Eric said. "Will you come home with me?"

Home. At that moment, Samuel realised what he'd been missing for the past twelve hours: home.

The home that was Eric's house, not his.

"Yes."

CHAPTER THIRTEEN

ERIC

"You know who it is, don't you," Eric asked Emily as they waited for Ethan to empty the stuff he'd forgotten to take out of his car for the journey to the airport.

Emily gave a small smile and nodded. "Yeah, I saw his car several times when he visited Zak about the custody case."

Eric blew out a breath. "I've made a mess of things, but can I ask a favour?"

"Always."

"Can you check up on him on occasion while I'm gone? Our relationship is…more than we planned and far more complex than you might realise."

"What do you mean?"

Eric ran his tongue along his bottom lip and sighed

again. "I'm…" Why was it difficult to explain who he was, especially to Emily? "I'm…"

"You're something you're not ready to tell me about, and that's fine. I have my suspicions, but you'll tell when you're ready."

Eric rubbed a hand over his face. "I'm a Daddy," he blurted, glad they were still at his house.

Emily smiled. "I had a feeling it was something along those lines, although I went more the BDSM route."

"How do you know about all that?"

"I have ears and eyes and the internet." She grinned. "Besides, I know you like taking care of people, so a Daddy kind of makes sense. I should've realised it earlier." She frowned. "That makes Samuel…"

"My boy."

Emily raised her eyebrows. "I thought…Never mind."

"Most people think Daddies are older, but it's not always the case. But going back to my favour. When I first came back, I thought I would help him experience the lifestyle and see how good a fit he was, then help him to find someone for himself." Eric felt his heart expand and briefly closed his eyes. "But he was much more than I'd bargained for. He's everything I've ever wanted, and now, I'm leaving him to fend for himself after having changed his life and made it difficult for him to manage alone. I'm selfish."

"You are the least selfish person on this planet, Eric Clarke! And don't you say otherwise. You didn't realise this would happen. It's not your fault, but we can try and mitigate the damage. It's only for two months."

"Two months is a long time to go without a Daddy when you've just found one."

"I can't be his Daddy, but I can check up on him as you said. I'll keep my eyes open. Make sure you keep in contact with him."

"Nothing will keep me from doing that." Eric beamed.

Emily enfolded him in her arms, holding him securely and making him feel less like the mess he was. It was a new feeling for him. He was usually calm and collected, and he needed to get back into that mindset to be able to last the next couple of months.

Pulling back, he gave his final bombshell, "I'm finishing up with all this. This is my last film."

Emily's mouth fell open. "Seriously?"

Eric nodded. "I couldn't understand why I hadn't arranged for another film after this one had finished, but I've had enough, Em."

"Enough of what?" Ethan asked, carrying a bag of stuff and dumping it in Eric's hallway.

"Hollywood."

"You're stopping? I thought you still enjoyed the acting?"

"I do. I can find a theatre or something around here I can do instead."

"Wow. I never thought I'd hear the day." Ethan slapped him on the back. "It will be great to have you around again."

Eric glanced at Emily, who had been silent during the conversation. She had tears in her eyes but a trembling smile on her face. He opened his arms, and she fell into them, sobbing, and he realised how much of a toll this must have been on them all. Staring at the ceiling, he pursed his lips. He *was* a selfish asshole. He should've been here for them.

Emily pulled away, wiping her face. "Now, don't you start cursing at yourself again. We've been spoilt having you as a brother, but we've missed you. There are plenty of years left to make it up, don't worry about it. Two months will be gone like that." She snapped her fingers. "Now, come on. We're going to be late."

Eleven hours later, he finally closed his front door behind him and slid to the floor. Exhausted didn't cover it. It was far too late to call Samuel, unfortunately, but he did send him a message to tell him he'd arrived and asking him to ring him when Samuel got up in the morning, regardless of the time. It would be something like two in the morning in New York, but he didn't care; he needed to hear his voice.

"What has happened to the Eric I know and love?" Emma shrieked as he walked through their front door.

"Nice to see you too, Emma."

"Don't give me that, mister. You look like crap. I bet your make-up artist is loving you at the minute."

He'd give her that one. Jenny was not happy with the bags under his eyes or the sallowness of his skin. "I'm fine. Just…homesick, I suppose."

He'd spoken to Vaughn a couple of days ago, explaining a little of his situation, but when it began to get convoluted, Vaughn had stopped him and invited him to dinner to spill his guts instead. It also meant his wife and daughter would be there, and Emma would get her two cents in, maybe even Kirsten, too.

Vaughn had a tricky personal situation—entirely of his own making, well, Emma's making—and it made their life difficult at times. But at home, where no one else could see them, they were so in love it was sickening, even for Eric.

"Come here. I think someone needs a hug."

Before he could reply, Emma folded her arms around him, reminiscent of the hugs he received from Emily, and he instantly released some tension. There was something about being held, which helped, and he finally began to understand why it helped littles and boys.

"Dinner's ready. Let's dig in. We can talk afterwards."

Eric grabbed the cutlery and wandered to the dining room where Vaughn and Carlie were placing glasses and napkins next to the placemats.

"Hey, I thought I heard you being grabbed by my wife."

"She was complimentary of my new look," he joked.

"I can imagine. As I'm certain, we'll hear all about it after dinner."

"I'm sure. Is Kirsten not joining us?"

"She went to see her friend in New Jersey for a couple of days. She said hello, though."

"And how are you, pumpkin?"

"Uncle Eric, I'm too old to be a pumpkin now. I'm seven," Carlie said, nose in the air.

"You *are* seven, I know. No one is too old to be called pumpkin, especially by an uncle who can still tickle her!" He mock-raced around the table, pretending to grab for her as she squealed and jumped away, laughing. He finally grabbed her and lifted her, pressing a kiss to her cheek. "You'll always be my pumpkin. Even when you're old and grey."

"I'm never getting old."

"Is that so?" he said, putting her down again.

She straightened her top, brushing it down carefully. "Yes. I'm staying young and beautiful forever."

"Then I wish you all the luck in the world, my dear pumpkin." He bowed to her.

"She'll need it with all of you around," Emma said, bringing two dishes in. "Vaughn, can you grab the other bowl, please."

"Sure." He kissed her cheek as he passed her and quickly returned with another serving dish.

Once they were all settled, conversation flowed as it always did when he'd met with his oldest friend. Every topic was covered, even those that ended up with heavy explanations for Carlie's benefit.

When his phone rang, he apologised and dug it out from his pocket. "Sorry, I've got to take this." He pushed his chair back and stood, wandering through the doorway to the living room and sinking onto the sofa.

"Hey, Samuel. How are you?" Eric's breath eased as his boyfriend's voice came over the line, strong and clear.

"I'm good. Long day, as always, but I thought I'd ring before I went to bed. How was your day?"

Eric frowned. Although Samuel's voice was strong,

it held a touch of trembling if Eric's hearing wasn't deceiving him. "Long." He chuckled. "The make-up team keeps complaining I'm not drinking enough, but if I drank anymore, I'd turn into a fish. Are you sleeping any better?" Samuel hummed on the other end, and Eric knew he was debating being truthful or not. "Sam, tell me the truth."

Samuel sighed. "Not really. These cases are taking longer to close than expected, and I'm trying to keep on top of them, but it's not easy, especially with new cases coming in as well. I'm all right, though."

He didn't sound all right. He sounded stressed as fuck. Eric closed his eyes and lowered his head. "What can I do, Samuel? How can I help?"

"You can't, Eric. I'm good. Honestly."

"Do you want me to ask if someone can give you some little time, a couple of hours or something?"

"No! Thank you, but…only you, Eric. I can't…" Samuel cleared his throat.

Eric stood, pacing the floor in front of the fireplace, cursing under his breath at being so far away from his boy. "I'm so sorry, Samuel. I've messed this up completely." He ran a hand through his hair, his chest constricting as he thought about Samuel suffering in silence and there being nothing Eric could do to help.

"You haven't messed anything up. You'll be back before you know it. I'm going to head for a shower, then bed. I've got an early morning tomorrow."

"Samuel…"

"It's fine, Eric. Have a good evening."

The phone clicked in his ear, and Eric glared at it as he pulled it away. He refrained from throwing it across the room, but only just. There had to be something he could do to help Samuel. If he could guarantee Samuel wouldn't need punishing during the time he was being little, he would've chanced doing it over a video call, but if punishment was required, Eric wouldn't be there to take care of him afterwards, and that broke all kinds of safety rules for the lifestyle.

Eric dropped into a chair, leaning his head on his crossed arms and breathing into the small space.

"What's wrong, Eric?"

Vaughn's voice startled him, and his head shot up. He laughed without mirth. "I have a *lot* to tell you."

"All right, but for the time being, come back and finish dinner. Once Carlie is in bed, we have all night."

Two hours later, Eric sat with a rare glass of wine and began to explain about Samuel. Vaughn and Emma already knew about his lifestyle, Vaughn being the one to help him find a decent club to keep his visits confidential. When he explained about the start of their relationship and Eric easing Samuel into the life, they were over the moon when it turned into something more.

"Unfortunately, I'm now three thousand miles

away, and he has no one to help him destress while I'm gone. I don't know how to help him from so far away."

"Have you asked anyone at the club?" Vaughn asked.

Eric shook his head. "No. We've been apart for a week, and I can tell Samuel is withdrawing from me further each time we talk. What are we going to be like after another nine weeks?"

He gulped his wine and slumped back in his chair.

"Well, I don't know the ins and outs of your relationship, but as it's new, I would suggest listening to Samuel and hearing what he has to say. You have to keep talking to him; otherwise, things will get worse, and he'll begin to lose faith in you." Emma tilted her head at him. "And if I'm reading you right, you love him."

Eric lifted his eyebrows and nodded slowly at her. "That I do. How it could happen after such a short time, I don't know. But he's everything I never expected to have. The reason I'm..." He rolled his lips inwards, stopping his words. He hadn't planned on telling them yet.

"The reason you're leaving the film industry?" Vaughn finished.

Eric flicked his gaze to Vaughn, noticing the curl to his lips. "How the fuck do you know me so well?"

"You're easy to read."

"For you, maybe."

Vaughn conceded the point with a nod of his head. "Going back to Samuel. I think your best bet would be to get counsel from the club. Someone there is bound to have some ideas you can use."

"It certainly wouldn't hurt to ask, I suppose."

"So, we only have you until early December. That's not long," Emma said with a pout. "You need to make sure you still visit."

"Of course, I will, and you can do the same."

"Nothing will keep us away."

Eric changed the subject, needing a reprieve. "How are things working out with your situation?"

Vaughn and Emma had decided when they first began seeing each other that Emma didn't want to be in the spotlight. She hated the media, the vultures, the whole big celebrity…everything. When her discomfort nearly ended their relationship, Vaughn had come up with an alternative plan. It meant they had been hiding their relationship for nine years, and the media still hadn't figured it out. How the hell they hadn't, Eric had no clue, but he could see it was taking its toll.

"We're managing, as always," Emma said, a tinge of sadness lilting her voice.

The conversation turned to more pleasant topics, namely the behind-the-scenes gossip of his and Vaughn's movie sets. When Eric told them about Don, Vaughn cursed a streak.

"I've heard so much about him. He needs taking

down. If only women were willing to stand up to him, he'd be out of a job quicker than anything."

"I agree, but the women have things to lose as well. It's not black and white, honey," Emma said, squeezing Vaughn's hand.

"I know. I hate this business sometimes."

"Don't we all?"

"At least you're getting out." Vaughn grinned.

"You know better than anyone that there's no 'getting out' of this job. I'll be hounded for the rest of my life. You would've thought they'd be fed up with me by now, especially with everything that's happened."

Emma stood, resting her hand on his shoulder as she passed. "Drama loves drama."

Vaughn nodded. "She's right. Until there is no more news, there will always be vultures." He pursed his lips. "Have you heard from them?"

Eric shook his head. "Greyson sent me some more information a few weeks back. They were still in Vegas and had appeared to have settled there. Until they find something new and shiny to follow, that is."

"I'm glad to see you're opening yourself up to Samuel, Eric. I've been worried for a long time that you wouldn't allow yourself the chance. Emily and Ethan are great, don't get me wrong, but you need something for yourself. Just you. And Samuel seems to be that."

"He is. As I said, he's everything."

Several hours later, he drove home, wishing he didn't have to get up early the following day, but he knew, the moment he stopped his routine, the harder it would be to get back into it. It had been bad enough getting back into it after being comfortable with Samuel, and even though he woke early to get to work, it was still later than Eric usually got up.

He sighed, his hands clenching on the wheel. Tomorrow, he needed to contact Infinity and see if there was someone he could ask for advice. Luckily, everyone was bound by strict confidentiality clauses, but he knew the owner would be careful in who he chose. Eric's wellbeing and career depended on it.

As for Samuel, Eric hoped the man could hang on for two months, but if he felt like Samuel was slipping, fuck the contracts, fuck the filming, fuck the director. He would leave everything in the dirt and fly back to catch him. He refused to let Samuel fall when it was his job to keep him safe, his job to keep him healthy, and his job to hold him near.

Daddy refused to let his boy suffer more than necessary.

Eric laughed at the joke Vaughn made as they

stood drinking glasses of expensive champagne—or in his case, sparkling water—at a red carpet event. His gaze scanned the room, dismissing several calls for his attention until he reached the man he had come to loathe more than anyone except his parents: Don.

"That asshole is at it again," he murmured, gaining Vaughn's interest with a slight tilt of his head in the man's direction.

Don had his hand around the waist of a petite, black-haired beauty, who barely came to his shoulders, and was talking to another man. The director had another woman's face cupped in his free hand and was moving it back and forth as if checking for imperfections. Eric watched as he let go, pointing to several places on the woman's face before throwing his head back in laughter.

The posture of the woman in question curled in as if to make herself smaller, and Eric cursed, shaking his head. "There needs to be something done about that man," he said, anger burning through his veins. "The way he treats everyone, but especially women, is disgraceful."

"You're right about that, but the man is a force to be reckoned with. Not many people will go up against him."

"You're looking at one who would. And will."

Eric focused on Vaughn, making it clear with a

look exactly what he planned once he was out of the business.

"Be careful, man. Just because you're not going to be working anymore doesn't mean he can't reach you."

Eric conceded the point. "He wouldn't be able to do much, but you're right. He could still hurt me in some areas."

It pained him to say, but he needed to think carefully before acting because he now had Samuel to consider. He refused to make any waves until he had explained and discussed it with him first. In some ways, he would've loved to be able to show Samuel this side of the business, the shitty schmoozing everyone does when they're supposed to be your best friends. In other ways, he was glad Samuel was nowhere near it all.

Throughout the night, his gaze continued to stray to the director, watching him interact with other people and noticing which women—and men—shrank away in fear or froze in their tracks. Sadly, it was a great deal.

As the man drew closer, Eric could catch wisps of conversation that boiled his blood, talking about women as if they were accessories. Eric mentally went through his options but reasoned he could do nothing but gather more information for when he may need it. Vaughn already knew about his "secret files," which detailed everything he'd ever heard or had proof of against certain members of the business, and so he kept up the inane chatter as Eric listened.

"I've had enough," Vaughn stated, settling his glass onto the tray of a passing waiter.

"You're not the only one."

They strode towards the doors of the main hotel event room, ignoring the calls of several people once more. Before they exited, someone bumped into Eric, and he grabbed them to keep them from falling.

"Sorry, I didn't see—"

"No problem. Accidents happen." Elsbeth smiled, though Eric could tell it was strained.

"Everything okay?"

"We're all good, aren't we, Elsbeth?"

Eric barely refrained from rolling his eyes when the director's voice came from behind him.

"Yes, Don."

The man slid an arm around her waist, and Eric watched as she stiffened before relaxing and offering a smile that didn't reach her eyes.

Eric narrowed his eyes but didn't say anything.

"You aren't leaving now, are you? The best part is still to come."

"Sorry, we have plans," Vaughn interjected before Eric could say something less than pleasant.

"Interesting. I hope Kirsten is keeping well, Vaughn?"

"She's doing well, thanks for asking."

"Glad to hear it." Don gave a leer in Elsbeth's direction, then held his palm out, indicating she should precede him. "We'll catch up another time, I'm sure. Enjoy your evening. I know I will."

Vaughn caught Eric's arm before he could go after the man, but it didn't stop him imagining grabbing hold of the asshole and punching him. In fact, it was satisfying and as good as if it had truly happened.

"Leave it," Vaughn murmured in his ear. "A fight for another day."

They collected their coats, continuing their conversation once they were safely ensconced in Eric's car.

"There will be a fight, Vaughn. I have so much evidence against the guy, I'm sure something could be done about him, as long as he didn't have so many pack dogs fighting his corner."

"And that right there is the problem. There are a lot of people who rely on him and won't let you take that from them. You go after him; you go after them. It will end up being an unfair fight."

Eric rested his elbow on the window, rubbing his fingers across his forehead. "If it was only me I needed to worry about, I'd go for it, but I can't chance it now that I have Samuel."

"Exactly my point."

Eric sighed. "I can pass the information onto someone who can use it. I don't know. I'll think about it."

Dropping Vaughn off, Eric meandered his way across the city to his apartment. When he was happily behind closed doors, he checked the time and sent a message to Samuel. They had missed each other a couple of times that week due to conflicting schedules, but he had usually been able to catch Samuel around his boy's lunchtime or in the evening. He refused to mess with Samuel's sleep pattern—he didn't sleep enough as it was—so he only sent a message at night because Samuel said the beep didn't wake him.

Stripping off his clothes, he threw them in the basket and traipsed to his bathroom. Shower and bed were his plan. Luckily, he had the following day off; therefore, he'd be able to catch up with Samuel a little more, hopefully. Unless the man was working, again.

Soon, he planned on helping Samuel to work better hours. Not for Eric's sake, but for Samuel's. He needed his little time, and when work happened, the time would reduce until there was nothing left. Eric refused to allow that to happen. Samuel's little time was as important as working.

CHAPTER FOURTEEN

SAMUEL

Samuel tucked the phone back into his pocket, ignoring the new message that popped up from Eric. He couldn't deal with it while he was trying to keep it together at his parents' house. He'd been without the man for eight weeks now, which felt like a lifetime.

"What do you think, Samuel?"

He blinked at Trent, having no idea what they were talking about, and shrugged as he stood, his whole body aching, and scurried to the back door for some fresh air. There was a hollowness inside him he couldn't fill no matter how he tried. An emptiness that widened the more time he spent apart from Eric.

Ignoring his mother, he trudged past her into the cold afternoon air. Shivering, he realised he should've brought his coat out, but he didn't want to go back in there and face them all again. Instead, he wrapped his arms around his waist and sat in the large wooden rocking chair that had been in the same place on the deck for as long as he could remember. How it was still in one piece after having five kids clambering all over it, he'd never know.

The chair was big enough for two people to sit, not comfortably, but not squashed either, so Samuel was able to tuck his legs beneath him for extra warmth. Once he was semi-content, he stared out across the soggy grass to the trees at the back of the garden. Sheltered as he was on the deck, he could only feel a slight breeze, but the tops of the trees were blowing wildly, mesmerising in their movement.

It felt good to not think about anything for a while.

A hand touching his shoulder made him jump, and he whipped his face around to see Carter staring at him with a creased forehead and downturned mouth while he held his swaddled, three-month-old daughter to his chest.

"Are you all right? You've been distant and distracted for weeks now."

Samuel cleared his throat and smiled, uncurling himself slowly from the chair and wishing he hadn't stayed in that position for so long when his legs filled with a tingling sensation. "Yeah, I'm good. Tired. You know what work's like."

"I do, but we've been working in the same business

for years, and I've never seen you like this before. You're looking gaunt, Samuel. What's wrong?"

Samuel stood, ready to be done with this conversation already. "Nothing. I'm going to help Mama." He brushed past his brother after giving Denise a stroke on her soft hair.

"Samuel, wait. I wasn't trying to get in your business. I wanted to let you know there are people here if you want to talk about anything. All of us will listen. I know we're siblings and prone to arguments and fighting, but beneath it all, we will help if you need it."

His throat thickened at the words, and tears pooled in his eyes, but he couldn't turn around, and he glanced to the side and nodded, hoping it was enough to show he'd heard. Entering the stifling house—hot since he'd been in the cold for too long—he bypassed everyone and dashed straight for the bathroom, locking the door behind him.

Staring at his reflection, all he saw was an old man with red-rimmed eyes. His skin was saggy, and although he'd lost weight, it, apparently, didn't make him appear any better; he looked more wrinkled than ever. He'd give his father a run for his money if someone were to guess which one of them was older. Despite the weight loss, his double chin was still visible. He had no idea what Eric had seen in him, but the movie star didn't need to worry about him anymore. Samuel would be fine on his own.

A knock sounded. "Samuel, Mama is putting lunch out."

He cleared his throat. "Okay, I'll be right there."

Quickly, splashing his face with water, he dried off and drifted back to the dining room, where more people had been added as their family grew. Instead of only immediate family now, Carter had Lia and their daughter, Trent had Max, and Luke had Casey. There was only him and Ava left single, as far as he knew, unless she had a boyfriend or girlfriend he didn't know about.

Leaning down to kiss his mother on the cheek and thank her for lunch, he slid into the chair next to his father as usual. He was cordial to his parents, but their relationship hadn't returned to where it had been before he'd found out their secret. They still hadn't mentioned anything to his siblings. It had been weeks since he'd found out the news about his older brother, but he hadn't properly dealt with it. Not with everything else that was being thrown at him. He was barely keeping up with the balancing act as it was.

Dinner was a rowdy event as always, but he kept mostly to himself, allowing others to take point. It wasn't vastly different from usual because Samuel was never exuberant in his conversation, but even he could tell he was quieter than normal.

"Samuel, can you help me with the plates, please?"

Inwardly, he winced, realizing some sort of vocal

communication would be required for him to survive the "talk" he knew was coming—his mother's words were a signal the rest of the family should stay away from the kitchen until told otherwise. Stacking the plates that had been passed to him, he followed his mother into the kitchen.

"I know we've talked this through, Samuel, but you can't go on like this. You'll make yourself ill."

"I'm fine, Mama. I have a lot on at work."

"Bullshit, Samuel Walker! That's not the only thing that's going on in your life. I'm your mother. I know these things."

Samuel clenched his jaw and glanced away, firming his resolve. "What more can I say until you talk to the others?" He pushed off the counter and rushed for the door.

"Samuel!" his mother cried after him.

He was sick of people lying to him, of keeping secrets, of bending the truth. Why couldn't people be honest? He'd always prided himself on being truthful and honourable, but what was the point when others weren't. He believed he'd discussed it enough with his parents, but he still didn't understand why they hadn't spoken to his siblings. It wasn't fair on him.

His house of cards was going to fall if he didn't get himself together, the thought reminding him of the card castle he'd made at Eric's one day. He shook his head.

Tugging his coat on, he exited the house without saying goodbye to anyone and climbed into his car. The journey home was quiet, except for the rush of traffic around him. When he parked, he opened the door to a freezing wind chill and rushed into his apartment building, sighing and lowering his shoulders when the heat enveloped him.

The phone he'd placed on the coffee table mocked him as he sat staring at the TV several long minutes later, which was showing some film with the sound turned down. He could feel the need to check in with Eric, a visceral pull towards him, but if he heard his voice, he knew he'd break, and he couldn't. Work tomorrow would be hell with more cases than he could handle, but he was determined to get through it; he wouldn't manage if he lost control now.

When Eric returned…*if* Eric returned, he would no doubt have forgotten about Samuel, so why bother delaying the inevitable. He would ignore him from now on; the man would soon get the picture.

Samuel would be fine, as he always was.

The day had gone to shit from the moment he walked through the doors of his office. Several requests had come through over the weekend asking Samuel for his professional opinion on their case. He spent several hours adding information to them before sending them back with Maggie to the relevant lawyers. It happened on occasion because he was the most experienced with family law, not that his wages showed that distinction.

Late morning, Gregory sent the Benedict file back to him with changes that needed to be made; he pushed aside his other cases to complete it. By early afternoon, it was finished and sent on its way, and he was able to get onto his own cases. Unfortunately, as soon as he opened the first file, Milton barged in the door demanding Samuel's attention.

Samuel felt his blood begin to boil as Milton droned on and on about what he needed Samuel to do for him. The more the man said, the more Samuel seethed.

"So, I need you to buy the ticket for me."

Milton stood in front of Samuel's desk with his arms crossed over his chest, looking at him with an expression of expectation. Samuel stared back at the man who had become the bane of his life and felt a tiny fissure develop in his personal wall.

"Do you know what, Milton?" Samuel stood, resting his fists on his desk as he leaned forward. "No...fuck no. I don't need to buy you anything anymore. You got more than you should've had through the divorce, and I've been stupid in letting you get away with this for the last…however long."

Milton's mouth was gaping, but Samuel was not done. He thought about everything he had given his ex-husband when he hadn't needed to and knew he'd made a rod for his own back. But not anymore.

"Enough is enough. You are a spoiled brat who needs someone to knock some sense into you. Go find yourself a Daddy or something. They'll have you in line before you knew what hit you. As for me, leave me the hell alone. I no longer want you in my office for *any* reason at all. You have no reason to be in contact with me, so get the fuck out!"

Samuel's voice had risen more and more as he spoke until the final words were yelled into the air between them, and Samuel's finger was pointed at the open office door. He couldn't find it in him to care that the whole floor had probably heard his words.

Milton stood there, arms by his side, expression shocked. Samuel had never spoken to him like that before if he excluded the time Eric had been in his bathroom. He pushed the thought aside. He couldn't deal with thoughts of Eric right now.

"Samuel—"

"No!" He couldn't help the betrayal from sounding in his voice. "You lost every right to say a word to me the moment you cheated on me with that asshole! I bet you haven't kept it in your pants for him either, have you?" He half-heartedly chuckled at the grimace that flew across Milton's face. "I don't give a damn anymore, Milton. Get the fuck out of my office and my life. If I see you here one more time, I *will* call security. I don't care who you're fucking."

Milton's shoulders lowered, but Samuel was past caring. He stared as a dejected Milton walked out of his office, hopefully for the last time. Dropping into his chair, his head fell into his hands, and he pressed against the corners of his eyes to stem the tears—not from losing Milton, he didn't care about that, but because he was tired and stressed and didn't see an end to it all.

A quiet knock sounded, and a whispered, "Samuel?"

He lifted his head to see Maggie inside his door. "Yes, Maggie. What can I do for you?"

She entered further, closing the door behind him. "Are you okay, Samuel?"

He leaned back in his chair, resting his head against the back, and blew out a breath towards the ceiling. "I will be if he listens to me. Although I probably shouldn't have done that here. No doubt I'll be receiving a visit from someone about the disruption."

"I wouldn't count on it, sir. Many people were tired of Milton swanning around the office. You've done them all a favour. But I meant, are you okay in regard to yourself? You've been tired and overworked lately. I hate seeing you like this."

Samuel sat upright again, leaning his elbows on his desk. "Yes, Maggie. I'm good. As you say, overworked, but it's nothing that won't get done eventually."

"All right. Well, if there's anything you need me to do, let me know."

"I will. Thank you, Maggie."

"I'll close the door behind me so you can get some peace." She chuckled.

"Thanks."

As soon as the door shut, he swivelled his chair towards the window, leaning back again and studying the raindrops on the windowpane. The weather was following his life, it seemed. A few weeks or months back, he remembered thinking the same thing. He rubbed at the headache forming in his temples, allowing himself a few minutes to wallow in his misery. Then, he inhaled deeply, turned back to his desk and set to work on digging through the mound before him. *Hopefully, tomorrow would be an easier day.*

The following day was *not*, in fact, an easier day. Samuel had been working until around midnight the day before and had stumbled home, only to be back at the office by six the next day. His workload had increased again, and he couldn't see the light at the end of the tunnel. For some reason, everyone seemed to need his attention more than usual, and his own cases were suffering for it.

He was deep into his workload, trying to finish up a couple of files so he could hand them back to the lawyers they belonged to when his door flew open unannounced, and Gregory came storming in with Maggie scuttling behind him an apology written all over her face.

"It's fine, Maggie."

She frowned but backed out of the office, closing the door behind her.

"What can I do for you, Gregory?" he said in as polite a voice as he could manage.

His mood was low, he was tired, and after the confrontation with Milton the previous day, he was pissed off. He could've done without seeing his ex-husband's boyfriend in his office for a few days.

"I've been through the Benedict file again. Where are the statements from the parents? We need them in the file, not floating somewhere around your office, Samuel!" Spittle flew from the man's mouth as he spoke, and Samuel grimaced.

He waited for a beat, inhaling and exhaling slowly before answering, "The statements are with Maggie to be copied as per your request last week. As soon as I finished what you asked for, the files were sent directly to you, and the statements were sent for copying. You will have them back as soon as Maggie has completed the task. Is there anything else?"

"What about the information you were getting from the companies involved?"

Samuel clenched his jaw, linking his fingers on the desk. "I wasn't told to gather that information. You said you were going to speak to them."

"Don't be stupid, Samuel! When will I have time to speak with them? That's your job." Samuel pinched the bridge of his nose, trying to keep calm. "And also, you need to contact the guardian of the child again. They want to provide additional information."

He supposed he should've seen it coming, but Samuel snapped at that moment. Standing, he pushed his chair back forcefully until it banged against the wall behind him, then circled his desk until he reached Gregory. Getting right into his face, he pressed a finger into his chest, making the man stumble back a step.

"No!" he bellowed, breathing heavily, glaring at the surprised lawyer. "No, I will not do any more fucking work on this case! I have literally done every single thing to get this case ready to go to trial. You have done fuck all except complain about what I've done. If you don't like what I'm providing, get someone else to fucking do it! I'm done!" He picked up a handful of papers and threw them at the man. "You treat me like shit and expect me to lay there and take it. Well, fuck you, Gregory!" he roared, the pounding in his ears loud enough to drown out any other sounds.

"Calm down and lower your voice, Samuel," Gregory hissed.

Samuel clenched his fists at the words. "I will *not* calm down!" He refused to be cowed anymore. "The only reason you are treating me this way is because of fucking Milton! The same way he comes to *me* for anything he needs, you do too. Why can't you both grow some balls and sort yourselves out, for fuck's sake?" He dragged his hands over his head, linking them at the back as he paced the office.

"You have no right to talk to me like this. I'm going to speak to—"

Samuel threw his hands in the air. "Do you know what, Gregory? Go tell whoever the fuck you want to! I don't give a rat's ass anymore. I'm doing three times the work of most of the people in this office because I'm a stupid asshole who won't refuse. I know more than I care to know about how you conduct your business, and you won't like what I know. But enough is enough. Tell whoever the fuck you want. I'm done."

He threw the door open, the metal handle banging against the wall and no doubt leaving an imprint. Indifferent to the crowd of lawyers and assistants crowding around his office, he waded his way through to the stairs instead of the lift. He needed to get out now; otherwise, he would explode.

His heart was racing, his body was slick with sweat, his limbs were trembling, but he managed to get to his car and, after a few seconds of breathing deeply to try and calm himself, was able to drive home. Once he was locked inside his apartment, he removed his shoes, jacket and tie, then wandered over to the window, attempting to loosen the tightness in his chest.

Rubbing the back of his neck, he tried to get his thoughts in order. Every time he closed his eyes, all he saw were jumbled images of his parents, Milton, Gregory, Eric, Maggie, his friends, work…it swirled around and around in his mind like a carousel.

He paced to the kitchen, grabbing a bottle of water, then strode back to the window, struggling to swallow the cold liquid, and instead pressed the wet container to his forehead to cool him down. Nausea roiled in his stomach, predicting a resurfacing of what little he'd managed to drink.

Uncaring that he, undoubtedly, didn't have a job to go back to, he was glad he no longer had Milton or Gregory to deal with. He thought about Eric, then pushed it all away. He'd not answered any messages for the past three days, so Eric wouldn't care about him now, anyway. His parents knew he wasn't happy with them, so they wouldn't bother him. His siblings had not been in contact, but they rarely did apart from the odd message every now and then between Sunday dinner visits.

All in all, no one was expecting him to call or visit. He had no one.

Watching the dreary day, his knees trembled with the weight of all he was holding, and he slid to the floor, the bottle rolling from his loose hand, and pressed his back into the corner of the room, pulling his knees in tight. He rested his elbows on his knees and folded his hands over his head, letting the tears come.

CHAPTER FIFTEEN

ERIC

"Hey, Eric!"

Eric inwardly groaned. "Oh, hi, Elsbeth. You on your way to the meeting, too?"

"Yeah. I'll walk with you if that's okay."

"Sure." Luckily, it was only a short trip across the car park to the building.

The crew had wrapped up the final scenes the previous week, but everyone was attending the final meeting to ensure everyone was happy with everything, questions were answered, and the schedule for what happened next was handed out. This would be the last time Eric would have to see Don for a long time, thankfully.

They entered the building, Eric holding the door open for Elsbeth with a small smile, which was returned with interest. He wished she would give up.

Even though she was annoyed with him when he'd taken her out for dinner that day so long ago, she still wanted him. He never understood the fascination. It had to be to do with money and fame, nothing else.

She wouldn't get anything from him now because he was leaving. Not that he'd told anyone that. He had a week left before he was heading home for good, and he couldn't wait.

"What are your plans after all this is over?"

Elsbeth's voice grated on his nerves as it echoed loudly around the large space, but he answered her, "I'm heading home for a bit." Elsbeth would not be the first to find out he wasn't coming back. He'd save that for the people who had earned the information.

"Oh. I thought you might stay around for Christmas. New York Christmases are supposed to be amazing."

"They are a sight to behold. I've seen many over the years, but I'd recommend staying to experience it if you haven't."

"I don't know anyone enough to spend time here. I'd be on my own."

"Being on your own isn't a bad thing sometimes. If it's a toss-up between being on your own but experiencing something new or being somewhere you don't want to be, I'll pick the new and alone every time."

They entered the meeting room to the raucous laughter of several crew members. Eric was a team player, but sometimes, just sometimes, certain groups of people rankled him. This particular group was Don's favourite and was called in for most of his films, but Eric hated the lot of them, probably because they were similar to Don.

He sat as far away from them as possible, Elsbeth sitting next to him, and pulled out his phone, putting it on silent before bringing up a brain-training puzzle game. He always had one on hand because a lot of his job was spent waiting for things to happen—although he sometimes played it while his make-up was being plastered on.

"Right, everyone. Thank you for coming," the producer, Wren, said, slapping a file onto the table in front of him. "We have roughly an hour here to finish up, then you're free to go." A cheer resounded from the whole room. "I know, I know, you love me." Wren grinned. "Anyway, here is the list of scheduled events for the moment. Please take note of your specific interview times and when your appearances are."

The sheets were passed around the table, and Eric glanced over his. It seemed he had been booked solid for the next week, which was to be expected. Wren knew he was leaving after that and had probably told everyone it was this week or never. He didn't mind. It would make the week go quicker, then he'd be on his way home to Samuel. He couldn't wait.

"Any questions or issues with the itinerary?"

Several members raised their hands, and Eric half-listened as he input the schedule onto his phone calendar.

His phone vibrated in his hand, a call coming through. Eric didn't usually answer calls that had unknown numbers on the display, but it was a UK number, and his instincts prickled at him.

He excused himself for a moment. "Hello?"

"Eric? It's Maggie."

Her voice sounded worried, which sent Eric's heart racing. "What's wrong?"

"Samuel is not doing well. I don't know what's happened between you, but I believe you are close. I would've called his family, but he had always told me he wanted to keep his work away from them."

"Maggie, hold on a minute." He popped his head back into the room. "I have to leave." Then he ran through the building. "Maggie, what's happened?" He stumbled towards his car, the hairs on his arms lifting as he envisioned Samuel being in the hospital or something worse.

"I think he's having a breakdown, Eric. The last two days have pushed him too far." She quickly detailed the visits of the asshole ex-husband and the dickwad ex-husband's boyfriend who had caused his boy to crack.

Having reached his car and climbed in while Maggie was talking, he was glad he was sitting down as a wave of dizziness swept over him. He was three thousand miles away! What the fuck was he going to do?

"I'm sorry. I wasn't sure who to call."

"It's fine, Maggie. I can't get there immediately, but I will ensure someone gets to Samuel within the next hour. As soon as I get a flight, I will be with him. Thank you for letting me know. I do appreciate it. You don't need to worry now; I'll take it from here." He sounded so much surer than he felt.

They hung up, and Eric leaned his head forward, breathing deeply to push back the light-headedness. When he was better, he slid his legs in and closed the car door, starting the engine before setting the phone into the holder to use his handsfree.

A knock on his window made him jump, and he turned his head to see a furious Don. He wound the window down.

"What the hell do you think you're doing? Get back into that meeting."

"No, sorry, family emergency."

"I don't give a damn, Eric. You have a schedule to adhere to. You're not going anywhere."

Eric stared at him. "And how exactly are you going to stop me?" He revved the engine and reversed, leaving Don standing there, shouting at him. Closing the window, he brushed the issue out of his mind and realised his first decision was who he needed to call first.

"Call Max Walker."

As the phone rang, he blew out a breath and pointed his car towards home. Luckily, Maggie had caught him before he'd had to turn his phone off for appearances; otherwise, he may not have received the call. The thought didn't fail to terrify him.

"Hello?"

"Max, it's Eric."

"Hey, man. How're things?"

"Not great. I need your help, but I also need you to keep it quiet."

"Sounds ominous. I can't guarantee I'll keep it quiet. It depends on the situation and if I feel it needs extra help."

Max's words made a smile curl Eric's mouth. Once a dominant, always a dominant despite his partner's less submissive tendencies. "That's all I ask, but while I'm explaining, I need you to keep this from Trent. For the moment. Once I've finished, we can discuss it. Please, Max. This is important. I've fucked up."

"All right. For the moment. Explain."

"You know I'm a Daddy, right?"

"Yes."

"Well, when I was last visiting, I stayed for a couple of weeks, and…I found a boy—a little."

"Okay, that's great news. I don't see where this is going."

"My boy is…Samuel. Trent's brother."

A low whistle came from the other side. "All right. What's happened?"

"Over those two weeks, I introduced him to being little, and he took to it like a duck to water. He's perfect for it, which I knew he would be. Unfortunately, I had to come back here. We spoke about different options, but Samuel was adamant he wouldn't have anyone else allowing him to be their boy while I was away. I didn't agree with it at first, but he persuaded me otherwise. This is where I've fucked up." He inhaled sharply, trying to keep his tears from falling. "His assistant has been on the phone. Samuel has had some sort of breakdown and left the office. She called me because she knew we were close, and Samuel had told her previously not to call his family about his work."

"Fucking hell, Eric!"

"I know! I honestly thought he'd be okay for two months. He's been hiding away for so long, but I thought with us able to talk every day, it would be all right. You're not the only one beating me up, Max."

"I know. I'm sorry, but you should've arranged for someone to give him his little time, even if it was me."

"I realise that now."

"Fuck! So, where is he? What's the plan?"

"I want you and Joey Kirkland to go around to his apartment. I'm going to call Joey in a minute. I need you both to get Samuel, whatever his state, to my house. It's where all his things are. He needs to be little;

he needs to have the decisions taken away from him so he can rest and recuperate."

"I've never been a Daddy, so I'm not entirely sure how to do this."

"Joey has been before. He tried it out for a few months before realising being a Daddy Dom was not his calling. He will be fine doing it, but I need you there as support for them both."

"I'm going to have to tell Trent."

"Why?"

"We need to get into Samuel's apartment, and I know Trent has a key."

"Fuck, I never thought about that. All right, but everyone else needs to be kept in the dark. I will have Emily meet you at my house with the key to the place. After that, you need to get her and Trent to leave. Samuel would not want Trent seeing him this way until he is in the right mind to make the choice himself."

Max sighed. "This is a fucking mess."

"Yes, it is, and one I intend never to make again."

"All right. Get Joey to ring me when he's on his way to Samuel's. I won't say anything to Trent until then; otherwise, he will want to storm in right now, and nothing I say will stop him."

"Thanks, Max. I appreciate this."

He ended the call and told his phone to call Joey.

"Joey Kirkland."

"Joey, it's Eric. I need your help."

By the time he'd finished bringing Joey up to speed on exactly how and what he needed him to do, Eric was in his apartment packing suitcases. He'd already booked a flight, which left in six hours. He stopped in the middle of his room, chest tightening, throat closing and called Vaughn.

"Fuck, Vaughn. I've screwed up big time," he choked.

Eric sank to his knees on the floor and cried.

He had no idea how long he'd spent on the floor when Vaughn turned up at his place. Eric had never been happier to see his friend. Vaughn pulled him into a hug and held him tightly.

"Don't you ever do that to me again, you asshole. You scared the shit out of me!" Vaughn's voice was rough and hoarse, and Eric could feel his body trembling. "I didn't hear a word of what you were trying to tell me through your tears. Now, stop making me think the worst and explain it all again so I can go and murder whoever hurt you."

"It's me you should murder, Vaughn. Samuel hasn't been doing well and has been hiding it from me. His assistant called me earlier telling me he's had some sort of breakdown. I've sent people to help him, and my flight is in five hours. I'm leaving, and I'm not coming back."

"Fuck!" Vaughn breathed.

"Yeah, I screwed up bad."

"It doesn't matter now. All that matters is that you're fixing it. You'll be there in no time." Vaughn blew out a breath. "What do you need me to do?"

"Can you help me think of ways to navigate the shitstorm that is heading my way about the film? I'm booked solid for appearances for the next week, including some that were supposed to be today."

"Forget about that for now. But yes, I will think of something to help you out. I know lawyers who can look into your contract and see where you stand. This is a family emergency; it can't be helped, but in the long term, it may be an issue."

They spent the next three hours packing two suitcases with essentials—the rest Vaughn said he would pack up and get shipped over to him. Eric wasn't bothered about most of it, to be honest. Everything could be bought if he needed something.

When Vaughn dropped him off at the airport, Eric had returned to his usual calm, disciplined self. He had learned patience over the years, and although it was difficult to think about Samuel suffering while Eric was travelling, every mile towards him was a mile closer to having him in his arms and never letting him go. Eric would be on his knees for a long time to come, begging for forgiveness.

Eric had spent the flight listening to ambient relaxation music through his headphones to help him keep calm. He hadn't been able to find out what was happening with Samuel before he boarded, but he knew his boy would be in good hands with Joey. Although Joey hadn't taken to the lifestyle, everyone who had been his boy, for however short a time, had said he was a good Daddy. He wished he could have had more information about Samuel's state of mind.

The moment Ethan picked him up from the airport, he knew he had plenty of explaining to do.

"I know you want me to talk, but can I make a phone call first?" he asked his brother.

Ethan nodded, his mouth pursed.

As they aimed towards the motorway, Eric dialled Max.

"Hey, Eric."

"How is he?"

"He's not too bad, to be honest. He's been alternating between sleeping and playing with the cuddly toys. He's not eaten a great deal, but Joey has managed to get some fluids into him."

Eric sighed, tension loosening his chest. "Thank you. I cannot thank you enough for this."

"No problem. We'll catch up when you get here, okay?"

"See you soon."

Hanging up, Eric dropped his head against the headrest and closed his eyes. He took several deep breaths before lifting his head and glancing over at Ethan.

"Okay, go," he said, giving Ethan permission to rant.

"Are you okay?" was what his brother asked.

"No. I will be when I get home, I hope."

"Care to tell me what this is all about? You don't usually call me to pick you up at four in the morning."

"There is a lot I need to explain."

He spent the rest of the journey describing his lifestyle to Ethan and what it meant to him and how things worked, then slowly worked towards the mess he'd made of his relationship. He told Ethan it was Samuel but asked him to keep it to himself for the moment because Samuel was a private person. Once he'd finished everything he could think of and answered all of Ethan's questions, they both lapsed into silence.

When they arrived in Cambridge, Eric felt himself tense up all over again. He was scared Samuel wouldn't want him now that Eric had messed up, and he wasn't sure how he felt about that. Samuel meant everything to him, and it was surprising to acknowledge after years of ensuring people stayed at arm's distance.

"Can you please drop me off, then head out again. I know that's horrible for me to ask, but I need you to do this. I'll catch up with you and Emily in a couple of days."

"Of course. Samuel needs to be your focus."

"Thanks."

Eric exited the car, grabbing his two suitcases, then carried them to the front door, which opened before he got there. His shoulders lowered when Joey appeared.

"He's sleeping at the moment."

Eric left the suitcases in the hallway and followed Joey up the stairs. "How has he been?"

Joey blew out a breath. "It's been a long twelve hours, put it that way."

"Thank you so much for this. I can't tell you how much I appreciate what you've done for him and me." Eric cupped Joey's shoulder.

"You're both welcome. He's an awesome boy when he lets himself out of his head." Joey stopped them before entering Eric's bedroom. "He knew I wasn't you, obviously, but he still followed my instructions, except for having a shower. I thought it might soothe him, but every time I suggest it, he tensed up and curled up with a cuddly toy instead. I'm not sure why."

"It could be because it was something we always

did together. He loves his rainstorm." Eric quirked the corner of his mouth.

"He's not eaten anything at all, but I managed to get plenty of milk inside him using the green beaker."

Eric raised his eyebrows. "The green one? The blue is usually his favourite."

Joey tilted his head. "It's making sense now. Anything that reminded him of you was discarded for something different. Did you play Lego with him by any chance?" Eric nodded. "Yeah, he wouldn't touch that. What about the blue dummy?" Eric nodded again. "Yeah, he's using the red one."

Eric's heart raced. "I don't know if that's a good thing, Joey. What if it means he doesn't want to see me?"

"Trust me, Eric. He wants you, and when you go in, you'll understand why I know that. He's in the bed in the nursery."

Eric stepped into the room hesitantly, his gaze immediately going to his boy and softening when he saw him curled up on the single bed, holding onto one of Eric's t-shirts and two cuddly toys. His gaze flicked to Max, who was uncurling himself carefully from beside the bed.

Max squeezed his shoulder as he went past, whispering in his ear, "We're heading out. There's food in the fridge, and we're at the end of the phone if you need anything. I'll speak with Trent, and we'll give you a couple of days. After that, no promises."

"Thank you," he mumbled back.

When the door closed behind them, Eric undressed to his t-shirt and briefs, then he scooted into bed beside Samuel, who still looked stressed in his sleep. Eric lay on his back as close to Samuel as he could get. He didn't want to pull Samuel to him and wake him from his slumber. Instead, he waited as patiently as he could and was rewarded when Samuel moved towards him in his sleep.

Eric's heart expanded as Samuel snuggled into Eric's side, and Eric lifted his arm over Samuel's head to allow him to nuzzle closer if he needed to. Within half an hour, Samuel was wrapped around him, his cuddlies squashed between them.

Despite being exhausted, Eric couldn't sleep. He watched over Samuel, seeing the tension on his boy's face ease and his body relax, the soft huffs of breath covering Eric's skin.

This was where he belonged. This was where they both belonged.

"Daddy?"

Samuel's voice was hoarse, and when Eric flicked his gaze to his boy, he saw tears pooling in his eyes.

"Yes, little one. I'm here." Eric tugged him closer.

"Dad-dy!" Samuel hiccupped, tears overflowing as he scrambled to get closer to Eric.

Eric tightened his arms around Samuel, eyes stinging with the threat of crying from the pain in his boy's voice. "Shh, it's okay, Sam. Everything will be okay now."

Samuel tried to get as close to Eric as he could, scrabbling to fit himself in Eric's arms while his sobs resounded around the room, breaking Eric's heart. Eric held him through it all, letting him cry it all out. "I'm so sorry, little one. I'm so sorry. I shouldn't have left you alone. I'm so sorry. I'm not going anywhere ever again," he whispered, again and again, running his hands over Samuel's back and head.

Once Samuel breathed easier, hopefully listening to the reassurances Eric provided, he felt Samuel tense up and braced for anger. Having been cracked open, he was sure Samuel would begin to reprimand Eric, which he did. Some were unintelligible, but most were words of betrayal that cut Eric deep, but he deserved every one of them, so he let him rant.

"Why did you leave me alone? Was I not good enough? You should've been here!" He flailed at Eric's shoulder, and he held him tighter. "You left me alone, Daddy!" The anger fell again, no doubt threatening to drop him back into the black hole, leaving him shaking. Eric refused to allow him to do so.

"I know. I know. I'm so sorry, Samuel. I promise it won't happen again. I promise I won't leave you anymore." Eric pressed kisses to his forehead and rubbed his hands over Samuel's body again, soft, gentle and settling.

Samuel's tears continued even as his body relaxed against Eric once more. Tiredness overwhelmed him until he slept, fitfully, clutching Eric's shirt.

CHAPTER SIXTEEN

SAMUEL

Samuel woke to a familiar scent and feeling as arms encased him in an embrace meant to settle and ease him, to allow him to know someone was there for him.

He couldn't believe Eric had come back and was there holding him; he must be dreaming. It didn't stop the tears from coursing down his cheeks; it didn't stop the sobs that left his body aching. His muscles were too weak to do much except tremble in Eric's arms, but there was no place he'd prefer to be at that moment. Everything else faded away because he knew Eric would take care of it all.

When the tears were all gone, he felt light as if everything was gone—not empty, light. A feeling he often felt when he was around Eric. It was the feeling that he didn't need to worry about anything because Eric would be there to see to it.

He tried to talk but found his mouth was too dry and coughed to clear it.

"It's all right, little one. Let me up for a moment, and I'll get you a drink. I don't want you to get dehydrated, and you've lost a lot of water."

Despite not wanting to let Eric out of his sight, Samuel lifted his arm and rolled to his back, grabbing his two cuddlies and his dummy. Before putting it in his mouth, he stared at the colour, frowning.

"Would you like the blue one?" Daddy whispered, pressing a kiss to his forehead.

Sam nodded, holding out the red one and smiling gently when the blue one was rubbed against his lips. He opened his mouth enough to take it between his teeth, then rolled over to his other side, hugging Cheeky-Boo and Darla to his chest. They had been his constant companion over the hours he'd been at Eric's house.

The time between leaving the office and waking to find Eric there was a bit of a blur. He recollected someone wrapping him in their arms that didn't smell of Eric but had the same calm demeanour, and when they had told him what to do, he'd obeyed because it had been easier than thinking for himself. He didn't remember the car journey they'd made, but he recalled crying when the scent of Eric enveloped him as he wandered around his house. He knew he'd slept a lot, too.

Joey—he remembered—had tried to feed him, which Samuel refused to do, knowing it probably wouldn't stay down, and instead had given him a drink and sat with him throughout the whole ordeal from what he gathered. Someone else had too, but Samuel couldn't remember who.

He knew he'd probably been a pain in the ass for Joey, but he couldn't stop himself. At the time, he hadn't believed Eric would return but couldn't stop himself from wanting to be in his house, relaxing and pretending all was fine. It didn't work out that way, though. Unfortunately, everything reminded him of what he'd lost—or thought he'd lost—and it made things worse.

The bed dipped again, and Sam rolled back, seeing Eric looking dishevelled and with red-rimmed eyes, holding out a blue beaker. Sam grinned, the dummy dropping from his mouth as he scooted himself up to rest against the cushioned headboard.

"Thank you, Daddy," he mumbled, bringing the spout to his mouth and drinking deeply.

"Not too much, little one. I don't want you being sick." Eric's hand cupped his own, gently guiding the beaker away from his mouth again. "You can have a little more in a minute. Do you need to use the bathroom?"

Until then, he would've said no, but as soon as Eric said the words, Sam needed to go. He nodded frantically and scooted off the bed, collapsing to the floor when his legs wouldn't hold him.

Eric caught him with an arm around his waist. "Easy now. Let's take it a step at a time. You're still weak from not eating. As soon as you're done in the bathroom, we'll get some breakfast."

"What time is it?"

"To be honest, I have no idea. My hours are all messed up, but whatever time it is, we're still having breakfast." He chuckled.

They stumbled to the bathroom, Eric heading to leave when Sam called out to him, "Stay!"

Eric turned back to him with a small smile and raised eyebrows. "Are you sure? I don't want to intrude."

"Stay," he said quieter but with a nod.

"Okay." Eric rested against the wall, leaning his head back against it but keeping his eyes on Sam.

Sam blushed as he peed, but it didn't stop him from going. He couldn't remember the last time he'd been. He flushed and washed his hands, Eric coming over to help him dry them.

"Food first, then shower, then relaxing some more. How does that sound?"

"Perfect." Eric turned away, but Sam frowned. "Daddy?" The word came so much easier now.

"Yes, Sam." He tilted his head in a way that showed he was listening to what Sam had to say, and Sam felt comfort in the gesture as well as a boost of confidence.

"Can I have a kiss?" he whispered, glancing at the floor.

Eric stepped closer, lifting Sam's chin with his index finger. "Of course, you can. I didn't want to assume you were ready. It's why I hadn't kissed you yet, but believe me, I want to." He leaned forward, pressing their lips together in a soft caress, setting butterflies adrift in Sam's stomach.

It was only brief, but Sam hadn't realised how much he'd needed that show of affection. "Thank you."

Eric chuckled and pressed a kiss to his nose. "You don't need to thank me, but you're welcome anyway. Come on, food!"

Following Eric out of the room and down the stairs, Sam studied his surroundings with brighter eyes. Whereas before Eric arrived, the place had seemed dark and deserted, now it was bright and full of life.

In the kitchen, Eric settled Sam's beaker, which Sam hadn't seen him pick up, on the table and strode to the fridge, opening the door. "Max said there was food ready for us, but I've no idea what they—ooh! We have pancakes! I would usually make pancakes fresh, but they don't taste too different if they're heated up." He glanced over his shoulder at Sam. "Pancakes?"

Sam nodded, clutching his hands together and wishing he'd brought one of his cuddlies with him. He didn't know what to do with himself.

"Sam? Would you like some colouring to do? Or something to read while I warm these up?"

Peering up at Eric from under his lashes, he nodded again and slid onto one of the chairs. Eric smiled and opened one of the drawers Sam knew held a variety of things for Sam to play with. Eric placed a colouring book, a box of pencils and a small square book in front of him.

Running a hand over Sam's head, Eric said, "There should be something there you'd like to do for the few minutes it will take me to make breakfast."

Sam was immediately drawn to the book, which was bright orange and had a tiger on the front of it. He ran his hand over the front, expecting it to be smooth but finding the tiger's fur had been replaced with soft, furry fabric. He lifted the cover, opening it to the first page and seeing an elephant whose trunk had been replaced with a bumpy card. He ran his nail up and down it, making a zipping noise at which he giggled. The next page showed a gorilla with big furry black patches on it. Sam rubbed his fingers across the material, closing his eyes and revelling in the softness.

A clink next to him had him opening his eyes. Eric

had placed a plastic plate next to him with triangular pieces of pancake on it. Sam couldn't see what was on the bottom of the plate, but he could see it had two ears as handles. He grinned at Eric and pushed the book aside.

"Can you wash your hands for me, please?" Eric asked, indicating the sink.

Sam hopped off the stool and washed up quickly, returning to his pancakes. He picked up his fork, speared a bite and shoved it in his mouth. As soon as he swallowed, his stomach growled as if thanking him for the food. Eric had spread some of the pancakes with a little chocolate spread and some with orange juice. It was lovely.

When the plate was empty, Eric asked him to wash his hands again—he was super sticky—and then Eric refilled his beaker, linked their fingers and tugged him towards the living room to their favourite sitting place. It was a large love seat that had been covered with a throw and several cushions, which made Sam feel like he was on a cloud when he sat on it.

Eric sat first, placing Sam's beaker on the little side table, then pulled Sam between his legs, repositioning them until they were both comfortable and could watch out the window to the row of trees swaying in the breeze.

"We have a lot to talk about, little one," Eric said.

Sam's heart jumped, and he finally realised something he must have pushed aside: Eric was back earlier than planned.

"Are you leaving again?" he croaked, tears pooling in his eyes again.

"No! No, not at all! I promise, little one. I promise I'm here to stay for as long as you'll have me." Eric cupped his face, bringing their lips together. "I'm not going anywhere."

Sam let out a huge sigh and snuggled back into his previous position. "Good. You're back early, though, aren't you?"

"Yes, but that doesn't matter. It's all sorted."

Sam closed his eyes, hoping that was true, but knowing there were probably some things Eric had left out. "I'm sorry for making you come back too soon."

"Trust me, I do not mind at all, little one. I do have some news." Eric's fingers skimmed across Sam's arms as he spoke. "I've finished with acting. I'm not going back again."

Sam lifted his head, eyes wide. "What? But you love it? Why are you stopping? It's not because of me, is it?" He tried to scramble upright, but Eric held him tight.

"Calm, little one. Calm. I do love acting, but I realised I hated the environment I was in. It is so vapid and fake, I couldn't stand it any longer. I'm happy with the decision."

Sam couldn't believe it. "What are you going to do?"

Eric shrugged. "Try out theatre around here or something. I don't know yet, but we'll figure it out."

Sam closed his eyes at the thought they would work it out together. "I am sorry this happened. I didn't mean for it to get so bad. I thought I was managing," he whispered into the silence, his focus on the movement of the trees as he tried to gather his thoughts.

"I do wish you would have told me, but I understand why you thought you couldn't. For future reference, you can tell me anything and everything, no matter how big or small it may seem. We're in this together, little one, and together, we will make this into whatever we want and need it to be. I'm all in. You and me. Together. If that's what you want."

Sam clambered up and straddled Eric's lap, wrapping his arms around Eric's shoulders and nuzzling into his neck. "Yes, please," he whispered, tears escaping, this time from happiness.

"Good." He smoothed a hand over Sam's back. "Now, the hard bit. You need to tell me everything, sweetheart. Everything that happened, everything you felt. We need to clear the air so we can figure out where to go from here. It's okay wanting to do this together, but to do that, we need to work out where the other person is coming from. I made the mistake of not talking to you properly about the potential pitfalls of not having little time before I left for New York, and I refuse to do that again."

Sam breathed in Eric's scent, then lifted his head. "Okay, but can we do one thing first?"

"What's that?"

"Can we have another nap? I'm tired."

Eric smiled. "That's a brilliant idea, little one. Shower, then sleep, then talk."

"Yes, please, Daddy."

They didn't spend as long in the shower as usual, but Sam enjoyed it, nonetheless. When they crept into the bed they usually used, it felt so big compared to what Sam had been sleeping on the past twenty-four hours. They wrapped themselves around each other and settled down.

Sam didn't fall asleep straight away. Despite telling Eric he was tired, he wasn't particularly, but he knew Eric had been up for too long. He looked exhausted; therefore, he'd told him he was tired to allow Eric to catch up on his sleep. Sam was content to breathe in the scent of the man who had come to mean so much to him. He was happy to listen to his heartbeat. He was satisfied to feel his skin against his own. He needed the reminder Eric was there.

Several hours later, after a hearty dinner, they sat huddled up on the sofa, ready to have a much-needed discussion. Samuel wasn't looking forward to it because it was going to expose a lot of his hidden issues and insecurities, but he'd promised Eric he would be honest. It was the least he could do after making Eric leave New York early, and no doubt, Eric would be getting in trouble for that, even if he told Samuel otherwise. Samuel might be a family lawyer, but he knew about contracts.

"Can you talk me through what happened while I was gone?" Eric asked, pressing his lips to Samuel's temple.

Despite sitting as they were, all cuddled together and wrapped tightly, Samuel felt like the lawyer, not the little. "Can I first say something I've realised? I think of myself as two people now. Is that a bad thing?" Samuel tipped his head to rest back, lifting his gaze to Eric's.

"What do you mean?"

"Well, like now, we're talking, and I feel like Samuel. When I'm little, I think of myself as Sam. Even when I'm thinking things through in my head, the different names indicate which frame of mind I'm in."

Eric smiled. "I don't see a problem with that unless you do, sweetheart. The two sides of your personality are different, and I think it's easier for you to separate them. If you were Samuel when you were little, you might struggle to get into the mindset and allow yourself to relax, and when you're Sam, you might not be able to answer lawyer-minded questions."

Samuel considered that and realised it made a lot of sense. "All right. I know we'd discussed me having a substitute Daddy while you were gone, but I knew I wouldn't be able to relax around someone who was not you. Okay, granted, I was fine with Joey, but…" He waved his hand. "Although I slipped into being little with you easily, I knew I wouldn't be able to do it with someone I didn't already trust in some ways. The fact you were known to family and friends went a long way to alleviate some of my fears."

"What fears?"

"Of being mocked and ridiculed. Of being a laughingstock of the law firm. I'm sure there are others hiding away in my psyche somewhere, but those were always at the forefront of my mind."

"Fair enough. What happened when I left?"

Samuel tucked his head under Eric's chin, not wanting to face him when he explained what had happened. "In the beginning, I found myself at a loose end. I'd spend my hours working like I had before I met you, but I'd lose the train of thought, go off on tangents. Every time I spoke to you, it centred me again." He took a deep breath. "Then work became inundated. I was sent cases that weren't mine, I was given extra cases to check over, and so on.

Maggie, bless her heart, tried to help me as much as she could, but there was only so much she could do. My own work was beginning to suffer. I know I should've said no, but I thought that if I was busier, the time would go faster, and you'd be home quicker."

Eric tightened his hold, resting his palm against the side of Samuel's head and keeping him in place. "I'm sorry, Samuel. I wish I'd known."

"It's okay now. We're sorting it." He turned his head slightly and pressed a kiss to Eric's chest before snuggling back in. "I went to dinner at my parents' on Sunday as usual. Mama didn't want to tell my siblings, so I left. Then Milton happened." He stared across the room at the blank TV screen. "Milton was his usual self-obsessed self. He came into the office demanding…I can't even remember what now. I was overworked and low on patience, and he tried the last of it. I said a lot of things that were a long time coming, but I shouldn't have. At least not in the office."

"Maybe not. Although that seems to be where he was always bothering you. Did he ever turn up at your apartment?"

Samuel shook his head. "No. It was always at work."

"It was inevitable then, I think."

"I still shouldn't have done it. Maggie tried to smooth things over by telling me everyone in the office would be glad to be rid of his presence, but I still felt like shit."

"That's understandable. Milton was in the wrong, but your personality doesn't allow you to be horrid. With or without reason. You tie yourself in knots when you are. I think that's why you're struggling with your parents so much. You hate the idea you're hurting them, but you can't stop it because you're hurting yourself."

"You're exactly right."

"How do you feel about this lifestyle?" Eric asked into the silence that had descended.

"About being a little and having a Daddy?" He felt Eric nod. "To begin with, I thought there was something wrong with me, but you helped me to realise there wasn't. As long as the participants are happy, it doesn't matter what goes on behind closed doors. I love having you take care of me. You certainly do a better job of it than I do myself."

"I love being able to take care of you. It eases something inside me, as I'm sure being little does for you."

"Yes."

"How did it get so bad for you?"

Samuel was silent for a time, trying to sort out his thoughts, though they were all jumbled. "Gregory came in demanding extra work from me and complaining about what had already been done. The problem was the case wasn't even my case. I was supposed to be helping him on it, but he passed everything to me to handle, but he got the credit for it all. I think having so many things balancing in the air finally overwhelmed me. The conversation with Mama, the argument with Milton, the argument with Gregory, it was too much. I couldn't think straight. I couldn't keep still."

"What did you do?" Eric asked when Samuel didn't continue.

"I drove home, paced the room for a while, then realised I had no one." He felt Eric tense at those words.

"No one?"

"I'd pushed Mama and Dad away, I'd walked out of work, I'd not be expected to be heard from by my siblings until the following Sunday dinner, and I hardly ever spoke to friends. And…" He breathed deeply. "I'd persuaded myself you would find someone else and didn't need me dragging you down," he finished on a whisper.

"Oh, Samuel."

Eric manhandled him until Samuel was straddling his thighs and facing him. Eric's eyes were sad, his face drawn. "You felt like you had no one to call because no one was expecting you to? Is that what you mean?"

Samuel nodded, tears welling and ready to spill at the merest thought of blinking. Unable to stop himself, he closed his eyes, allowing the tears to fall. Then he opened them again and stared at Eric. "But then you came."

"I'll always be here for you." He wiped the tears from Samuel's face, cupping his jaw and bringing his face close for a kiss. "I'm yours, and you're mine. If you agree to it, that is?"

"Yes."

Samuel closed the gap, melding their lips and feeling like he had come home. His home wasn't a place; it was a person. This person. His Daddy.

He opened for Eric to take possession of his mouth, relaxing against him and enjoying the closeness he'd been missing for what seemed like forever. Eric sat upright, sliding his hands up Samuel's back to clasp the back of his head while his tongue danced alongside Samuel's. They were breathing heavily, loud panting heard throughout the room when Eric finally pulled back.

"I missed you so much."

"You, too." Samuel remembered what Eric had said at the beginning of their conversation. "Are you leaving acting?"

Eric settled back on the arm of the sofa, taking Samuel down with him. He fit so perfectly against Eric as if he was made to be there; at least that was what Samuel felt.

"I don't want to leave acting altogether. I'd love to

try and find something here I could do. I was thinking as an acting coach or teacher or something. Even playing at the theatre. I don't know yet. I *do* know I don't want to be part of the film industry anymore. There is so much faking and fawning going on that I've had enough of it all. I want to be *me*. I don't want to be Eric, the actor, all the time. I'm tired." He chuckled. "I'm twenty-four, and I'm tired. Go figure."

"Everyone can get tired of something if they've lost the joy of doing it."

"Have you lost the joy of being a lawyer?"

"God, no! I love it. I don't like some of the people I work for. It's time for a change of scenery." He'd been thinking about it for a while but had always thought it was too much hassle to change firms, but his life was getting worse, so it was something he needed to consider.

"Or you could start your own firm?"

"Huh. I hadn't thought of that."

"Something to consider." Eric cleared his throat. "But now, I think it's time for hot chocolate."

"Any reason why?" Samuel asked as he made a colossal effort to get off Eric's lap.

"There is no reason needed for hot chocolate, especially if they contain marshmallows."

"I'll remember that the next time you tell me I've had too much hot chocolate."

Eric clutched his chest. "Oh no! I've given you the perfect excuse."

Samuel smiled, then frowned when a phone started ringing. Eric sighed, heading to the kitchen where he'd left his phone.

"I should be grateful for small mercies," he mumbled when Samuel entered the room.

"Why?"

"I left New York before my contract was officially over. I expected to have had several phone calls before now, berating me for it. I'm assuming Vaughn was able to hold them off. Unfortunately, it seems the silent time is over." The phone started ringing again. This time, Eric grinned and answered.

"Vaughn, hey." His smile dimmed. "Yes, I figured, thanks." He listened, then sighed. "Okay. I knew it was coming. I'll sort out a lawyer from here, and we can get them to talk and pass the info between them." Eric glanced at him and winked. "I have inside knowledge." He bit the inside of his cheek, staring intently at Samuel. "I don't know…All right." He lifted the phone from his ear. "Vaughn would like to talk to you. Is that okay?"

Samuel's stomach fluttered, but he nodded, taking the phone. "Hello?"

"Samuel? Hi. I'm Eric's best friend, Vaughn. Don't tell him I told you this, but he's the best person anyone could wish for. If you admit that, I will deny it to my grave. I wanted to say that he can sometimes be distant from other people. I don't know if you're the same, but between you and I, he needs to reclaim his life. His parents took so much from him, but the ability to care deeply for those around him—friends, not you—has been taken away too. You will both need them during the coming months. Grab hold of them and hold tight. Do you hear me?"

Samuel gazed into Eric's eyes and gave the only answer he could, "I will do everything I can."

CHAPTER SEVENTEEN

ERIC

"God, I don't know if I want to do this," Samuel mumbled as he paced in the living room, wringing his hands together.

"It will be fine. Everyone will be great about everything. They are here for you. We need to explain, and everything will go back to the way it was before."

"But what will they think of me needing therapy?"

"It doesn't matter what they think, but even if it does, they will be fine with it. You're getting the help you need to figure out what you want from life. There is nothing wrong with that."

Eric tried to reassure him every time Samuel voiced one of his fears, but it was difficult to do when he felt so guilty over being the reason this happened in the first place. If Eric had put his foot down and demanded Samuel have some little time, this might not have happened. It was something Eric had to come to terms with.

A knock sounded, and Samuel stopped pacing and stared in the direction of the front door with his eyes widening.

"It will be fine, I promise." Eric stood, heading to the door, leaving Samuel to calm or whittle himself further, whichever he chose to do. Opening the door to their visitors, he smiled, indicating for them to enter. They were all looking sombre, and he couldn't have that.

"Before I take you to see him, you need to understand something. He is such a strong man, but he's also fragile. Please accept what he is going to tell you as fact. You can ask questions, by all means, but don't belittle him or me when we explain."

"That's a big ask," Carter said, his gaze boring into Eric.

"It is, but he's your brother. In that case, it shouldn't be hard at all."

Eric received nods from Samuel's siblings and led them to the living room. As soon as he entered, he strode over to Samuel, standing in front of him. "I'm here. I'm not going anywhere."

Samuel gazed into his eyes and nodded, a small smile curling his mouth, then they turned to his family, who had found seats around the room that was plenty big enough for their five visitors and themselves.

Eric led Samuel over to the two-seater sofa and sat down beside him, clasping their hands together to hopefully keep Samuel tethered.

"How are you, Sammy?" Trent asked, leaning forward in his seat, a pained look on his face.

Samuel squeezed Eric's hand, then answered, "I'm doing better. A lot better."

"Can you tell us what happened?" Carter asked.

Clearing his throat, Samuel glanced at Eric. "I think to explain that, I have to go explain something else first. Though some of you may know."

"You can tell us anything, Sammy. Nothing will push us away," Trent said.

Samuel smiled and blew out a breath. "Okay. I am what's called a little, and Eric is my Daddy."

Eric barely contained his laughter when Samuel threw the information out like a missile. Glancing around at their visitors, he saw some faces of under-standing, some of confusion, and he knew this was going to get uncomfortable.

"What's a little?" Ava asked.

Samuel squeezed his hand again, and Eric gave him some relief. "A little is someone who regresses to a younger age and gives control over to their Daddy, in this case, allowing them to take care of everything that needs to be done. It allows the little to wipe themselves free of the responsibility of anything other than what their Daddy tells them to do. Does that make sense?"

"So, Sammy—" Ava began.

"Sam. My little is called Sam," Samuel interrupted.

"Sorry. So, Sam gets to play while you do all the heavy lifting?" Ava finished, a twinkle sparkling in her eye.

"Exactly."

"Hey! I do some heavy lifting!" Samuel raised his eyebrows and pouted.

"I know you do, sweetheart, and I wouldn't have it any other way." Eric released his hand and wrapped his arm around him, pulling him closer to settle against him.

"I can totally see it," murmured Carter.

"Why didn't I see it before?" Luke remarked.

"So, what happened after that?" Carter asked.

Eric held Samuel as he went through the same information as he had done when he'd explained everything to Eric, although missing out a few bits his siblings didn't need to know. There were grumbles about Milton and Gregory, with Carter letting out a few choice words on occasion. All in all, everyone was supportive and caring, even when it came to telling them about his therapy sessions, which was exactly what Samuel needed.

When Samuel had poured his heart out, Eric could feel his boy flagging.

"Right. I'm afraid that's all we have time for today. I need to get my boy rested up for visit number two."

"Is that Mama and Dad?"

Samuel nodded and stood, accepting embraces and whispered words from each of his brothers and sister. "Thanks, everyone. I'm sorry I worried you."

"Well, I'm sure they worried you enough growing up. It's entirely fair, I say." Max grinned. Samuel pulled him into a hug again, and Eric heard the words of thanks coming from Samuel. "Take care of yourself. Forget these lot." Max waved at the crowd.

"I try, but they're a little hard to forget," Samuel joked.

Once they left, Eric dragged Samuel to the kitchen for sustenance. While he made some sandwiches, he settled Samuel with his playing cards and retrieved Cheeky-Boo from his hiding place. Samuel hadn't wanted that information to get into the hands of his siblings.

By the time lunch was ready, Samuel had created a masterpiece of card building. It was so magnificent that Eric was worried it would come tumbling down with even a small breath in the wrong direction.

"Whoa, little one. That's fantastic! I need to get a photo." He pulled out his phone and snapped a few shots, one with Sam smiling so widely, Eric was afraid he'd dislocate his jaw. "Is Cheeky-Boo helping to knock it down, or are we keeping it up?" He didn't think it would last long because even a small breeze would collapse it all.

"You and me, Daddy! Big breath."

Samuel inhaled, puffing his cheeks out, and Eric followed suit. When Samuel started blowing, Eric did, too, but slightly less forceful, allowing Samuel to do most of the work. As he thought, only a little air knocked it flying. Samuel cheered, and Eric laughed as the cards went sliding across the table and onto the floor.

"Right, let's get this cleared away, and we can eat. I'm starving."

After lunch, Eric got Samuel settled in the dining room with his Lego box, which had been emptied all over the surface—so he could find all the pieces he needed apparently—while Eric cleaned their dishes. The afternoon visitors were going to be more difficult to get through, but he knew Samuel was strong enough.

Before too long, it was time, and Eric told Samuel he could leave the Lego on the table for later. Eric led Samuel's parents into the living room and offered them a seat before sitting next to Samuel.

"Are you okay, Samuel?" his mother asked.

"Yes, Mama. I…" He glanced at Eric and took a deep breath. "I have a lot to talk to you about."

"We have things to explain to you, too, if you'd like to hear them?"

Samuel gazed at his father for what seemed like an eternity, then he stood from the sofa and rounded the coffee table, dropping to the seat beside his parents. "I'm so sorry, Mama, Dad. I didn't mean it! I know you'd never do something for no reason. It took me by surprise, and I didn't know what to do about it. It seemed like you were leaving the burden all on me when you should be sharing it with everyone. But it's your choice at the end of the day."

"Hush, now. You have nothing to be sorry for. You were right. We should have told you. I'm sorry we didn't. We thought we were doing the right thing." Mr Walker had tears running unchecked down his cheeks as he stared at his son.

"A lot of things have happened lately, and no one thing is to blame. Everything altogether is," Eric said.

Samuel embraced his father, then his mother and came back to sit with Eric, climbing in his lap. Eric spared a glance to his parents but saw only happiness. They went through the whole conversation they'd had with Samuel's siblings, explaining how the Daddy and little relationship worked, what had happened with Samuel at work and with Milton and Gregory. By the end, Samuel was exhausted; even his parents could see it.

"We're going to head out, but thank you so much for talking to us. I hope to see you at the family dinners now, Eric. You and your siblings are welcome to join us anytime you want. There is always enough food."

"Thank you, Mrs Walker."

"Oh, I think you can call me Catherine now, dear."

Samuel sagged against him as Eric closed the door. "Come on. I think you deserve a rainstorm."

Eric sat on Samuel's sofa staring at the blank TV, waiting for Samuel to return from his first therapy appointment. They had spoken about it throughout the weekend, and Samuel had decided to go ahead with it, much to Eric's relief. When they contacted a recommended therapist that morning to ask if she had space, Dr Amanda Bagworth confirmed she had and had a cancellation for that day if Samuel had wanted to take it. Samuel had agreed but hadn't wanted Eric to go with him, which was why he'd been sitting in the same position since his boy had left.

His stomach roiled and pitched as he thought about what Samuel had been put through while Eric had been off galivanting in New York. From what he'd managed to gather from Samuel's words, it had been hell for him, and the images of what could've happened swirled in his head on repeat.

After everything Eric had made him suffer, Samuel still wanted Eric. It was mind-blowing. He knew he wouldn't have been so quick to allow Samuel back into his life if roles had been reversed.

How did other Daddies get through the separation, or did they stay single until they could commit completely? Is that what Eric did wrong?

Taking his phone from his pocket, he hesitated. There was no one he knew he could call and ask. Joey would've been the nearest thing, but he had only been in one Daddy relationship. He was literally on his own. Unless…He dialled a number he had never used before.

"Good afternoon, Mr Clarke. How can I help you today?"

"How did…? Never mind. I would like to have a discussion with another Daddy if possible. Completely confidential. I…I need some advice."

"Is this the number we can reach you on?" the man on the other side of the phone asked.

"It is."

"We'll be in touch."

The phone line went dead, and Eric pulled it from his ear to stare at it. He should've realised by now these people were some of the best around, and nothing got past them.

Anonymity was the top end of the spectrum when it came to providing for and protecting their members. Their technology was high-end, their results undeniable. In all the years he'd been using the service, he had never been disappointed.

They knew so much information about you, it was scary to think about sometimes. It had taken Eric a long time to agree to them having that much detail about his life. In the end, though, he had needed their clubs, so after months of checking them out as far as he could, he'd signed up.

His thoughts returned to his predicament. Could he be enough for Samuel? Could he be what Samuel needed? What happened if they got deeper into their relationship and they broke up? What would that do to Samuel?

His phone rang, startling him. The display showed a withheld number, and he answered.

"Eric? My name is Andy. I was asked to give you a call by Anonymity?"

"Hi, Andy. Thanks for calling."

"No problem. How can I help?"

Eric blew out a breath. "This is difficult for me to admit, but I messed up, and although my relationship is back on track, I can't help thinking I'm going to do something else wrong."

"That is a difficult situation to be in. If you're willing, can you give me a bit more background info so I can see where you're coming from?"

Without revealing identities or any info that would identify either one of them, Eric explained what had happened and the outcome. "I'm not sure if I'm the right person for him."

"If your boy is not happy with the situation, I'm sure he will tell you. And if you're not sure whether he would, that conversation is sorely needed in my opinion."

"I agree. I feel so…"

"Guilty."

Eric nodded his head, although the other man couldn't see him. "Yeah."

Andy sighed. "You're going to need to forgive yourself. While you believe you're not worthy of him, I believe your boy will tell you. Both of you have gone through a difficult time and have come out the other side, not intact, but strong. Communication is always important. I know you learned that in your training."

"I did, and I do. I wonder…whether I'm right for him because, although I care deeply for him, I don't know if he feels the same."

"Communication, as I said. You don't have to proclaim your undying love today, but you need to get on the same page. Otherwise, this will become a bigger thing in your head and will begin to affect other areas of your life."

They spoke for a few more minutes before Eric began to feel a bit better.

"I'll talk to him as soon as he's back unless he's too

exposed. Thank you, Andy. Even having a sounding board has helped."

"You're welcome. If you need me again, get in contact with Anonymity again. They know how to reach me."

"I appreciate it."

After he hung up, he began to think about his parents. In some ways, he'd let Samuel down like Eric's parents had let Eric down. The semantics were different, but the premise was there.

The front door opened as Eric's phone rang again. He ignored his phone for the moment and strode over to the man.

"Hey, are you okay?" He wanted to check in with him before Eric touched him at all. He wasn't sure how sensitive Samuel would be after a session that appeared as if it had drained him.

"Daddy, can I sleep?" Sam said in a small voice.

Eric's heart ached at the broken sound. He enfolded Sam in his arms and held him securely, hoping his nearness helped to ground him. "Of course, you can sleep. Let's get you a glass of milk before bed." He began to steer Sam to the kitchen when Sam protested.

"No, home. I mean, your house." Sam's cheeks heated as he dropped his gaze.

"Sure. Let's go."

Eric grabbed Sam's things and wrapped his arm

around Sam's shoulders, touching him constantly to show him Eric was still there. He opened the car door, helping Sam in, then clicked the seatbelt closed before shutting the door and hopping around the car to the driver's seat. Once they were on their way, Eric entwined their fingers, resting them on Sam's thigh. Every now and then, Eric squeezed Sam's hand, but he remained silent, leaving Sam with his thoughts.

Eric guided Sam straight up the stairs to the bedroom when they arrived. He decided against a shower despite knowing Sam loved them and undressed his boy, checking his body language the whole time. When Eric had him down to his boxers, he lifted the covers back and directed Sam to lie down before tucking him in. He strode across to the mini-fridge, removing a small carton of milk with a straw and returned to Sam. Pointing the straw at Sam's mouth, Eric's muscles unclenched a little when Sam began to suck, drinking it all down.

Pulling it away when it was empty, Eric ran a hand over Sam's head as his eyelids fluttered closed. After Sam was emitting deep, even breaths, Eric rose from his kneeling position and stepped away. He closed the bedroom door and descended the stairs, intent on getting some dinner in the oven so Sam could have something to eat when he woke.

His phone rang from his pocket, and he pulled it

out, seeing another withheld number. He shook his head but decided to answer.

"Hello?"

"Is that Eric Clarke?"

"Can I ask who's calling?"

"My name is Bradford Jenkins from Jenkins and Sumner Attorneys. We have been trying to contact you regarding a breach of contract between yourself and Lynx Films. We need to arrange a meeting."

Eric rolled his eyes, having known it was coming. "I'm sorry, Mr Jenkins, but I'm in England at the moment. There is no way I will be travelling in the near future due to a family situation, which was the reason I was pulled away from my responsibilities."

"The meeting does not have to take place in person. We are happy to undertake a video conference."

"Be that as it may, before I confirm any meeting, I will be hiring a lawyer. Please email me your details so I can pass them along. My lawyer will then be in contact."

"Of course. I'll send it right away. Have a good day, Mr Clarke."

Eric didn't reply. He hung up the phone and placed it on the table before turning back to dinner preparations. His mind whirled around the options he had. Firstly, he needed to find a lawyer who dealt with this type of case; he'd have to ask Samuel if he knew of anyone. If not, he'd have to ask friends. He was sure one of them would know someone who could help.

He had put lasagne in the oven when his phone rang again. Wanting nothing more than to ignore it but knowing he better not, he swiped it from the table and glared at it before smiling and setting it to speakerphone.

"Hey, sis."

"Hey, you. How are you doing?" Emily's concerned voice filled the kitchen, and Eric relaxed a little more.

"I'm good. Samuel had his first therapy session today and is currently asleep, so I'm cooking dinner."

"You're good to him. I'm glad you two are together. On paper, you might look a little shaky, but in reality, you're perfect for each other."

"Thanks. I would like to think so, too," he answered, a smile gracing his mouth.

"So, why don't you?"

"Huh?" Eric had no idea what she was getting at.

"Why don't you think you're perfect for each other?"

That was his sister, blunt as always.

"I do. I..." He sighed, resting his hands on the counter and staring out of the window above the sink. "He deserves better than me, Emily. I let him down, and he shouldn't forgive me for that. My actions literally broke him." His throat constricted the rest of his words.

"Oh, Eric." Emily exhaled. "You are so hellbent on being everything for someone that you focus on what you don't do for them instead of what you do for them. You've given Samuel his freedom—"

"At what cost? His sanity?" Eric interrupted.

"Eric—"

"Can you say I haven't hurt him? Can you tell me that my actions didn't cause this?" Eric paused. "No, because they did. He is now in therapy because of me!"

"No, I'm not."

Samuel's voice was sharp across the space of the kitchen, and Eric whirled around to face him.

"Samuel—"

"*You* are not the one to have caused this. *You* have done nothing except support me even when you weren't here. *You* allowed me to be who I wanted to be. *You* gave me everything. Don't ever say you caused this because you didn't. *I* caused this. And I will do my damnedest to never do it again."

The only sounds in the kitchen were the oven's fan and their heavy breathing as they stared at each other across the space.

Eric was so shocked by Samuel's statement he didn't know how to react. He barely heard his sister saying she was hanging up. Why would Samuel think *he* was the cause of it all?

He must have said it out loud because Samuel said, "Because I knew what I was doing to myself, and I let it happen. I could've stopped it at any time, but I thought I could manage. I thought I was a superhero. But since this happened, I realised something. I'm not. I'm me. And by allowing myself to remember that, I can do what I need to do and let go of the things I cannot manage." He quirked the corner of his mouth. "I realised a lot during the hour session today."

"So I see."

Eric swiped a hand across his forehead, still not wholly convinced he had nothing to do with what happened to his boy.

Samuel stepped forward, sliding his arms around Eric's waist and fitting his head under his chin like he always loved to do. "You have helped me so much, Eric. I cannot thank you enough, and even though I know you don't believe me, you need to understand what you *have* given me." His boy pulled back. "Your love. Your respect. Your understanding. You have given me as much as I have given you, I'm sure."

Eric inhaled deeply. "I love you so fucking much, Samuel. It will take some time for me to believe that I didn't hurt you, but I love you. I can't live without you."

Samuel's smile lit up the room. "I—"

The oven timer went off, and they both laughed. Eric held up a finger to Samuel before removing the dinner to stop it from getting charred, then turned back to his boy, his love.

"I love you, Eric. To the moon and back."

Eric slanted his mouth over Samuel's as soon as the last word left his lips. Sliding his hands down to Samuel's hips, he pulled him closer, their cocks hardening at the contact. Holding tight to their future, they sealed their love with a kiss. And a bit more.

CHAPTER EIGHTEEN

SAMUEL

Samuel was nervous as hell. After their declarations of love earlier that week, they'd sat down and talked everything through. Every little bit of information they could think of to make sure they were both on the same page and starting fresh instead of allowing what happened before to grow bigger. They'd spoken about their fears as well, and each had tried to alleviate the other's. It had helped. At least, Samuel thought it had.

The other thing they had agreed upon, although more reluctantly on Samuel's part, but not out and out refusal, was that Samuel would try to be more of a little when they were out with their friends. The whole social mingling was unsettling, to begin with, but Samuel was determined to make their friends part of their lives, as was Eric. Neither had let the group of people close to them, afraid they were going to get hurt in one way or another, but they had decided to try their hardest. So far, that had consisted of spending an evening with Ethan and Emily and spending some time with Trent and Max.

They were starting slowly. Or at least they had been.

Today was Sean and Asher's wedding to which they were both invited. Hence the reason Eric wanted to try something new. Crush was closed to the public all day as the whole event was taking place within the walls of the bar. Samuel was looking forward to it because, secretly, he loved weddings. He was as sappy as ever when it came to all aspects of it. No doubt he'd even cry at some point, though he'd try and hide it from Eric.

Eric had mentioned Samuel being little for part of the event. Initially, Samuel had refused outright, but with some discussion, Samuel had agreed he would try, mainly at the reception, where Eric could take over sorting his food, drink and other needs. He'd put his foot down at a beaker, though.

"Are you ready, sweetheart?"

Samuel faced Eric, his breath catching at the sight of the man in a black suit, black shirt and white tie. "Wow! Seeing the pictures of you like this didn't do you justice!"

The suit fit like a glove, and his shiny black shoes

topped off the look. Having his hair slicked back and his movie-star looks fully on display, Samuel's heart started to race. He licked his lips, his breathing increasing.

"Fuck, little one. Don't look at me like that. We'll be late for the wedding."

Samuel blinked rapidly, trying to erase the sight from his mind, but it didn't work. Not when every blink brought the picture back to him again. "Sorry. I'm ready. Let's go." He rushed past Eric and raced for the stairs, Eric's chuckles floating down behind him.

Having a few seconds reprieve, he took deep breaths, trying to calm himself. "Later, Samuel. Later."

"Definitely, later," Eric's voice whispered from beside him.

Samuel gasped at the heat flickering in his gaze but swallowed and nodded.

Crush was decked out as it had been for Max and Trent's wedding but with a slightly different colour scheme. As it got closer to the time when the wedding would start, Samuel and Eric took their seats, Eric linking their hands together on his lap. Samuel ducked his head, and heat crept into his cheeks.

Eric snickered and pressed a kiss to Samuel's temple. "I love you, little one."

Samuel smiled at his lap, squeezing Eric's hand in response before looking around the room. There were a lot more couples within their group of friends now, and he loved seeing how they interacted with each other. It was one of the reasons he'd always felt out of place, but now he had Eric, and it gave him the ability to see things clearer. No one was left out for being single, the opposite, in fact.

The wedding march sounded, and everything began. Samuel's small smile stayed on his lips for the entire thing, and eventually, he gave in to the urge and rested his head on Eric's shoulder, sighing with happiness.

Despite being a hard-assed lawyer when the need arose, he was a total sap when it came to romance, and he found he loved it even more when Eric did things when he wasn't expecting them. Surprises had never been his favourite, but recently, that had changed.

Life was good. Now, he needed to get through the meal.

"If at any point you want me to stop, tell me. All right?"

Eric was as concerned as Samuel, and that helped to calm him. Knowing that Eric wouldn't push him in any way made it easier to accept the idea.

"I will."

"I love you, little one." Eric kissed him chastely.

"I love you…Daddy," he whispered the last word, but the smile he was rewarded with made the butterflies in his stomach worthwhile.

Samuel glanced around the table at the other six

occupants. They were all people he knew in some way or another, not enough to call friends, but acquaintances, definitely. He had no idea how they were going to react to…whatever Eric was planning on doing for him. They had gone through ideas of what Eric might be able to do for Samuel without it being too obvious, but now he was here, and despite the nervousness he was feeling, he found himself willing to give Eric more leeway than he had originally thought.

Eric poured a glass of water for him into a tumbler, and a short, sharp feeling of annoyance that it wasn't his beaker went through him. He hadn't expected that, but he pushed it aside and accepted the drink with a smile. When the food arrived, Eric cut up his food while Samuel watched his own hands in his lap, then he focused on eating it. By the time he was halfway done, Samuel had relaxed again.

"You're doing brilliantly, Sam. Thank you for allowing me to do this."

Samuel finished his mouthful, wiping his face with his napkin. "It's actually easier than I expected it to be. I keep thinking people are looking at me, but they're probably staring at the movie star by my side." He grinned, feeling lighter by the minute.

"Nah, I'm old news." Eric laughed. "No one cares about a washout."

Samuel nudged his shoulder with his own. "No, you're not."

"Hey, lovebirds. How's it hanging?" Trent turned up at Samuel's side, crouching between their chairs. "I wanted to make sure you were okay," he said, examining Eric.

"Why wouldn't I be?"

"Well, you have a complete wedding sap for a boyfriend. I imagine everything has been romantic as shit coming from his mouth." Trent snorted even as he tried to keep a straight face.

Samuel casually shoved his elbow backwards without looking and managed to knock Trent off-balance, ending up with him on his ass. The guests surrounding them burst out in laughter, including Trent himself.

"Good aim!" Max sidled up, holding up a high five, which Samuel reciprocated. "I'm going to leave you on your ass because you obviously deserved it." He glanced at them. "What did he do this time?"

"Oh, he was being his usual brotherly self."

"Hey, I was being kind!" Trent protested as he pulled himself to standing.

"Your version of kind and mine differ slightly, Mr Walker."

"Damn right, Mr Walker."

"Shut up. God, you Walker siblings are a nightmare!" Max complained, turning away from them and waving over his head. "I'm heading to the sane table."

"There's a sane table? Where? I want to see this

fantasy!" Trent scampered after his husband, the sounds of chuckling following him.

"They're a right comedy act, aren't they?" Eric said, smiling fondly.

"That and some."

When the food was finished, and the tables were pushed closer to the edge of the room to make way for a dance floor, Samuel felt completely relaxed. He wasn't little in his usual sense of the word, but he was comfortably in between, allowing Eric to do and get things for him but also retaining some of his independence. It was the perfect balance for their first outing.

Eric stood, holding out his hand. "Would you like to dance?"

"I'd love to, but I will warn you I haven't done this in a while."

Samuel slid his arms around Eric's neck and rested his head against his shoulder, enjoying the scent of his man. Cologne and a slight tease of sweat were filling his nostrils with every breath, and it was as intoxicating as it always had been. He intended to have fun with his Daddy that night.

Sean and Asher said goodnight not long after, heading off for their honeymoon to the Isle of Wight, and Eric and Samuel left shortly after they did. When they finally arrived home—or Eric's house—Samuel zipped up the stairs to the bedroom.

"Daddy, I need you!" he called as he went.

Eric's laughter floated up the stairs.

Sam undressed as fast as he could manage and jumped onto the bed, giggling breathlessly as he bounced several times. He lay sprawled across the covers, waiting with bated breath for Eric to enter. When he did, he laughed, leaning against the door-frame and crossing his arms over his chest.

"Eager, are we?" He smirked.

"Yes! Please, Daddy!" Sam squirmed against the covers that were slowly warming to the heat of his skin.

"Not yet, little one. Rainstorm time."

Sam began to pout, then paused. "Okay!" He clambered off the bed, rushing towards the bathroom and nearly tripping over his feet.

"Slow down! You're going to hurt yourself, and then we'll end up in A&E instead of a bed."

Sam huffed and frowned but slowed down to a fast walk. As he was already naked, he walked directly under the nozzles, which sprayed warm water on him. He lifted his arms out to the sides and turned in a circle, his eyes closed and his head facing the ceiling. He had no idea why this shower felt so good, but he loved every minute he was in it.

Hands slid along his waist as he spun, holding him steady and allowing him to spin faster. He chuckled, then fell against Eric, his head continuing to spin though he was still.

"Dizzy," he puffed.

"Yeah, I bet. Hold still for a few minutes. Your head will catch up."

Eric smoothed his fingers up and down his back, each time moving lower and lower until he was ending the caress with a gentle squeeze of his ass. Each time he did it, Sam's hips bucked forward, his rapidly hardening cock pressing against Eric's thigh.

Sam blinked away the droplets of water and glanced up at Eric, seeing a small smile on his Daddy's face. "I love you, Daddy."

"I love you, too, little one."

Eric leaned down and joined their lips, licking into Sam's mouth immediately. Sam dropped his head back and held tight around Eric's waist, succumbing to the sensual exploration. Sam's whimpers were muffled by the noisy spray hitting the floor, but he was sure Eric would feel them through his chest.

Eric's finger went lower, following the path of Sam's crack and stroking over his entrance. Sam jerked, not sure if he wanted to move forward and receive friction from Eric's body or backwards and feel his finger. Eric removed his hand briefly, reaching for something behind Sam he couldn't see, then returned to his previous position. His mouth deepening the kiss even as his finger began penetrating Sam. The lube—which must've been what Eric had reached for—helped ease the way, and soon one finger became two.

Sam pulled away from the kiss, gasping for air as

he nuzzled his face into Eric's neck and concentrated on the sensations Eric was providing. His dick was rubbing between them, and he could feel Eric's cock, sliding against his skin. Sam wanted more.

"More, please!"

"Be patient, little one. Another couple of minutes, and I'll give you what you need," Eric crooned into his ear.

Sam licked at the water dribbling along Eric's skin, keeping up the gentle thrusts while Eric prepared him fully. Eric's fingers withdrew, and Sam whimpered, his body following.

"All right, Sam. Time to get out and get dry."

"But Daddy—"

"No arguments. We can't do what I want to do to you in here, so get to it."

Sam pouted but followed the instructions. He didn't want to get out; he'd been more than comfortable staying there. Eric dried him off while he stood pursing his lips.

"Right! Onto the bed, little one. Hands and knees, please."

Sam scrambled to do as Eric said, eager for more even if he couldn't have it in his rainstorm. When he was in the right position, he lowered to his elbows instead of his hands because he was a little wobbly.

"Look at you. So eager for Daddy."

Sam glanced over his shoulder, seeing Eric staring

at his ass. He felt the flush of embarrassment heat his face and turned his head back to the headboard. The bed dipped, then Sam felt warm hands skim across the skin of his ass and up his spine before moving back down again. Eric did this several times, and Sam could feel the goosebumps rising and lowering with the movement. He shivered several times, squirming with the need to move but worried if he did, Eric would stop.

"So beautiful. So responsive."

His hands gripped the sheets as Eric's hands clasped his ass, widening his cheeks and blowing a breath across his taint. A hot, wet tongue laved up his crack, and his breath caught at the sensation making his channel clench.

Sam bit his bottom lip, trying to keep from moaning loudly, but a yell turned into a moan when a loud smack rent the air, and heat bloomed across his right ass cheek. Sam dropped his head onto the covers, swallowing hard against the arousal that speared through him from the spank.

"Did you like that, little one? It's something we discussed earlier this week but haven't put into action yet." His hands smoothed over Sam's heated cheek before another smack startled Sam into bucking forward again. "Hmm, yeah, I think someone likes it from the sounds I'm receiving."

Eric fastened his mouth onto Sam's pucker, sucking

and licking at it like he had done the first time they'd been together. Sam's mouth was wide open, trying to fill his lungs with enough air to breathe without passing out—he didn't want to miss any of what Eric was giving him.

"Do you know," he sucked, "that you," he licked, "were amazing today?" He licked and nipped and sucked, then encircled Sam's cock from beneath, stroking him in time with his ministrations. As his tongue began to push forward past the rim of muscles, Eric smacked his ass again. As heat bloomed throughout his body, his channel tightened around the tongue, sending flickers of fire along his spine.

Sam felt himself leaking, and Eric swiped a hand across the tip of his cock, using it to ease his actions.

"Please, Daddy. Please!" Sam couldn't hold back his chants anymore. He wanted everything Eric could give him.

Eric lifted his head, the cool air suddenly washing over Sam's exposed ass. "Are you ready for me, little one?"

"Yes! God, yes, please!" Sam pushed back, peering over his shoulder to watch Eric as he knelt behind him.

He felt the blunt head of Eric's cock resting against his hole and groaned, pushing back, wanting more. Bearing down, his eyelids fluttered as Eric slid inside him, completing him in a way he would never have imagined someone doing so before. Sam took more and more until Eric was fully seated, Eric's arms bracketing his body, Eric's front covering Sam's back.

"You doing okay?" Eric whispered, pressing a kiss behind Sam's ear and several more down his neck and across his shoulders.

"Yes. Definitely, yes. Please move, Daddy. I need you."

"All right, little one. Your wish is my command."

The heat disappeared from his back, and Eric took hold of his hips. His Daddy withdrew slowly, and Sam bit his lip against the drag along his insides. It was an amazing feeling. Eric powered forward again, still slower than Sam wanted, then withdrew again. The grip tightened on Sam's hips, and he braced himself, knowing what was coming.

Eric's hips snapped forward, pushing Sam towards the headboard, and the slap of their skin meeting broke the otherwise silent room.

"Fuck, yes, Daddy."

"You've got a dirty mouth when you're aroused," Eric groaned. "It sounds hot. Those dirty words coming from such a lovely boy."

"Please, Daddy. Oh God, please!"

"You're going to make Daddy come, little one."

Eric's hips slapped against Sam's ass, and Sam braced himself to stop his forward momentum, wanting to feel every bit of him.

Samuel moaned. "Fuck! Oh, God! Can I come, Daddy? Please?"

"Wrap your hand around your cock and make yourself come. Come for Daddy." Eric's voice was more of a growl than anything else.

Samuel moved one arm to support him, then spat into his hand and wrapped it around his shaft, stroking frantically and twisting at the top. His orgasm was rolling down his spine, the tingles advertising the impending release.

"Fuck, yes! Come for me, Sam." Eric's voice flowed over him, and just like that, he released, coating his hand in his sticky fluid. Seconds later, he felt Eric tighten his grip and press close, groaning as the heated come coated his insides.

Eric pulled free and helped Samuel to his side, his knees complaining about being on them as long as he had been.

"Sorry, I should've thought about you being uncomfortable."

Eric rubbed a hand over Samuel's stomach, then pressed a kiss to his temple and rose from the bed. When he came back, he was carrying a cloth, which he used to clean Samuel up. Then he chuckled.

"We need to change the sheets, I'm afraid."

Samuel groaned and rolled to his back, not wanting to move more than he had to, but he refused to make Eric change them by himself. Dragging himself upright, he wriggled on his ass a little, smiling when he felt the twinge. He loved that feeling as much as the fucking itself. The tell-tale reminder he'd had Eric inside him.

"What are you smiling at, little one?" Eric came to stand in front of him, a small smile on his face.

"I like being able to feel you afterwards," he whispered self-consciously, heat invading his cheeks.

Eric leaned down and cupped Samuel's jaw, lifting his head to meet his gaze. "I love the idea that you can feel me," he murmured, taking Samuel's lips in another desperate kiss before pulling away again. "God, you make me crazy."

Samuel grinned. "Likewise."

They changed the bedding, then snuggled under the cool covers, Samuel wrapping himself around Eric to keep warm.

"Thank you for everything," he said.

Eric dropped a kiss on his head, tightening his grip, then whispered, "Thank *you*."

Samuel had been on tenterhooks for the whole of Sunday despite having visited his family and bringing Eric along. They had decided Eric would attend this

Sunday, then see how Emily and Ethan would feel about it. He was sure Ethan would be fine, but he didn't know with Emily; he got the feeling she was a little on the shy side when it came to meeting new people.

When his family had mentioned work, he'd told them he was going back that week, and there he was hiding out in his car when he should be strolling across the car park to the office. He would. He needed a minute.

His thoughts had veered back and forth as to what would happen when he arrived that morning. He'd had no notifications from the company or messages from people that he had been fired. Maggie had been in touch a few times, but she hadn't mentioned anything either. Who knew?

He inhaled deeply, reminding himself if he lost his job, he could always get another one. At least, that was what Eric kept telling him.

As if his thoughts conjured him, Samuel received a message from him.

You'll be fine. Just walk in there, head held high. You have nothing to be ashamed of. I love you no matter what happens today. x

A smile crept across his face, but it was the encouragement he needed. He climbed out of the car, locking it behind him, and strode into work. Nothing extreme happened when he turned up. Nobody came after him. Nobody gave him sly glances. He took that as a good indicator. Maggie enveloped him in a hug when he arrived at his office, and he smiled and returned the embrace.

"How are you?" she asked as they entered his office, which looked the same as usual, except for the mess he'd left when he'd walked out last time.

"I'm good, actually. How are things around here? I was expecting to face the firing squad." He circled his desk, resting his briefcase on the surface before pulling his chair back.

"No one is out for you, Samuel."

Samuel jerked his head towards the door when Peter, one of the senior partners, entered his office.

"Good morning, Peter." He strode towards the man, holding out his hand.

"How are you doing, Samuel?" Peter held his hand for a moment, then released him, replacing his hands in his trouser pockets. It was the same stance he'd seen the man use every day, and it settled him some. If he was going to be fired, he'd have expected to see some different body language from him.

"I'm doing a lot better now, thanks. I'm sorry for—"

"Don't be. You did us all a favour despite the dramatic event."

Samuel frowned. "What do you mean?"

Peter raised his eyebrows at Maggie. "Did you not tell him?"

Maggie shook her head. "I didn't think it was my place, sir."

Peter tilted his head at her, and Maggie's cheeks flushed. Interesting. Then he returned his gaze to Samuel. "I'd had no idea what Gregory had been up to during his hours working here. I honestly thought he'd been an asset to the company, but when I was told what he'd been doing and that you were the one who had done most of his work, especially on the Benedict case, there was an internal review of him, and we decided to let him go."

Samuel's eyebrows raised as he stared at the man. "Wow. I never expected that."

Peter shrugged. "There is no point in having people who are not team players. This office needs to run like clockwork, and if someone else is being over-worked because one person can't be bothered to do it, then we need to release them. As for Milton, well, he's been barred from the premises. He wouldn't need to be here anyway, now that Gregory is gone."

Samuel blew out a breath, lowering his shoulders as relief flowed through him. "Regardless, I do apologise for my behaviour. I didn't expect to lose control like that."

Peter waved his hand through the air as if casting

his words aside. "Don't worry about it. I'm glad you've had a breather. You work damn hard here, and I, and the other partners, appreciate it. All I need from you is your agreement that you will begin to refuse a case if you do not have time for it. I will be getting Maggie to promise to tell me if she sees you taking on too much. We need you here in one piece, Samuel."

"Thank you, and yes, I will be careful with my workload from now on. No extra-curricular cases."

"Glad to hear it. Well, I'll leave you to your day. Make sure you come to me if you need anything at all."

With that, he swept out of the room, closing the door behind him. Samuel stared after him, not sure what to think about the words of a man he had barely seen before that day. His vision blurred, and he felt himself being guided somewhere before he was pulled onto a soft surface, which he realised was the sofa. A glass of water was pushed into his hands, and he drank slowly.

He came back to himself properly when a scent he recognised enveloped him. He turned and burrowed himself in Eric's arms, breathing deeply.

"Well, aren't you the hero of the hour, little one," he whispered.

CHAPTER NINETEEN

ERIC

Eric was vibrating with as much excitement as his boy on Christmas Day. They had arranged with Ethan and Emily that they would come and visit them in the late morning, then all four of them would head to Samuel's parents' house for Christmas lunch and stay through the afternoon. But the morning was for him and his boy.

Eric woke before Samuel despite the boy being so excited he could hardly sleep the previous night. Or it was because he hadn't been able to sleep. It had taken two orgasms before Samuel had drifted off, and even then, it was fitfully for a while. Once he had finally calmed, Eric had crept out of bed and arranged all the presents under the tree they'd eventually set up in the living room, right next to the window.

Samuel had found a new favourite place to sit...in

the loveseat by that window, where he could watch the trees and see the Christmas tree without having to move a muscle.

Resting his head on his hand, he watched Samuel sleep. The stress of the months before seemed to have vanished over the last couple of weeks, and he was sure a lot of it had to do with the reconciliation at his work. The two main symptoms of Samuel's stress were no longer an issue, which had helped him to finish his work on time.

Thinking about work, had Eric remembering his most recent phone call with his lawyer. When Eric had explained to Samuel about the film company threatening to sue him for breach of contract, Samuel had passed him over to a friend of a friend, Ryan Richardson. Ryan had been fighting in his corner for the past few weeks, and they were slowly making headway. The film company's lawyers were trying to fine him for not attending the necessary appearances, but Ryan was fighting back with a family emergency, and Eric had agreed to some appearances and interviews via video unless the journalists wanted to visit Cambridge.

He had no inclination to fly halfway across the world to attend events he didn't need to. Naturally, he would for the premiere, but he planned on taking Samuel with him for that, although he hadn't discussed it with him yet.

Samuel snuffled and turned onto his side, facing

Eric, and he couldn't resist reaching out and skimming a finger along his cheek. He couldn't believe he'd figured himself out quickly enough to make sure he didn't lose the man currently lying next to him.

"Daddy?" The sleepy voice made him smile.

"Yes, sweetheart?"

"Is it time to get up?" Samuel rubbed his face against the pillow, and Eric waited for him to wake a little more and for it to register what day it was. He laughed when Samuel's eyes darted open, and a grin spread across his face. "It's Christmas!" Samuel called into the silence of the morning.

"Yes, it is."

Samuel sat upright, the covers pooling around his waist, and his eyes widened when he saw the box at the bottom of the bed. He flicked his gaze to Eric's, and Eric knew what he was asking.

"I thought we could start a new tradition. This is your first gift, which you can open before doing anything else."

Samuel scrambled across the bed, reaching for the shiny silver box with a gold bow and pulling it towards him. "What is it?" he asked.

Eric chuckled. "Why don't you open it and find out?"

Samuel gently caressed the box before pulling on the bow and unravelling it. Pushing the bow off, he lifted the lid and set it aside. The white tissue paper inside was carefully unfolded, and Samuel laughed when he saw what was lying inside.

"Pyjamas!"

Eric grinned. "Not just any pyjamas, Samuel. Christmas pyjamas."

"They have Christmas lights all over them." Samuel pulled the top and bottom set from the box and held them up. "Festive."

"I thought so." Eric reached down beside the bed and brought his pyjamas from under the bed where he'd hidden them the night before. "We can match while we're eating breakfast and opening the rest of the gifts." Samuel's hand covered his mouth, and he giggled. "What?" Eric held his hands out in front of him.

"The movie star is going to wear Christmas pyjamas?"

"Of course, I am."

"I don't believe it."

Eric climbed off the bed, the sheets slipping off his naked body and exposing him to Samuel's gaze. A small gasp sounded, and Eric threw a grin over his shoulder. He pulled the trousers on, followed by the long-sleeved top and held his hands out to his sides.

Samuel chuckled. "You look very Christmassy."

"Thank you. Your turn."

He rose from the bed, his cheeks colouring as his own body became visible, and tugged on the pyjamas. Eric thought he looked adorable. When he was dressed, Eric rounded the bed and pulled him into his arms.

"Merry Christmas, sweetheart."

Samuel lifted his head and smiled. "Merry Christmas, Daddy."

Eric dropped his lips to Samuel's, tasting his boy for the first time on Christmas morning. He pulled back seconds later, not wanting to postpone the excitement for too long.

"Breakfast first or presents first?"

Samuel bit his bottom lip and smiled. "Presents," he whispered.

Eric grinned. "Presents, it is, but we are going to get a drink first at least."

They descended down the stairs, and Eric watched as Samuel's eyes widened at the sight of the presents under the tree.

"When did they get here?"

Eric shrugged, his face neutral. "Santa must've brought them."

Samuel rolled his eyes but shuffled over and sat on the sofa.

"I'm going to grab us some drinks. Don't open anything yet. I want to get some photos for our first Christmas together."

He strode into the kitchen, grabbing Sam's beaker and a glass for himself. He filled them with milk, grabbed two bananas and wandered back to see Samuel, who hadn't moved from his position.

When Eric sank into the seat next to him, Samuel turned his face to him. "I can't believe we're here."

Eric tilted his head, frowning. "What do you mean?"

"I never thought I would ever be here. When I was with Milton," he grimaced, "we never celebrated Christmas at home. We always went to his parents or my parents. If anyone visited our place, there wouldn't be any decorations up. They wouldn't have thought it was anywhere close to Christmas." He glanced around. "This is…beautiful and magical. I love everything about it."

Eric placed the cups on the coffee table and turned towards Samuel, cupping his jaw. "You deserve this, sweetheart. You have so much love to give and deserve to be given so much love. It's about time you had something for you. Or us. This is our new Christmas. We can make our own traditions as we already have. Ethan and Emily will be here later, then we're going to your parents' house. If we find it doesn't work, we'll change things. Or if we decide we want to do some different things, we can discuss it. We make our own happiness, sweetie. I've learned that if nothing else these past few months."

"I want that. So much. New traditions. You. Family. Love." Samuel inhaled deeply, then sighed it out with a smile.

Eric wrapped his arms around his boy. "I'm so glad you're happy, little one."

"Daddy?"

"Yes, sweetheart?"

"Can I open a present now?"

Eric chuckled. "Have a quick sip of milk first because you've not had anything to drink yet, then yes, you can open the presents."

Samuel reached for his beaker, sucking the liquid through the holes while his eyes strayed to the boxes waiting for his attention. Eric could tell he was eager to get started, and he wondered how long he would restrain himself.

It wasn't long.

Samuel drank every bit of his drink, then slipped to the floor, reaching for the first present and checking the label. He wouldn't find any that didn't belong to him. Eric had spoiled his boy rotten and would continue to do so as long as Samuel would allow him to.

The paper tore quickly, and Samuel gasped as an interactive watch came into view. He knew Samuel had a watch he wore regularly, but Eric thought it might be a good gift for him so he could use it for a variety of things, not just checking the time. As far as Eric was concerned, anything Samuel didn't want could get donated to someone. A win, win situation.

"I've been looking at one of these for a while, but I never knew what to do with it. They were all so confusing, I wasn't sure what to choose."

"You can do a lot with this. I can show you how to work it. It's not too difficult."

"Thank you. It's perfect."

Samuel opened a few more gifts before his stomach growled, making them both laugh.

"Come on. Let's go grab some breakfast before you eat the gifts instead of opening them. Do you want to grab your new colouring book and pens?"

"Yeah!"

Samuel reached for the large, chunky book containing pictures of Christmassy things and followed Eric into the kitchen. He settled himself at his usual place, scooting his seat in close to the table and opened his book, beaming as he flicked through them.

Eric smiled gently and set about grabbing some eggs and bread to make soldiers; he'd found out Samuel loved dunking his toast into the runny eggs. He wanted this day to be as special as possible for his boy, especially after everything he'd been through the past few weeks.

"Oh! Cheeky-Boo!" Samuel suddenly shouted, scraping his chair back and rushing from the room.

Eric shook his head and chuckled. Samuel had started leaving his favourite monkey on the bedside table, and he'd obviously been too distracted that morning to remember to grab him. Samuel's footsteps thudded up and down the stairs before he came rushing back into the room and dropping himself back onto his seat. He held one arm around his cuddly while steadying the book with his hand and coloured with his other hand. Eric reached for his phone, turned the sound off and took a picture of his boy, so content in his task.

The size of Eric's heart grew more every time he glanced in Samuel's direction. He had never felt so content, so at ease as he did in his presence.

When the eggs and soldiers were ready, he asked Samuel to tidy and clean up, then they ate their breakfast talking about what mischief their siblings would be getting up to that day. Samuel knew there would no doubt be gag gifts, as was the usual case with his brothers and sisters. Luke was the usual recipient, but anyone could get anything at any time. Eric made a note to be careful when opening any potential gifts.

By the time Ethan and Emily arrived, Samuel had opened all his gifts and surprised Eric with some he'd hidden at some point.

"Happy Christmas!" Ethan shouted as he strode into the room with an armful of presents, depositing them on one of the other sofas.

"I'm sure he's already drunk," Emily said, shuffling in behind him.

"I am not. It's a day to be happy, is it not?" Ethan sat down on the floor next to Samuel, picking up one of the horses Eric had bought him. "Hey, buddy. Do you want to play with these, or would you like to open some more presents?"

Ethan grinned at the boy, and Eric felt tears gathering in his eyes. To see his family not only accepting him and Samuel but interacting with Sam as a little was overwhelming. When they first spoke in more detail about being together, Eric had never believed this could be possible. Samuel wasn't comfortable being completely little around his own family, but he was getting more relaxed around Eric's siblings. He'd anticipated some people being unsure of how to act around them, but most had been great.

It helped a little to have Max, Trent and Joey in the lifestyle in a small way because they were able to talk things through with them when they were unsure about anything.

"Can we play for a bit?" Sam asked hesitantly.

"Of course! Let's go over here, so we have more room."

Ethan stood, collecting a few of Sam's toys and carrying them over to the rug in front of the fireplace. He sat down, cross-legged and waved Sam over. With a small glance at Eric, who nodded and smiled back,

Sam laid on his stomach next to Ethan.

"Don't forget a cushion, sweetheart." Eric grabbed a small one and threw it over to them, hitting Ethan in the face. "Shot!" Eric lifted his arms in victory.

"Hey!" Ethan grumbled, passing the pillow to Sam. "That's not kind."

He watched them for a few minutes more, and, not wanting to intrude and make Sam uncomfortable, he picked up Sam's empty beaker and trailed into the kitchen to make drinks.

Emily followed behind, setting a couple of plates on the table. "Sam's in good hands with Ethan. He's a big kid and will have great fun playing with Sam."

Eric grinned. "Yeah. I need to get Samuel at peace with the idea of going to visit a club. I think he'd have a great time mixing with some other boys there. We could find someone to have playdates outside of the place too."

"Just be careful, yeah. You know from experience that your status will make you prey to a lot of people."

"I know." Eric nodded his head, listening to the boil of the kettle. "In some ways, it will work against us, but I'm hoping there are some decent people around that will be able to see past what they might get out of it, except for friendship."

"There are. It's finding them." Emily changed the subject. "How's Vaughn, Emma and Carlie?"

"I've not spoken to them today yet. I'm going to

save it until a little later this afternoon because I'm sure Carlie will be too engrossed in her toys to be any kind of conversationalist."

Emily chuckled. "Yeah, I remember you two being the same. I'd hardly see you after the presents were opened." She hesitated. "Mum sent me a message," she admitted.

Eric paused in his stirring of the milk. He had been expecting something from them himself, in all honesty, but nothing had come through as of yet. "Oh? What did she have to say?"

"Merry Christmas." He could hear the tinge of sadness in her voice. "Literally, just that."

"I'm sorry for everything that happened, Emily. I'm sure you miss them."

"No, don't do that." She came to stand next to him. "It's not your fault. It's theirs." She sighed. "I don't miss them as such. I miss who I thought they were. I miss what I thought we *all* were together. But I much prefer what we have now—with no lies between us—than what I thought we had then."

Eric left the spoon in the cup and turned to Emily, enfolding her in his arms. As big as he was, he towered over her, but she was still his big sister, always looking out for him. "I love what we all have here, too."

He squeezed her again, then let her go, finishing up the drinks as they chatted about the visit to Samuel's parents' that afternoon. When they returned to the living room, Eric stopped and stared at the sight of his brother and his boy playing with the horses, cowboys and cars, along with some empty boxes as buildings set up around them. Both were on their stomachs, completely intent on their game, and it warmed Eric's heart again.

"Told you," Emily whispered as she shuffled past, placing Ethan's drink on the table while she kept hers and curled her legs underneath her as she sat on the sofa.

Eric carried on walking, sitting a little closer to Sam, but not too close as to interrupt their play. Sam's beaker waited on the table for when Sam wanted something or when Eric thought he needed a drink.

"Have you decided what you're going to do with yourself now you're unemployed?" Emily asked with a grin.

"If you didn't have a drink in your hand, I'd throw this cushion at you," he remarked with a smile before he shrugged. "I've not decided completely. I thought I'd think about it over Christmas and New Year, then come up with some options with Samuel's help. Once we have them, I'll start making calls."

"Is there anything you can think of off the top of your head?"

"I'd been thinking about being an acting coach of some sort. Giving lessons or something. I don't know exactly, but it would make sense to use my skills in that way."

"What about acting yourself, though? I know you love it."

Eric nodded in agreement. "The theatre? I could work on a pantomime. That would be fun. Not too much of a fan of musicals, so not those, but other theatre performances possibly."

"Sounds like a good idea. You should check out the local colleges and universities, too. I bet they're crying out for people to help them with lessons."

"You could do video lessons or something similar," Ethan said, sitting up, then bum-shuffling across the floor to reach for his drink.

"That's an idea."

He noticed Sam rolling to his side and quickly stood to help him, knowing getting up was not as easy for him as it was for the rest of them. The age difference was something they were going to have to face eventually, and he knew it was something that already bothered Samuel at times.

After a brief drink break, Ethan persuaded Sam to open the rest of his presents. He received several more horse items, much to Sam's pleasure, plus an interactive drawing tablet, which, when it was drawn on, provided rainbow colour lines.

Before long, it was time to head to Samuel's parents' house, so they dressed in respectable

Christmas clothes, and Eric drove them over. There were a handful of cars in the driveway and on the street, so Eric knew most, if not all, of the people were already present.

They all climbed out of the car, and when Eric stood next to Samuel, he noticed his boy was trembling. He pulled him into his arms. "What's the matter?" he whispered into his ear.

Samuel burrowed his face into Eric's neck. "I want to be little, but I'm scared."

"Scared of what?"

"That they'll laugh at me."

Eric hugged him tighter. "You know they won't, Samuel." He swallowed hard and decided to say what he'd been holding back for several days. "Okay, listen. Let's go in there as we are. I have a change of clothes, plus a few other bits in a bag we can take in with us. If you feel comfortable, we can start slow. Playing with something or doing some colouring. If you start to feel more comfortable, we could change your clothes, or something smaller. We can go at your speed, Samuel. If you're not ready, we won't."

Eric counted to five breaths before Samuel answered, "Okay."

His heart raced. "You're sure?"

Samuel nodded. "I'm nervous, but I want to try, even if it's only something small." He stared into Eric's eyes. "I want to be little. It's Christmas Day, and I want to stop feeling like I have to do grownup stuff."

Eric chuckled at his perturbed tone. "I'm afraid, even little boys have to do things they don't want to do on occasion." Samuel pouted, and Eric laughed again. "Come on, Sam. Let's go wish your family a Happy Christmas." He grabbed the bag and linked their fingers together, heading over to where Ethan and Emily were waiting.

Samuel didn't knock; he opened the door and shouted a greeting. Within seconds, Samuel's mother came bounding towards them and enfolded her son in her arms.

"Merry Christmas, Samu…Sam," she said with a catch in her voice. "I hope you got spoilt this morning."

"Yes, I did. Ethan and Emily brought me some amazing presents, and Eri—" Samuel glanced at Eric and inhaled, letting it out slowly. "Daddy bought me some horses and colouring books, and he found a carousel for me!"

Sam's voice got louder and more excited with every word. Eric could see the expression of joy on Samuel's mother's face as she listened intently to her son's speech. After Sam finished, his cheeks were rosy, and he was breathing heavily, but his eyes sparkled.

"That is wonderful!" Catherine clapped her hands together and pressed them to her mouth, tears shining in her eyes. Turning to him, she dragged him into a hug. "Thank you for bringing him back to us," she whispered.

Eric nodded, unable to say anything through the lump in his throat. When they pulled away, he indicated his siblings and croaked, "This is Emily and Ethan."

Catherine embraced them the same way she had done her son and him, telling them they were part of the family now and could come and go as they pleased.

"Come on, let's go see the others. I love that this house is full of people again."

The rest of the day was spent laughing, joking and getting to know everyone. Emily and Ethan fit in without any issues, not that he thought there would have been. There was a moment of sadness when Samuel's parents brought Charles Junior into the discussion. After having had a big family meeting where their parents had come clean about a few home truths, they were trying to talk more about the boy they'd lost before he'd had a chance to live. And it *was* sad, but it was also a happy time for remembering there was another one of them somewhere in the universe.

When they finally arrived back at Eric's stuffed full of Christmas dinner, mince pies and desserts, Eric was ready to sit down and not move for a few hours.

"We're going to head straight off, little bro," Ethan

said, pulling him into a hug and clapping him on his back. "Merry Christmas. I'm glad you're home to stay." He gave a small smile before heading to Samuel.

"Don't mind him. He's missed you more than you probably realise," Emily explained as she hugged him tightly. "Let me know how he takes the final gift," she whispered.

"Will do."

Eric clasped Samuel's hand as they waved goodbye before turning towards the house and pulling Samuel along with him.

Laughter sounded behind him. "Where are we going in such a hurry?"

"Be patient, little one."

He unlocked the door, removed their coats and shoes, then got them situated on the sofa with drinks before he twisted to face Samuel. "I have two more gifts for you."

"You do?" Sam's eyes lit up.

"Yes, the first is this." He pulled an envelope from one of the drawers in the coffee table and handed it to his boy.

Sam took it and carefully opened it. The card had a picture of a golden brown horse with a blonde-coloured mane. Sam smiled at it, then unfolded it, reading the words aloud, "You are invited to the Ranch Horse Sanctuary for the opportunity to learn about horses and, if you wish, to receive riding lessons." He looked at Eric, eyes wide. "I can't! Daddy, I'm scared!"

"Hush, little one." He wrapped his arms around his boy, holding him close and calming him before explaining what it was. "I'm sorry. I should've said this before, but it would've given the gift away. There is no pressure for this. This sanctuary is for horses who help people with healing and for children who need soft and gentle horses. All the horses there have been trained to be calm and gentle with the people around them. I thought we could go and have a look. We don't have to go anywhere near them if you don't want to, but with a little bit of courage, you can grow to love them more than you already do." He tilted Sam's head up and pressed a kiss to his forehead before saying, "Wouldn't you like to ride one, one day?"

Sam didn't say anything for a moment. "Yeah, I would."

"Then why not let me help you try. I will be there every step of the way because I have no idea how to look after a horse, so I need to learn as well."

"I supposed we could go and see them, but if I don't like it, we can leave, can't we?"

"Of course. I'm so proud of you for being brave and having a go. Even if it doesn't work out, at least you've tried."

They stayed close for a moment, then Eric slipped his hand into his pocket. Pulling out the object that had been burning a hole in his pocket for the last few hours, he held it up for Sam to see.

"Would you like to move in with me?"

Sam climbed onto his lap and kissed him. "Yes, Daddy!"

ONE YEAR LATER

SAMUEL

S am waved his hand at his Daddy, who was sitting on the fence of the paddock he was currently riding around, holding his phone up as if he was taking a photo. The horse beneath him was a gorgeous chestnut colour and was so gentle in her movements, Sam wasn't afraid at all.

It had taken Samuel several months to get used to being around horses, but every week for the last year, Eric had taken him to the horse sanctuary, and Sam had managed to get past his fear for the most part. It was still a bit scary when the horses moved fast, but he was learning it didn't mean they were going to hurt him.

The whole process of taking care of a horse was now ingrained in his brain, and he loved what the place had managed to achieve with him. He was also impressed with their whole setup and had recommended them to families for helping their child to settle if they were struggling. It didn't always help them, but for some families, it did. Helping one was better than helping none in his book.

"Time to bring him in now, Sam," called Beverly, the owner.

He inhaled, then gently lead Dozer to where he should go, smiling wide when the horse listened to his silent instructions.

After he had dismounted and given the reins to Beverly, he skipped over to Eric and threw his arms around him. "That horse is gorgeous! I loved it!"

"I'm glad you're having fun, Sam." He pressed a kiss to Sam's temple as Sam's eyes closed in delight. He loved that small expression of tenderness Eric did, probably unconsciously. "We need to get you wrapped up again; otherwise, you will get a cold." He lifted Sam's coat and helped him get it on, zipping it up for him as soon as it was in place. "Are you going to put your gloves on this time?"

"Nope," Sam said, shaking his head. "My hands aren't cold."

Eric lifted his eyebrows, knowing as well as Sam did that his hands were freezing, but he didn't want to wear them. They were itchy, and he couldn't feel his Daddy's hands when he wore them. "All right." Eric tucked them into Sam's coat pockets again.

"Well done, Sam. You did brilliant work out there today." Beverly returned to them, her hands covered with leather gloves. Sam wondered if they would be better for him than the fabric ones. He'd have to ask Daddy later.

"Thank you," he replied, ducking his head. "I love Dozer."

"I'm glad to hear it. He's there for you to ride whenever you want to, okay."

"Really?"

She nodded and glanced at Eric, who Sam saw nod. "Dozer is yours, sweetie." She smiled at him.

Sam's mouth dropped open, and his gaze flicked from Beverly to Eric and back several times. "What?" he whispered, a hand covering his mouth.

"Dozer belongs to you. He's your horse, Sam. He will be kept here where we can look after him when you can't, and you can come and visit whenever you want to and ride him, look after him, feed him. Everything we've taught you to do."

Tears dripped down Sam's cheek. "I never believed I'd be able to have a horse!" he cried, ducking his head into Eric's coat and holding on tightly.

"You've done so well, little one. I'm so proud of you. Happy birthday."

Sam cried into Eric's coat as Eric steered them somewhere. When he finally stopped with the tears, his eyes felt raw, and his chest and throat hurt. "Thank you," he croaked to the chorus of neighing from all around him.

"You're welcome, little one."

Eric narrowed his eyes, then firmed his lips. Sam frowned as Eric fumbled in his coat pocket, muttering, then pulling off his gloves before rummaging again. He pulled out a small box, inhaled and dropped to one knee. Sam gasped.

"You have shown me what bravery means. It wasn't standing up to those who have hurt you. It wasn't putting your foot down when people tried to walk all over you. Although those are good examples. For me, you have shown me that bravery means to be true to yourself and what you want. To go after what you need in your life. To forgive even those who have hurt you beyond what you thought you could endure. Without your bravery, we wouldn't be where we are today. I would love for you to keep teaching me, to keep showing me how to live life to the fullest, finding enjoyment in every little piece of every minute of the day. With that in mind, Samuel, will you marry me?"

Tears were once again flowing down Samuel's cheeks, and he could barely say a word. He managed a hoarse, "Yes," and began sobbing his heart out. He felt Eric place the ring on his finger, then they were holding each other so tightly, Samuel could hardly breathe.

He was getting married!

"I see it's good news then." Jonah's deep voice sounded from behind Sam, and he lifted his head to look at him.

Jonah and Hayden Cross had been the first Daddy and little they had befriended at Chalice when they visited the place. It had taken a little while for Sam to get his membership to the place, and he had been so nervous the first time he'd attended. The place was huge, but it had many different rooms where different things happened, and occasionally, there was a Daddy night. They had attended that the first time because they didn't know anyone else in the area.

When Jonah and Hayden had sat down beside them and started talking, Sam and Hayden had been inseparable. The past year had been a whirlwind of playdates, nights out, dinners at each other's houses and more.

Sam had also managed to balance being a little in more places. He was little most of the time when he wasn't working, although new places were different for them. They were always cautious at first, then slowly introduced more of his little into the surroundings. It worked for them, and that was the main thing. Eric refused to live by other people's rules and made sure they were both happy with the situation before seeing if there was anything else Sam wanted to try.

"I have a horse!"

Eric and Jonah started laughing, and Sam couldn't

figure out why. His cheeks heated as he realised he'd shouted out about the horse and not the engagement.

"And I'm engaged!" he added.

"I see that. Congratulations. On both the horse and the ring."

"Daddy! Are we still going for a playdate with Sam and Eric?" Hayden visibly bounced at Jonah's side, clinging to his Daddy's hand and arm as if to keep him tethered.

"I don't know, Hayden. They might want to celebrate."

"No!" Sam glanced at Daddy and saw his smile and nod. "Please come. I want to show Hayden my new horse and doll."

"All right, then. If you're sure, Eric," Jonah said.

"Yeah, it's not a problem. It might wear them both out a little more."

"I'm sure the horse riding has done that anyway, but yeah. They can both have a nap in the car on the way home."

"Come on, then. Let's head home. Warm milk and a cookie might be the snack for today."

"What about my birthday cake, Daddy?" Sam clasped his hands together in front of him. He'd been looking forward to seeing his surprise cake. He had no idea what it could be.

"What birthday cake? I didn't know it was your birthday?" Eric frowned, hands on his hips.

"Daddy!" Sam giggled.

"I think it's my cake, anyway," said Jonah.

"No! It's mine!" He laughed.

"We'll see," Eric said with a smile. He turned to Jonah. "We'll see you there."

"See you in a bit."

Eric opened the car door for Sam, who climbed in without hesitation. He was so excited. They didn't know enough people to have a birthday party for littles, but they were going to see his parents for dinner that evening. Despite turning forty-five, Sam had never felt so young and so happy. He put it down to the fact he was with Eric, who was so much younger than he was.

The age difference no longer bothered him. He could see how it might—and did—bother some people, but to those who mattered, they were a match made in heaven, and Sam agreed.

Much to Sam's amazement, he did nap on the hour-long journey home. He hadn't thought he would be able to, being so excited and everything, but he was gone within seconds, Daddy told him with a laugh when they arrived home.

Sam jumped out of the car and raced towards the house, which had been decorated with balloons and streamers before they'd rushed to the sanctuary. He fluttered his fingers through the streamers as he went past and waited for Eric on the porch, staring at and playing with the ring on his finger.

"You're so eager."

"It's my birthday, Daddy!"

Eric chuckled. "I know, sweetheart."

"Can we have a cookie for a snack? I did sleep in the car."

"Yes, you can have a cookie, but first, we need to jump into the rainstorm and get ourselves clean for our visitors, okay?"

"Yep!" Sam called as he raced up the stairs.

Since he'd been living with Eric, he'd lost a lot of his excess weight and had a lot more energy because he had someone else to look after him. He'd had to buy a whole new wardrobe when his work clothes had started falling off him. Now, he wasn't as self-conscious when he was naked with Eric. They'd also found he didn't need to drink coffee anymore either. His new energy levels had helped him not have to drink the awful stuff, and he stuck to milk, water and the occasional cup of tea.

He threw all his clothes in the washing basket and stepped into the bathroom, wanting to shower quickly, so he was ready for his friend. Hayden was great fun, although he had even more energy than Sam did, which was saying something.

"You are eager," Eric said with a chuckle. "I couldn't see your heels for dust."

"Daddy!" Sam laughed.

"Come here, little one. I need a hug from the birthday boy."

Sam went willingly into his Daddy's arms, wrapping himself around him and resting his head on Eric's shoulder. "Thank you for everything, Daddy," he whispered.

"You're welcome, Sam." He kissed his temple. "I'm so glad you agreed to marry me. I want to spend the rest of my life making your life as happy as possible."

"You're already succeeding then. I love you."

"I love you."

The past year had been a whirlwind. Eric had been to court with the film company, but the case had been dismissed when evidence had been provided of Eric's family emergency from several witnesses and the added information that he had offered to do the interviews via video, but Lynx Films had declined. The case had been closed because the company had not been willing to bend when Eric tried to provide an alternative to the necessary interviews.

Not just that, but damning evidence had come to light about the director's personal and professional behaviour, which had sunk the man's career. No one could find out where the information had come from, but as soon as some had come to light, women and men had been backing it up with their own versions of events.

Eric tenderly washed Sam, soaping him all over

before spraying him off, then dropping to his knees and giving Sam a different birthday gift. Once his mind had come back online, they dried off and dressed in some party clothes, which for Eric was jeans and a t-shirt, and for Sam was shorts and a t-shirt.

They wandered down the stairs, hand in hand, as the doorbell rang. Sam skipped over to the door, opening it wide for Jonah and Hayden to come in.

"Hayden!"

"Sam!"

"Anyone would've thought they hadn't seen each other for weeks," Jonah stated, shaking his head at the pair of them.

Sam grabbed Hayden's hand, pulling him towards the living room. "Wait until you see what I've got," he said.

"Wow. Those horses have real cowboy dolls to ride them."

"And a cowgirl, look!" Sam held up the cowgirl, who had slightly longer hair than the other two.

"A family of cowboys…girls…Daddy?" Hayden shouted.

Jonah's head poked inside the door. "Yes, Hayden?"

"What do you call it when you have cowboys *and* cowgirls? Cowpersons doesn't sound right," he grumbled.

"I don't think there is a collective name for them,

Hayden. You might have to call them cowboys and cowgirls."

Sam saw Hayden frown, then shake his head and carry on talking to Sam. "I don't think that's right. There should be a name that talks about them all."

"We can think of one," Sam suggested. "Cowpeople?"

"Hmm. I don't know. We might have to keep thinking."

"Do you want to play with them while we think?"

"Yeah!"

They laid on their stomachs, making space for the horses' paddocks and where the people could live— Sam had a small house that could be used as a ranch. He had no idea how long they'd been playing before Eric came in and told them to tidy away and wash their hands for a snack.

Having learned their lesson several months ago, they tidied away quickly, washed their hands and ran into the kitchen.

"Slow down, you two," Eric said.

"Sorry, Daddy." Sam ducked his head, but his eyes went wide when he saw the table. "A horse!" he yelled when he saw the cake on the surface. "Oh my! It's in the shape of a horse!" He stepped closer, not wanting to get too close and knock it over.

"Wow. I don't think that shout could've been any louder. Do you, Jonah?"

Jonah shook his head. "Nope. That is the loudest birthday shout ever."

"I will do a louder one on my birthday," Hayden declared.

"Sit down, then. Sam, you have to decide. Would you like to cut up your horse cake now and have some cake for a snack, or would you prefer a cookie instead?" Eric asked, placing a beaker in front of each of the boys. He picked up two mugs, giving one to Jonah.

"Ohh! The cake looks so pretty, but I want cake!"

"Me too," said Hayden.

Sam covered his face, then mumbled, "Cake."

"What was that, Sam?"

He lifted his head, and pouting, said, "Cake, please."

"Cake, it is." Eric brought over the slices of cake once he'd cut it, and the boys dug in, each moaning with how tasty the chocolate cake with vanilla buttercream tasted.

When they had both finished, Eric shooed them back into the living room to play. Sam had no idea when Eric and Jonah had joined them, but he eventually became aware of their conversation surrounding him as he played with his friend.

Life could not get much better than this, he thought, smiling at his ring.

Would you like to read more about Crush? Pre-order Lawful Attraction now—it's coming June 3 and is the final in the series!

Sign up to my newsletter to get a free **BONUS SCENE** from Love Scene and the Crush prequel short story, Love Conquers.

If you have a moment, would you write a review for Love Scene please? Reviews help other readers decide whether they would like to read the book, and therefore, are also important for authors.

LAWFUL ATTRACTION

CRUSH SERIES BOOK 9

An **MM** romance about life, love, family and beating the odds, especially when it involves a police officer and a dancer.

There's a fine line between protecting and stalking...

Logan has unwavering loyalty to the law, and when he finds Bastien in a precarious situation, his protective instincts flare up to an all-time high. His need to help overshadows everything else, including his sense. Unfortunately, the dancer doesn't want his help.

What Bastien does for a living doesn't mean he has no morals. He has to live, and his wages and tips don't always cover everything. He's glad he doesn't have anyone who relies on him because he can barely make ends meet working all the hours of the day. When a so-called friend turns on him, who does he have left?

Can they put their differences aside and realise what is right in front of them?

ORDER HERE:

https://readerlinks.com/l/1793155

I am Elouise East but feel free to call me Elli. I write sweet and steamy connections in gay romance. I also touch on taboo stories under the name Elouise R East.

Books that tell the stories where friendship and family are the focal point - be it blood family or chosen - is very important to me. That's why I include a variety of personalities, talents, ages, situations and abilities as I believe a story needs, or a character needs. I want my characters to be real, to be relatable, to be free to have whatever views they tell me they have. And trust me, most of the time, I do not have *any* say in the matter!

My characters come to life on the page for me as well as my readers. Their stories unfold in front of me, and I have very little input into how they want to be shown. Just like real life, the lives of my characters change with every choice, every interaction and every conversation. And I wouldn't have it any other way.

I write books that are emotionally realistic, even if liberties are taken with other aspects of my stories. I don't know any other way to write. It comes from deep inside.

Who am I? A single parent to two children who make life worth living. An avid reader who still devours every book she can get her hands on. A student of learning about any subject that takes her fancy. An author of books she would read herself. And a romantic at heart who loves anything cheesy.

Who's in?

Stalk me here… ;-)
WEBSITE: https://elouiseeast.com/
NEWSLETTER: https://elouiseeast.com/newsletter
LINKTREE: https://linktr.ee/elouiseeastauthor

BOOKS BY ELOUISE EAST

CRUSH

First Kiss

Instant Desire

Primary Seduction

Deep Down

A Crush for Christmas

Life Support

Covert Strength

Love Scene

Lawful Attraction

JUST A LITTLE CRUSH

Star-Crossed

He's Behind You

A Special Love (newsletter story)

DADDY

Love Me, Daddy

Soothe Me, Daddy

Spoil Me, Daddy

<u>DARK & DIVERGENT</u>

A Biker Make Three

Forbidden Temptation

Too Many Secrets

<u>CHARMED</u>

Treehouse Whispers

Rhythm Inside (Heard it in a Love Song Anthology)